KU-307-834

Paddy Clarke
Ha Ha Ha

Paddy Clarke
Ha Ha Ha

Roddy Doyle

Secker & Warburg
London

First published in Great Britain 1991
by Martin Secker & Warburg Limited
an imprint of Reed Consumer Books Ltd
Michelin House, 81 Fulham Road, London SW3 6RB
and Auckland, Melbourne, Singapore and Toronto

Copyright © Roddy Doyle 1993
The author has asserted his moral rights

A CIP catalogue record for this book
is available from the British Library

ISBN 0 436 20159 3

Reprinted 1993 (four times), 1994
First printed in Australia 1993
by Griffin Paperbacks

Long Gone Lonesome Blues
Words and Music by Hank Williams
Copyright © 1950 (renewed 1978) Acuff-Rose Music
Incorporated, USA. Acuff-Rose Opryland Music
Limited, London W1. Reproduced by permission.
All Rights Reserved. International Copyright Secured.

I'll Never Get Out of This World Alive
Words and Music by Fred Rose and Hank Williams
Copyright © 1952 Milene Music Incorporated & Hiriam Music,
USA. Acuff-Rose Opryland Music Limited, London W1.
Reproduced by permission of Music Sales Limited.
All Rights Reserved. International Copyright Secured.

Bachelor Boy
Words and Music by Bruce Welch and Cliff Richard
Copyright © 1962. Reproduced by permission of EMI Music
Publishing Ltd trading as Elstree Music,
London WC2H 0EA.

This book is dedicated to

Rory

We were coming down our road. Kevin stopped at a gate and bashed it with his stick. It was Missis Quigley's gate; she was always looking out the window but she never did anything.

—Quigley!

—Quigley!

—Quigley Quigley Quigley!

Liam and Aidan turned down their cul-de-sac. We said nothing; they said nothing. Liam and Aidan had a dead mother. Missis O'Connell was her name.

—It'd be brilliant, wouldn't it? I said.

—Yeah, said Kevin. —Cool.

We were talking about having a dead ma. Sinbad, my little brother, started crying. Liam was in my class in school. He dirtied his trousers one day – the smell of it rushed at us like the blast of heat when an oven door was opened – and the master did nothing. He didn't shout or slam his desk with his leather or anything. He told us to fold our arms and go asleep and when we did he carried Liam out of the class. He didn't come back for ages and Liam didn't come back at all.

James O'Keefe whispered, —If I did a gick in me pants he'd kill me!

—Yeah.

—It's not fair, said James O'Keefe. —So it's not.

The master, Mister Hennessey, hated James O'Keefe. He'd be writing something on the board with his back to us and he'd say, —O'Keefe, I know you're up to something down there. Don't let me catch you. He said it one morning and James O'Keefe wasn't even in. He was at home with the mumps.

Henno brought Liam to the teachers' toilet and cleaned him up and then he brought him to the headmaster's office and the headmaster brought him to his auntie's in his car because there was no one at home in his own house. Liam's auntie's house was in Raheny.

—He used up two rolls of toilet paper, Liam told us.

—And he gave me a shilling.

—He did not; show us it.

—There.

—That's only threepence.

—I spent the rest, said Liam.

He got the remains of a packet of Toffo out of his pocket and showed it to us.

—There, he said.

—Give us one.

—There's only four left, said Liam; he was putting the packet back in his pocket.

—Ah, said Kevin.

He pushed Liam.

Liam went home.

Today, we were coming home from the building site. We'd got a load of six-inch nails and a few bits of plank for making boats, and we'd been pushing bricks into a trench full of wet cement when Aidan started running away. We could hear his asthma, and we all ran as well. We were being chased. I had to wait for Sinbad. I looked back and there was no one after us but I didn't say anything. I grabbed Sinbad's hand and ran and caught up with the rest of them. We stopped when we got out of the fields onto the end of the road. We laughed. We roared through the gap in the hedge. We got into the gap and looked to see if there was anyone coming to get us. Sinbad's sleeve was caught in the thorns.

—The man's coming! said Kevin, and he slid through the gap.

We left Sinbad stuck in the hedge and pretended we'd run away. We heard him snivelling. We crouched behind the gate pillars of the last house before the road stopped at the hedge, O'Driscoll's.

—Patrick——, Sinbad whinged.

—Sin-bahhhd——, said Kevin.

Aidan had his knuckles in his mouth. Liam threw a stone at the hedge.

—I'm telling Mammy, said Sinbad.

I gave up. I got Sinbad out of the hedge and made him wipe his nose on my sleeve. We were going home for our dinner; shepherd's pie on a Tuesday.

Liam and Aidan's da howled at the moon. Late at night, in his back garden; not every night, only sometimes. I'd never heard him but Kevin said he had. My ma said that he did it because he missed his wife.

—Missis O'Connell?

—That's right.

My da agreed with her.

—He's grieving, said my mother. —The poor man.

Kevin's father said that Mister O'Connell howled because he was drunk. He never called him Mister O'Connell; he called him the Tinker.

—Will you look who's talking, said my mother when I told her that. And then she said, —Don't listen to him, Patrick; he's codding you. Sure, where would he get drunk? There's no pubs in Barrytown.

—There's three in Raheny, I said.

—That's miles away, she said. —Poor Mister O'Connell. No more talk about it.

Kevin told Liam that he saw his da looking up at the moon and howling like a werewolf.

Liam said he was a liar.

Kevin dared him to say that again but he didn't.

Our dinner wasn't ready and Sinbad had left one of his shoes back in the building site. We'd been told never to play there so he told our ma that he didn't know where it was. She smacked the back of his legs. She held onto his arm but he still kept ahead of her so she wasn't really getting him properly. He still cried though, and she stopped.

Sinbad was a great crier.

—You're costing me a blessed fortune, she told Sinbad.

She was nearly crying as well.

She said we'd have to go out and find the shoe after dinner, the both of us, because I was supposed to have been looking after him.

We'd have to go out in the dark, through the gap, over the fields, into the muck and the trenches and the watchmen. She told us to wash our hands. I closed the bathroom door and I got Sinbad back for it; I gave him a dead leg.

I had to keep an eye on Deirdre in the pram while our ma put clean socks on Sinbad. She wiped his nose and looked at his eyes for ages and pushed the tears away with her knuckle.

—There, there; good boy.

I was afraid she'd ask him what was wrong with him and he'd tell her. I rocked the pram the way she always did it.

We lit fires. We were always lighting fires.

I took off my jumper so there wouldn't be a smell of smoke off it. It was cold now but that didn't matter as much. I looked for somewhere clean to put the jumper. We were at the building site. The building site kept changing, the fenced-in part of it where they kept the diggers and the bricks and the shed the builders sat in and drank tea. There was always

4

a pile of bread crusts outside the shed door, huge batch crusts with jam stains on the edges. We were looking through the wire fence at a seagull trying to pick up one of the crusts – it was too long for the seagull's beak; he should have grabbed it in the middle – when another crust came flying out the shed door and hit the side of the seagull's head. We heard the roars of the men's laughing from inside the shed.

We'd go down to the building site and it wouldn't be there any more, just a square patch of muck and broken bricks and tyre marks. There was a new road where there'd been wet cement the last time we were there and the new site was at the end of the road. We went over to where we'd written our names with sticks in the cement, but they'd been smoothed over; they'd gone.

—Ah gick, said Kevin.

Our names were all around Barrytown, on the roads and paths. You had to do it at night when they were all gone home, except the watchmen. Then when they saw the names in the morning it was too late, the cement was hard. Only our christian names, just in case the builders ever went from door to door up Barrytown Road looking for the boys who'd been writing their names in their wet cement.

There wasn't only one building site; there were loads of them, all different types of houses.

We wrote Liam's name and address with a black marker on a new plastered wall inside one of the houses. Nothing happened.

My ma once smelt the smoke off me. She saw my hands first. She grabbed one of them.

—Look at your hands, she said. —Your fingernails! My God, Patrick, you must be in mourning for the cat.

Then she smelt me.

—What have you been up to?

—Putting out a fire.

She killed me. The worst part was waiting to see if she'd tell my da when he came home.

Kevin had the matches, a box of Swan ones. I loved those boxes. We'd made a small wigwam out of planks and sticks and we'd brought two cardboard boxes with us from behind the shops. The boxes were ripped up and under the wood. Wood by itself took too long to get going. It was still daytime. Kevin lit a match. Me and Liam looked around to see if there was anyone coming. There was no one else with us. Aidan was staying in his auntie's house. Sinbad was in hospital because he had to get his tonsils out. Kevin put the match under the cardboard, waited for it to grab the flame and let go of the match. We watched the fire eat the cardboard. Then we ran for cover.

I couldn't really use matches properly. The match broke or it wouldn't light or I'd pull it along the wrong side of the box; or it would light and I'd get rid of it too quickly.

We waited behind one of the houses. When the watchman came we'd run. We were near the hedge, the escape route. Kevin said that they couldn't do anything to you if they didn't catch you on the building site. If they grabbed us or hit us out on the road we could bring them to court. We couldn't see the fire properly. We waited. It wasn't a house yet, just some of the walls. It was a line of six houses joined together. The Corporation were building the houses here. We waited for a while. I'd forgotten my jumper.

—Oh, oh.

—What?

—Oh janey.

—What?

—Emergency, emergency.

We crawled around the side of the house; not all the way because it was taking too long. There was a barrel over near where I'd put my jumper. I ran for cover. I crouched behind the barrel and breathed in and out real hard, getting ready to go. I looked back; Kevin stood up properly, looked around and got back down again.

—Okay, he hissed.

I took a last breath and came out from behind the barrel and dashed for the jumper. No one shouted. I made a noise like bombs exploding as I grabbed the jumper off the bricks. I slid back behind the barrel.

The fire was going well, loads of smoke. I got a stone and threw it at the fire. Kevin stood up again and scouted for a watchman. The coast was clear and he signalled me to come. I charged, crouched down and got to the side of the house. Kevin patted me on the back. So did Liam.

I tied the jumper around my waist. I put the sleeves in a double knot.

—Come on, men.

Kevin ran out from behind our cover; we followed him and danced around the fire.

—Woo woo woo woo woo –

We put our hands to our mouths and did the Indian stuff.

—Hii-yaa-yaa-yaa-yaa-yaa-yaa –

Kevin kicked the fire at me but the pile just fell. It wasn't much of a fire now. I stopped dancing. So did Kevin and Liam. Kevin pushed and pulled Liam to the fire.

—Lay off!

I helped Kevin. Liam got serious, so we stopped. We were sweating. I had an idea.

—The watchman is a bas-stard!

We ran back to behind the house and laughed. We all joined in.

—The watchman is a bas-stard! The watchman is a bas-stard!

We heard something; Kevin did.

We escaped, dashed across the remains of the field. I

7

zigzagged, head down, so no bullets would get me. I fell through the gap into the ditch. We had a fight, just pushing. Liam missed my shoulder and punched my ear and it stung, so he had to let me hit him in the ear back. He put his hands in his pockets so he wouldn't try to stop me.

We got out of the ditch cos the midgeys were landing on our faces.

Sinbad wouldn't put the lighter fuel in his mouth.

—It's halibut oil, I told him.

—It isn't, he said.

He squirmed but I held onto him. We were in the school yard, in the shed.

I liked halibut oil. When you cracked the plastic with your teeth the oil spread over the inside of your mouth, like ink through blotting paper. It was warm; I liked it. The plastic was nice as well.

It was Monday; Henno was in charge of the yard, but he always stayed over at the far side watching whoever was playing handball. He was mad; if he'd come over to our side, the shed, he'd have caught loads of us in the act. If a teacher caught five fellas smoking or doing serious messing he got a bonus in his wages; that was what Fluke Cassidy said and his uncle was a teacher. But Henno only watched handball and sometimes he took his jacket and his jumper off and played it as well. He was brilliant. When he hit the ball you couldn't see it till it hit the wall; it was like a bullet. He had a sticker in his car: Live Longer, Play Handball.

Sinbad's lips had disappeared because he was pressing them shut so hard; we couldn't get his mouth open. Kevin pressed the fuel capsule against his mouth but it wouldn't go in. I pinched Sinbad's arm; no good. This was terrible; in front of the others, I couldn't sort out my little brother. I got the hair above his ear and pulled it up; I lifted him: I just wanted to hurt him. His eyes were closed now as well but the tears were getting out. I held his nose. He gasped and Kevin shoved the capsule half-way into his mouth. Then Liam lit it with the match.

We said we'd get Liam to light it, me and Kevin, just in case we got caught.

It went like a dragon.

I preferred magnifying glasses to matches. We spent afternoons burning little piles of cut grass. I loved watching the grass change colour. I loved it when the flame began to race through the grass. You had more control with a magnifying glass. It was easier but it took more skill. If the sun stayed out long enough you could saw through a sheet of paper and not have to touch it, just put down a stone in each corner to stop it from blowing away. We'd have a race; burn, blow it out, burn, blow it out. Last to burn the paper completely in half had to let the other fella burn his hand. We'd draw a man on the paper and burn holes in him; in his hands and his feet, like Jesus. We drew long hair on him. We left his mickey till last.

We cut roads through the nettles. My ma wanted to know what I was doing going out wearing my duffel coat and mittens on a lovely nice day.

—We're doing the nettles, I told her.

The nettles were huge; giant ones. The hives from their stings were colossal, and they itched for ages after they'd stopped stinging. They took up a big corner of the field behind the shops. Nothing else grew there, just the nettles. After we hacked them over with a sideways swing of our sticks and hurleys we had to mash them down. Juice from the nettles flew up. We built roads right through the nettles, a road each because of the swinging sticks and hurleys. When we were going home the roads had met and there were no nettles left. The hurleys were green and I had two stings on my face; I'd taken off my balaclava because my head was itchy.

I was looking at crumbs. My da put his hand on the magnifying glass and I let him take it. He looked at the hairs on his hand.

—Who gave you this? he said.

—You.

—Oh, that's right; I did.

He handed it back.

—Good man.

He pressed his thumb down hard on the kitchen table.

—See if you can see the print, he said.

I wasn't sure.

—The fingerprint, he said. —The thumb.

I shifted my chair over closer to him and held the glass over where his thumb had been. We both looked through the glass. All I could see was the yellow and red dots of the table-top, bigger.

—See anything? he said.

—No.

—Come on, he said.

I followed him into the living room.

—Where are you two going when your dinner's just ready? said my ma.

—Back in a sec, said my da.

He put his hand on my shoulder. We went to the window.

—Get up there till we see.

He dragged the armchair over for me to stand on.

—Now.

He hauled up the venetian blinds. He spoke to them.

—Out of the way and let the duck see the rabbit.

He locked the cord and held it for a while to make sure that both sides of the blinds stayed up.

He pressed his thumb on the glass.

—Now, look.

The smudge became lines, curved tracks.

—Do yours now, he said.

I pressed my thumb on the glass, hard. He held me so I didn't fall off the chair.

I looked.

—Are they the same? he said.

—Yours is bigger.

—Besides that.

I said nothing; I wasn't sure.

—They're all different, he said. —No one's fingerprints are the same as someone else's. Did you know that?

—No.

—Well, now you do.

A few days later Napoleon Solo found fingerprints on his briefcase.

I looked up at my father.

—Told you, he said.

We didn't do the barn. We didn't put it on fire.

The barn had been left behind. When the Corporation bought Donnelly's farm he bought a new one near Swords. He moved everything out there except his house and the barn, and the smell. The smell was really bad on wet days. The rain freshened up the pigshite that had been lying there for years. The barn was huge and green, and great when it was full of hay. We crept in from the back before the new houses were built. It was dangerous. Donnelly had a gun and a one-eyed dog. Cecil, the dog's name was. Donnelly had a mad brother as well, Uncle Eddie. He was in charge of the chickens and the pigs. He raked the stones and pebbles of the driveway in front of the house every time a car or a tractor went over them and messed them up. Uncle Eddie walked by our house one day when my ma was painting the gate.

—God love him, she said to herself but loud enough for me to hear her.

My ma mentioned Uncle Eddie when we were having our dinner one day.

—God love him, I said, and my da smacked my shoulder.

Uncle Eddie had two eyes but he was a bit like Cecil because one of them was closed over. My da said that it went that way because it got caught in a draught when Uncle Eddie was looking through a keyhole.

When you were doing a funny face or pretending you had a stammer and the wind changed or someone thumped your back you stayed that way for ever. Declan Fanning – he was fourteen and his parents were thinking of sending him off to boarding school because he smoked – he had a stammer and he got it because he was jeering someone with a stammer and someone else thumped him in the back.

Uncle Eddie didn't have a stammer but he could only say two words, Grand, grand.

We were at mass and the Donnellys were behind us and Father Moloney said, —You may be seated.

We were getting up from our knees and Uncle Eddie went, —Grand, grand.

Sinbad burst out laughing. I looked at my da to make sure that he didn't think it was me.

You could climb up the bales of hay, right up into the barn. We dived down from one level to another level of bales. We never hurt ourselves; it was brilliant. Liam and Aidan said that their Uncle Mick, their ma's brother, had a barn like Donnelly's barn.

—Where? I said.

They didn't know.

—Where is it?

—The country.

We saw mice. I never saw any, but I heard them. I said I saw them. Kevin saw loads of them. I saw a squashed rat. The marks of the tyre were on it. We tried to light it but it wouldn't go.

We were up in the top of the barn. Uncle Eddie came in. He didn't know we were there. We held our breaths. Uncle Eddie walked around in a circle twice and went back out. There was a block of sunlight at the door. It was one of those big corrugated-iron doors that slid across. The whole barn was corrugated iron. We were so high up we could touch the roof.

The barn became surrounded by skeleton houses. The road outside was being widened and there were pyramids of huge pipes at the top of the road, up at the seafront. The road was going to be a main road to the airport. Kevin's sister, Philomena, said that the barn looked like the houses' mother looking after them. We said she was a spa, but it did; it did look like the houses' ma.

Three fire brigades came out from town to put the fire out but they weren't able to. The whole road was flooded from all the water. It happened during the night. The fire was gone when we got up the next morning and our ma said we couldn't go near the barn and she kept an eye on us to make sure we didn't. I got up into the apple tree but I couldn't see anything. It wasn't much of a tree and it was full of leaves. It only ever grew scabby apples.

They found a box of matches outside the barn; that was what we heard. Missis Parker from the cottages told our ma. Mister Parker worked for Donnelly; drove the tractor and went to the pictures with Uncle Eddie every Saturday afternoon.

—They'll dust them for fingerprints, I told my ma.

—Yes. That's right.

—They'll dust them for fingerprints, I told Sinbad. —And if they find your fingerprints on the matches they'll come and arrest you and put you in the Artane Boys Band.

Sinbad didn't believe me but he did believe me as well.

—They'll make you play the triangle because of your lips, I told him.

His eyes went all wet; I hated him.

Uncle Eddie was burnt to death in the fire; we heard that as well. Missis Byrne from two houses up told my ma. She whispered it and they blessed themselves.

—Maybe it's for the best, said Missis Byrne.

—Yes, said my ma.

I was dying to get down to the barn to see Uncle Eddie, if they hadn't taken him away. My ma made us have a picnic in the garden. My da came home from work. He went to work in the train. My ma got up out of the picnic so she could talk to him without us hearing. I knew what she was telling him, about Uncle Eddie.

—Was he? said my da.

My ma nodded.

—He never told me that when he came up the road with me there. All he said was Grand grand.

There was a gap and then they burst out laughing, the two of them.

He wasn't dead at all. He wasn't even hurt.

The barn was never green again. It was bent and buckled. The roof was crooked like the lid of a can. It swung and creaked. The big door was put leaning against the yard wall. It was all black. One of the walls was gone. The black on the walls fell off and the whole thing became brown and rusty.

Everyone said that someone from the new Corporation houses had done it. Later, about a year after, Kevin said he'd

14

done it. But he didn't. He was in Courtown in a caravan on his holidays when it happened. I didn't say anything.

On a nice day we could see the specks of dust in the air under the roof. Sometimes I'd go home and it was in my hair. On windy days big dead chunks fell off. The ground under the roof was red. The barn was nibbled away.

Sinbad promised.

My ma pushed his hair back from his forehead and combed her fingers through it to keep it on top of his head. She was nearly crying as well.

—I've tried everything, she told him. —Now, promise again.

—I promise, said Sinbad.

My ma started to untie his hands. I was crying as well.

She tied his hands to the chair to stop him from picking the scabs on his lips. He'd screamed. His face had gone red, then purple, and one of the screams went on for ever; he didn't breathe in. Sinbad's lips were covered in scabs because of the lighter fuel. For two weeks it had looked like he had no lips.

She held his hands at his sides but she let him stand up.

—Let's see your tongue, she said.

She was checking to see that he wasn't telling a lie.

—Okay, Francis, she said. —No spots.

Francis was Sinbad. He put his tongue back in.

She let go of his hands but he didn't go anywhere. I went over to where they were.

You ran down the jetty and jumped and shouted Voyage To The Bottom Of The Sea, and whoever got the most words out before they hit the water won. No one ever won. I once got as far as the second The but Kevin, the ref, said that my bum had gone into the water before I got to Of. We threw stones at each other, to miss.

I hid behind the sideboard when the Seaview was being swallowed by a giant jellyfish; it was terrible. I didn't mind it at first and I put my fingers in my ears when my da told my ma that it was ridiculous. But when the jellyfish kind of surrounded the submarine I crawled over to the sideboard. I'd been lying on my tummy in front of the telly. I didn't cry. My ma said that the jellyfish had gone but I didn't come back out till I heard the ads. She brought me to bed after it and stayed with me for a while. Sinbad was asleep. I got up for a drink of water. She said she wouldn't let me watch it next week but she forgot. Anyway, the next week it was back to normal again, about a mad scientist who'd invented a new torpedo. Admiral Nelson gave him a box that sent him bashing into the periscope.

—That's the stuff, said my da.

He didn't see it; he just heard it. He didn't look up from his book. I didn't like that; he was jeering me. My ma was knitting. I was the only one let up to watch it. I told Sinbad it was brilliant but I wouldn't tell him why.

I was in the water down at the seafront, with Edward Swanwick. He didn't go to the same school as most of us. He went to Belvedere in town.

—Nothing but the best for the Swanwicks, said my da when my ma told him that she'd seen Missis Swanwick buying margarine instead of butter in the shop.

She laughed.

Edward Swanwick had to wear a blazer and tie and he had to play rugby. He said he hated it but he came home on his own in the train every day so it wasn't too bad.

We were flinging water at each other. We'd stopped laughing cos we'd been doing it for ages. The tide was going out so we'd be getting out in a minute. Edward Swanwick pushed his hands out and sent a wave towards me and there was a jellyfish in it. A huge see-through one with pink veins

16

and a purple middle. I lifted my arms way up and started to move but it still rubbed my side. I screamed. I pushed through the water to the steps. I felt the jellyfish hit my back; I thought I did. I yelled again; I couldn't help it. It was rocky and uneven down at the seafront, not like the beach. I got to the steps and grabbed the bar.

—It's a Portuguese man of war, said Edward Swanwick.

He was coming back to the steps a long way, around the jellyfish.

I got onto the second step. I looked for marks. Jellyfish stings didn't hurt until you got out of the water. There was a pink lash on the side of my belly; I could see it. I was out of the water.

—I'm going to get you, I told Edward Swanwick.

—It's a Portuguese man of war, said Edward Swanwick.

—Look at it.

I showed him my wound.

He was up on the platform now, looking over the railing at the jellyfish.

I took my togs off without bothering with the towel. There was no one else. The jellyfish was still floating there, like a runny umbrella. Edward Swanwick was hunting for stones. He went down some of the steps to reach for some but he wouldn't get back into the water. I couldn't get my T-shirt down over my back and chest because I was wet. It was stuck on my shoulders.

—Their stings are poisonous, said Edward Swanwick.

I had my T-shirt on now. I lifted it to make sure the mark was still there. I thought it was beginning to get sore. I wrung out my togs over the railing. Edward Swanwick was plopping stones near the jellyfish.

—Hit it.

He missed.

—You're a big spa, I told him.

I wrapped my togs in my towel. It was a big soft bath one. I shouldn't have had it.

I ran all the way, up Barrytown Road, all the way, past the cottages where there was a ghost and an old woman with a smell and no teeth, past the shops; I started to cry when I was three gates away from our house; around the back, in the kitchen door.

Ma was feeding the baby.

—What's wrong with you, Patrick?

She looked down for a cut on my leg. I got my T-shirt out to show her. I was really crying now. I wanted a hug and ointment and a bandage.

—A jelly – a Portuguese man of war got me, I told her.

She touched my side.

—There?

—Ouch! No, look; the mark across. It's highly poisonous.

—I can't see – . Oh, now I do.

I pulled my T-shirt down. I tucked it into my pants.

—What should we do? she asked me. —Will I go next door and phone for an ambulance?

—No; ointment –

—Okay, so. That'll mend it. Have I time for me to finish feeding Deirdre and Cathy before we put it on?

—Yeah.

—Great.

I pressed my hand hard into my side to keep the mark there.

The seafront was a pumping station. There was a platform behind it with loads of steps down to it. When there was a spring tide the water spread over the platform. There were more steps down to the water. There were steps on the other side of the pumping station as well but it was always cold over there and the rocks were bigger and sharper. It was hard to get past them to the water. The jetty wasn't really a jetty.

It was a pipe covered in cement. The cement wasn't smooth.
There were bits of stone and rock sticking out of it. You
couldn't dash along to the end. You had to watch your step
and not put your foot down too hard. It was hard to play
properly down at the seafront. There was too much seaweed,
slime and rocks; you always had to keep your eyes down
searching under the water. All you could really do was swim.

I was good at swimming.

Sinbad wouldn't get in unless our ma was with him.

Kevin once dived off the jetty and split his head. He had to
go into Jervis Street for stitches. He went in a taxi with his
ma and his sister.

Some of us weren't allowed to swim down at the seafront.
If you cut your toe on a rock you'd get polio. A boy from
Barrytown Drive, Seán Rickard, died and it was supposed to
have been because he'd swallowed a mouthful of the seafront
water. Someone else said he'd swallowed a gobstopper and it
got caught in his windpipe.

—He was by himself in his bedroom, said Aidan. —And
he couldn't slap his back to get it up.

—Why didn't he go down to the kitchen?

—He couldn't breathe.

—I can slap mine, look it.

We looked at Kevin thumping his back.

—Not hard enough, said Aidan.

We all tried it.

—It's a load of rubbish, said my ma. —Don't mind them.
She spoke softer.

—The poor little lad had leukaemia.

—What's leukaemia?

—A disease.

—Can you get it from swallowing water?

—No.

—How?

—Not from water.

—Sea water?

—No kind of water.

The seafront water was grand, my da said. The Corporation experts had tested it and it was perfect.

—There, said my mother.

My Granda Finnegan, her father, worked in the Corporation.

The teacher we had before Henno, Miss Watkins, brought in a tea-towel with the Proclamation of Independence on it because it was fifty years after 1916. It had the writing part in the middle and the seven men who'd signed it around the sides. She stuck it up over the blackboard and let us up to see it one by one. Some of the boys blessed themselves in front of it.

—*Nach bhfuil sé go h'álainn*,* lads? she kept saying after every couple of boys went past.

—*Tá*,** we said back.

I looked at the names at the bottom. Thomas J. Clarke was the first one. Clarke, like my name.

Miss Watkins got her *bata**** and read the proclamation out for us and pointed at each word.

—In this supreme hour the Irish nation must, by its valour and discipline, and by the readiness of its children to sacrifice themselves for the common good, prove itself worthy of the august destiny to which it is called. Signed on behalf of the provisional government, Thomas J. Clarke, Seán Mac-Diarmada, Thomas MacDonagh, P. H. Pearse, Eamonn Ceannt, James Connolly, Joseph Plunkett.

Miss Watkins started clapping, so we did as well. We

* Isn't it lovely?   ** Yes.   *** Stick.

started laughing. She stared at us and we stopped but we kept clapping.

I turned back to James O'Keefe.

—Thomas Clarke is my granda. Pass it on.

Miss Watkins rapped the blackboard with the bata.

—*Seasaígí suas.**

She made us march in step beside our desks.

—*Clé – deas – clé deas – clé –***

The walls of the prefab wobbled. The prefabs were behind the school. You could crawl under them. The varnish at the front of them was all flaky because of the sun; you could peel it off. We didn't get a room in the proper school, the cement one, until a year after this, when we got changed to Henno. We loved marching. We could feel the boards hopping under us. We put so much effort into slamming our feet down that we couldn't keep in time. She made us do this a couple of times a day, when she said we were looking lazy.

While we marched this time Miss Watkins read the proclamation.

—Irishmen and Irishwomen: In the name of God and of the dead generations from which she receives her old tradition of nationhood, Ireland, through us, summons her children to her flag and strikes for her freedom.

She had to stop. It wasn't proper marching any more. She hit the blackboard.

—*Suígí síos.****

She looked annoyed and disappointed.

Kevin put his hand up.

—Miss?

—*Sea?*****

* Stand up.   **Left – right – left right – left –
*** Sit down.   **** Yes.

21

—Paddy Clarke said his granda's Thomas Clarke on the tea-towel, Miss.

—Did he now?

—Yes, Miss.

—Patrick Clarke.

—Yes, Miss.

—Stand up till we see you.

It took ages for me to get out of my desk.

—Your grandfather is Thomas Clarke?

I smiled.

—Is he?

—Yes, Miss.

—This man here?

She pointed at Thomas Clarke in one of the corners of the tea-towel. He looked like a granda.

—Yes, Miss.

—Where does he live, tell us?

—Clontarf, Miss.

—Where?

—Clontarf, Miss.

—Come up here to me, Patrick Clarke.

The only noise was me on the floorboards.

She pointed to a bit of writing under Thomas Clarke's head.

—Read that for us, Patrick Clarke.

—Ex – eh – executed by the British on 3 May, 1916.

—What does Executed mean, Dermot Grimes who's picking his nose and doesn't think I can see him?

—Kilt, Miss.

—That's right. And this is your grandfather who lives in Clontarf, is it, Patrick Clarke?

—Yes, Miss.

I pretended to look at the picture again.

—I'll ask you again, Patrick Clarke. Is this man your grandfather?

—No, Miss.

She gave me three on each hand.

When I got back to the desk I couldn't put the seat down; my hands couldn't do anything. James O'Keefe pushed the seat down for me with his foot. It made a bang; I thought she'd get me again. I put my hands under my legs. I didn't crouch: she wouldn't let us. The pain was like my hands had dropped off; it would soon become more of a wet sting. The palms were beginning to sweat like mad. There was no noise. I looked over at Kevin. I grinned but my teeth chattered. I saw Liam turn round at the front of the row, waiting for Kevin to look his way, waiting to grin for him.

I liked my Granda Clarke, much more than Granda Finnegan. Granda Clarke's wife, my Grandma, wasn't alive any more.

—She's up in heaven, he said, —having a great time.

He gave me half a crown when we went to see him or when he came to see us. He once came on a bike.

I was messing through the drawers in the sideboard one night when Mart and Market was on the television. The bottom drawer was so full of photographs that when I was sliding the drawer back in some of the photographs on the top of the pile fell out the back onto the floor under the sideboard. I got them out from under there. One of them was of Granda and Grandma Clarke. We hadn't been to his house in ages.

—Dad?

—Yes, son?

—When are we going to Granda Clarke's?

My da looked like he'd lost something, then found it, but it wasn't what he'd wanted.

He sat up. He looked at me for a while.

—Granda Clarke's dead, he said. —Do you not remember?
—No.
I couldn't.
He picked me up.

My da's hands were big. The fingers were long. They weren't fat. I could make out the bone under the skin and the flesh. He had one of his hands dangling over the chair. He was holding his book with his other hand. His nails were clean – except for one – and the white bits at the top were longer than mine. The wrinkles at his knuckles were a bit like the design of a wall, the cement between the bricks up and across. There weren't many other wrinkles but the pores were like hollows, with a hair for every pore. Dark hair. Hair came out from under his cuff.

The Naked and the Dead. That was what the book was called. There was a soldier on the cover with his uniform on. His face was dirty. He was American.

—What's it about?
He looked at the cover.
—War, he said.
—Is it any good? I said.
—Yes, it is, he said. —It's very good.
I nodded at the cover.
—Is he in it?
—Yes.
—What's he like?
—I haven't got to him. I'll let you know.

World War Three Looms Near.

I got the paper every day for my da when he'd get home from work, and at the same time on Saturdays. Ma gave me the money; the Evening Press.

World War Three Looms Near.

—Does Looms mean Coming? I asked my ma.

—I think so, she said. —Why?

—World War Three's coming near, I told her. —Look.

She looked at the headline.

—Oh dear, she said. —That's just newspapers. They exaggerate things.

—Will we be in the war? I asked her.

—No, she said.

—Why not?

—Because there won't be one, she said.

—Were you alive in World War Two? I asked her.

—Yes, she said. —Indeed I was.

She was making the dinner; she put on her busy look.

—What was it like?

—It wasn't too bad, she said. —You'd have been disappointed, Patrick. Ireland wasn't really in the war.

—Why not?

—Oh, it's complicated; we just weren't. Your daddy will tell you.

I was waiting for him. He came in the back door.

—Look.

World War Three Looms Near.

He read it.

—World War Three looms near, he said. —Looms, no less.

He didn't seem fussed.

—Have you your gun ready, Patrick? he said.

—Ma said there won't be a war, I said.

—She's right.

—Why?

He sometimes liked these questions, and sometimes he didn't. When he did he folded his legs if he was sitting down and leaned a bit to the side into his chair. That was what he did now, leaned nearer to me. I couldn't hear him for the first bit because it had been what I'd hoped he'd do – fold his legs and lean over – and it had happened the way I'd wanted it to.

——between the Israelis and the Arabs, I heard.

—Why?

—They don't like one another, he said, —basically. The same old story, I'm afraid.

—Why does the paper say about World War Three? I asked him.

—To sell papers, first, he said. —A headline like that sells papers. But as well, the Americans are backing the Jews and the Russians are backing the Arabs.

—The Jews are the Israelis.

—Yeah, that's it.

—Who are the Arabs?

—Everyone else. All their neighbours. Jordan, Syria –

—Egypt.

—Good man, you know your stuff.

—The Holy Family went to Egypt when Herod was after them.

—That's right. There's always work for carpenters.

I didn't get it, fully, what he'd said, but it was the kind of thing that Ma didn't like him saying. She wasn't there though, so I laughed.

—And the Jews are winning, said my da. —Against all the odds. Good luck to them.

—Jews go to mass on Saturdays, I told my da.

—That's right, he said. —In synagogues.

—They don't believe in Jesus.

—That's right.

—Why don't they?

—Ah now.

I waited.

—People believe different things.

26

I wanted more than that.

—Some believe in God, others don't.

—Communists don't, I said.

—That's right, he said. —Who told you that?

—Mister Hennessey.

—Good man, Mister Hennessey, he said.

I knew by the way he said the next thing that it was a part of a poem; he did that sometimes.

—And still they gazed and still their wonder grew that one small head could carry all it knew. Some people believe that Jesus was the son of God and others don't.

—You do, don't you?

—Yes, he said. —I do. Why? Was Mister Hennessey asking you?

—No, I said.

His face changed.

—The Israelis are a great people, he said. —Hitler tried to exterminate them, nearly did, and look at them now. Out-numbered, out-gunned, out-everythinged and they're still winning. Sometimes I think we should move there, to Israel. Would you like that, Patrick?

—I don't know. Yeah, I might.

I knew where Israel was. It was shaped like an arrow.

—It's hot there, I said.

—Ummm.

—It snows in the winter though.

—Yep. A nice mix. Not like here, all rain.

—They don't wear shoes, I said.

—Do they not?

—Sandals.

—Like what's his name, your man –

—Terence Long.

—That's right. Terence Long.

We both laughed.

—Terence Long —
Terence Long —
Wears no socks —
What a pong.
—Poor oul' Terence, said my da. —Up the Israelis, anyway.
—What was World War Two like? I asked him.
—Long, he said.
I knew the dates.
—I was a kid when it started, he said. —And I was nearly finished with school when it ended.
—Six years.
—Yep. Long ones.
—Mister Hennessey said he never saw a banana till he was eighteen.
—I'd believe him.
—Luke Cassidy got into trouble. He asked him what the monkeys ate during the war.
—What happened to him? said Da when he'd stopped laughing.
—He hit him.
He said nothing.
—Six.
—Rough.
—Luke didn't even think it up for himself. Kevin Conroy told him to say it.
—Serves him right then.
—He was crying.
—All because of bananas.
—Kevin's brother's joining the F.C.A., I said.
—Is that right? That'll straighten his back for him.
I didn't get it. His back was straight already.
—Were you ever in it?
—The F.C.A.?

28

—Yeah.
—No.
—During the –
—My father was in the L.D.F.
—What's that?
—Local Defence Force.
—Did he have a gun?
—I suppose so. Not at home; I think anyway.
—I'm going to join them when I'm old enough. Can I?
—The F.C.A.?
—Yeah. Can I?
—Sure.
—Was Ireland ever in a war?
—No.
—What about the Battle of Clontarf?
He laughed, I waited.
—That wasn't really a war, he said.
—What was it then?
—A battle.
—What's the difference?
—Well, let's ——Wars are long –
—And battles are short.
—Yes.
—Why was Brian Boru in a tent?
—He was praying.
—In a tent though. You don't pray in a tent.
—I'm hungry, he said. —What about yourself?
—Yeah.
—What are we having; any idea?
—Mince.
—Righto.
—How goes gas kill you?
—It poisons you.
—How?

—You're not supposed to breathe it. Your lungs can't cope. Why?

—The Jews, I said.

—Oh, he said. —Yes.

—If Ireland was in a war would you go into the army?

—It won't be.

—It might be, I said.

—No, he said. —I don't think so.

—World War Three looms near, I said.

—Don't mind that, he said.

—Would you?

—Yes, he said.

—So would I.

—Good. And Francis.

—He's too young, I said. —They wouldn't let him.

—There won't be a war, he said. —Don't worry.

—I'm not, I said.

—Good.

—We were in a war against the English, weren't we?

—Yes.

—That was a war, I said.

—Well, it wasn't really——I suppose it was.

—We won.

—Yes. We murdered them. We gave them a hiding they'll never forget.

We laughed.

We had our dinner. It was lovely. The mince wasn't too runny. I sat in the chair beside Da, Sinbad's chair. Sinbad said nothing.

—It's not Adidas. It's Ad-dee-das.

—It's not. It's Adidas.

—It isn't. It's eee.

—i.

—eee.

—i.

—Spa-face; it's eeeeeeee.

—i i i i i i i.

None of us had Adidas football boots. We were all getting them for Christmas. I wanted the ones with the screw-on studs. I put that in my letter to Santy but I didn't believe in him. I only wrote to him because my ma told me to, because Sinbad was writing to him. Sinbad wanted a sleigh. Ma was helping him to write his letter. Mine was finished. It was in the envelope but she wouldn't let me lick the flap yet because Sinbad's letter had to go in as well. It wasn't fair. I wanted an envelope of my own.

—Stop whinging, she said.

—I'm not whinging.

—Yes, you are; stop it.

I wasn't whinging. Putting two letters in one envelope was stupid. Santy would think it was only one letter and he'd just bring Sinbad's present and not mine. I didn't believe in him anyway. Only kids believed in him. If she said I was whinging again I'd say that, and then she'd have to spend all day making Sinbad believe in him again.

—I don't know if Santy brings sleighs to Ireland, she told Sinbad.

—Why doesn't he?

—Because there's hardly ever any snow, she said. —You wouldn't get a chance to use it.

—There's snow in winter, said Sinbad.

—Only sometimes.

—Up the mountains.

—That's miles away, she said. —Miles.

—In the car.

She didn't lose her temper. I stopped waiting. I went into the kitchen. If you held an envelope over the steam coming

31

out of a kettle you could open it, and close it again without anyone knowing. I needed a chair to plug in the kettle. I checked to make sure that there was enough water in it, over the element. I didn't just lift it up and weigh it; I took the lid off and looked in. I got off the chair and put it back. I didn't need the chair any more.

I went back to the living room. Sinbad still wanted the sleigh.

—He should bring you what you want, he said.

—He does, love, said my ma.

—Then –

—But he doesn't want you to be disappointed, she said. — He wants to give the children presents that they'll be able to play with all the time.

Her voice hadn't changed; she wasn't going to bully him.

I went back to the kitchen. I took my letter out of the envelope and put it on the table, well away from the round wet mark that the milk bottle had left. I licked the gummy part of the flap and stuck it down. I pressed hard. The steam was coming out of the kettle spout now. I waited. I wanted the gum to be dry. More steam; it was singing out now. I held the envelope enough into the steam so I wouldn't scald my fingers. It was too close; the envelope was getting wet. I raised my hand. I brought the envelope over and across the steam. Not for too long; the envelope was beginning to droop, like it was going asleep. I got the chair and pulled the plug out and put it back right beside the tea caddy where it had been before I'd plugged it in. There were Japanese birds on the caddy with their tails all tied together and in their mouths. The envelope was soggy, a bit. I brought it out into the back garden. I got my thumb nail in under the flap. A little bit lifted. I held it up. It had worked. I pressed the gum bit. It was still sticky. It worked. I went back in; it was cold and windy and getting dark. I wasn't afraid of the dark, only

32

when it was windy as well. I put my letter back in the envelope.

Sinbad was finishing his letter.

—L.e.g.o., my ma was spelling it for him.

He was no good at joining the letters. She let me put his letter into the envelope. I folded it separate and slid it in beside mine.

When my da came home from work he stuck the letter up the chimney. He was crouched over; he was making sure we couldn't see properly.

—Did you get that letter, Santa?

He yelled it up the chimney.

—Yes, indeed, he said in a deep voice that was supposed to be Santy's.

I looked at Sinbad. He believed it was Santy talking. He looked at my ma. I didn't.

—Will you be able to manage all those presents? my da yelled up the chimney.

—We'll see, he said back. —Most of them. Bye bye now. I've other houses to visit. Bye bye.

—Say bye bye to Santa, lads, said my ma.

Sinbad said bye bye and I had to as well. My da got back from the chimney so we could say it properly.

My hot water bottle was red, Manchester United's colour. Sinbad's was green. I loved the smell off the bottle. I put hot water in it and emptied it and smelled it; I put my nose to the hole, nearly in it. Lovely. You didn't just fill it with water – my ma showed me; you had to lie the bottle on its side and slowly pour the water in or else air got trapped and the rubber rotted and burst. I jumped on Sinbad's bottle. Nothing happened. I didn't do it again. Sometimes when nothing happened it was really getting ready to happen.

*

33

Liam and Aidan's house was darker than ours, the inside. That was because of the sun, not because it was scruffy dirty. It wasn't dirty, the way a lot of people said it was; it was just that all the chairs and things were bursting and falling apart. Messing on the sofa was great because it was full of hollows, and nobody ever told us to get off it. We got up on the arm, onto the back and jumped. Two of us would get onto the back and have a duel.

I liked their house. It was better for playing in. All the doors were open; there was nowhere we couldn't go into. Once, we were playing hide and seek and Mister O'Connell came into the kitchen and opened the press beside the cooker and I was in there. He took out a bag of biscuits and then he closed the door real quietly; he said nothing. Then he opened the door again and whispered did I want a biscuit.

They were broken biscuits, a brown bag of them; there was nothing wrong with them except that they were broken. My ma never bought them.

Some of the boys in school had mothers that worked in Cadbury's. Mine or Kevin's didn't and Aidan and Liam's ma was dead. Ian McEvoy's ma did; not all year, before Easter and Christmas. Sometimes Ian McEvoy had an Easter egg for his lunch; the chocolate was perfect, just the egg was the wrong shape. My ma said that Missis McEvoy only worked in Cadbury's because she had to.

I didn't understand.

—Your daddy has a better job than Ian's daddy, she said. Then she said, —Don't say anything to Ian, sure you won't.

The McEvoys lived on our road.

—My da has a better job than yours!

—He does not!

—He does so.

—He doesn't.

—He does.

34

—Prove it.

—Your ma only works in Cadbury's because she has to!

He didn't know what I meant. I didn't either, not really.

—Because she has to! Because she has to!

I gave him a shove. He shoved me back. I held onto the curtain with one of my hands and pushed him hard with the other one. One leg slipped off the back off the sofa and he fell. I won. I slid down into the sofa.

—Champi-on! Champi-on! Champi-on!

I liked sitting in the hollow, just back away from where the shape of the spring was. The material was great; it was like the designs had been left alone and the rest of the material had been cut with a little lawn mower. The designs, flowers, felt like stiff grass or the back of my head after I got a haircut. The material didn't have any colour but when the light was on you could see that the flowers used to be coloured. We all sat in it when we watched the television; there was loads of room and brilliant fights. Mister O'Connell never told us to get out or stay quiet.

The kitchen table was the same as ours but that was all. They had all different chairs; ours were all the same, wood with a red seat. Once when I called for Liam they were having their tea when I knocked on the kitchen door. Mister O'Connell shouted for me to come in. He was sitting at the side of the table, where me and Sinbad sat, not the end where my da sat. Aidan was sitting there. He got up and put on the kettle and he sat down again where my ma always sat.

I didn't like that.

He made the breakfasts and dinners and everything, Mister O'Connell did. They had crisps every lunch; all I ever had was sandwiches. I hardly ever ate them. I put them in the shelf under my desk; banana, ham, cheese, jam. Sometimes I ate one of them but I shoved the rest under the desk. I knew when it was getting too full in there when I saw the inkwell

35

beginning to bob, being lifted by the pile of sandwiches underneath it. I waited till Henno had gone out – he was always going out; he said he knew what we got up to when his back was turned so not to try anything, and we kind of believed him – and I got the bin from beside his desk and brought it down to my desk. I unloaded the packs of sandwiches. Everyone watched. Some of the sandwiches were in tinfoil, but the ones that weren't, that were just in plastic bags or the cover of the pan, they were brilliant, especially the ones near the back. Stuff was growing all over them, green and blue and yellow. Kevin dared James O'Keefe to eat one of them but he wouldn't.

—Chicken.

—You eat one.

—Got you first.

—I'll eat one if you eat one.

—Chicken.

I squeezed a tinfoil pack and it piled into one end and began to break through the foil. It was like in a film. Everyone wanted to look. Dermot Kelly fell off his desk and his head hit the seat. I got the bin back up to Henno's desk before he started screaming.

The bin was one of those straw ones, and it was full of old sandwiches. The smell of them crept through the room and got stronger and stronger, and it was only eleven o'clock in the morning: three hours to go.

Mister O'Connell made brilliant dinners. Chips and burgers; he didn't make them, he brought them home. All the way from town in the train, cos there was no chipper in Barrytown then.

—God love them, said my ma when my da told her about the smell of chips and vinegar that Mister O'Connell had brought with him onto the train.

He made them mash. He shovelled out the middle of the

36

mountain till it was like a volcano and then he dropped in a big lump of butter, and covered it up. He did that to every plate. He made them rasher sandwiches. He gave them a can of Ambrosia Creamed Rice each and he let them eat it out of the can. They never got salad.

Sinbad ate nothing. All he ever ate was bread and jam. My ma tried to make him eat his dinner; she said she wouldn't let him leave the table till he was finished. My da lost his temper and shouted at him.

—Don't shout at him, Paddy, my ma said to my da, not to us; we weren't supposed to hear it.

—He's provoking me, said my da.

—You'll only make it worse, she said, louder now.

—You have him spoiled; that's the problem.

He stood up.

—I'm going in now to read my paper. And if that plate isn't empty when I come back I'll let you have what for.

Sinbad was scrunched up in his chair looking at the plate, staring at the food to go away.

My ma went after my da to talk to him more. I helped Sinbad eat his dinner. He kept dropping it out of his mouth onto the plate and the table.

He made Sinbad sit there for an hour until he was ready to inspect the plate. It was empty; in me and in the bin.

—That's more like it, said my da.

Sinbad went to bed.

He was like that, our da. He'd be mean now and again, really mean for no reason. He wouldn't let us watch the television and the next minute he'd be sitting on the floor beside us watching it with us, never for long though. He was always busy. He said. But he mostly sat in his chair.

I polished everything in the house on Sunday mornings before we went to mass. My ma gave me a cloth, usually part of a pair of old pyjamas. I started upstairs in their bedroom. I polished the dressing table and straightened her brushes. I wiped the top of the headrest. There was always loads of dust up there. It always left a mark on the cloth. I wiped as much of the picture of Jesus with his heart showing as I could reach. Jesus had his head tilted sideways, a bit like a kitten. The picture had my ma and da's names and the date they got married – the twenty-fifth of July, nineteen fifty-seven – and the dates of all our birthdays, except my youngest sister that my ma was only after having. The names were written in by Father Moloney. My name was the first; Patrick Joseph. Then my sister that had died; Angela Mary. She was dead before she came out of my ma. Then Sinbad; Francis David. Then my sister; Catherine Angela. There was a place left for my new sister. Her name was Deirdre. I was the oldest; the same name as my da. There was room for six more names. I wiped the stairs, all the way down, including the rails. I cleaned all the ornaments in the drawing room. I never broke anything. There was an old music box; you turned a key at the back and it played a song. There was a picture of sailors at the front. The felt material at the back was wearing away. It was my ma's. I didn't do the kitchen.

Aidan and Liam's auntie, the one that lived in Raheny, she cleaned their house. Sometimes they stayed with her. She had three children but they were much older than Aidan and Liam. Her husband cut the grass for the Corporation. He did the verges on our road twice a year. He had a huge red nose like a sponge with little lumps growing all over it. Liam said it looked even better close up.

—Do you remember your ma? I asked him.

—Yeah.

—What?

He said nothing. He just breathed.

His auntie was nice. She walked from side to side. She said God the cold or God the heat, depending on what the weather was like. When she walked across the kitchen she went Tea tea tea tea tea. When she heard the Angelus at six o'clock she'd go into the television and all the way she'd be saying The News the News the News the News. She had big veins like roots curling up the side and the back of her legs. She made biscuits, huge big slabs; they were gorgeous, even when they were stale.

They had another auntie that wasn't really their auntie. That was what Kevin told us anyway; he heard his ma and da talking about it. She was Mister O'Connell's girlfriend, although she wasn't a girl at all; she'd been a woman for ages. Her name was Margaret and Aidan liked her and Liam didn't. She always gave them a packet of Clarnico Iced Caramels when she came to the house and she made sure that the white and pink ones were divided evenly between them, even though they tasted the same. She made stew and apple crumble. Liam said she farted once when he was sitting beside her, during The Fugitive.

—Ladies can't fart.

—They can so.

—No, they can't; prove it.

—My granny always farts, said Ian McEvoy.

—Old ones can; not young ones.

—Margaret's old, said Liam.

—Beans beans good for the heart!

The more you eat the more you fart!

She fell asleep once in their house. Liam thought she was falling against him – they were watching the television – but she was only leaning. She snored. Mister O'Connell held her nose and she snorted and stopped.

During the holidays, after Christmas Day, Liam and Aidan went to Raheny to their real auntie's and we didn't see them for ages. It was because Margaret had moved into the house with Mister O'Connell. They had an empty bedroom in their house. Their house was the exact same shape as ours; Liam and Aidan had the same bedroom and they'd no sisters so there was one room left over. She was in that one.

—No, she isn't, said Kevin.

Liam and Aidan's auntie, the real one, had taken them away. She'd gone to their house in the middle of the night. She had a letter from the Guards saying that she could take them, because Margaret was staying in the house and she shouldn't have been. That was what we all heard. I made up a bit; she'd put Liam and Aidan into the back of their uncle's Corporation lorry. It was great hearing that after I'd thought it up. I believed the rest of it though.

Their uncle had given us a go on the back of the lorry once. But he made us get off because we kept standing up and he said it was dangerous and he wasn't insured if one of us fell off and smacked our heads off the road.

We walked to Raheny. It took a long time because there was no one looking after the E.S.B. pylon depot so we climbed in and had a mess. There were all pyramids of poles in there, for the wires, and a smell of tar. We tried to break the lock of the shed but we couldn't. We didn't really want to break it; we were just pretending we did, me and Kevin. We were going to Liam and Aidan's auntie's.

We got there. She lived in one of the cottages near the police station.

—Are Liam and Aidan coming out? I asked.

She'd answered the door.

—They're out already, she said. —So they are. Down at the pond. They're breaking the ice for the ducks.

We went up to St Anne's. They weren't at the pond. They were up in a tree. Liam was way up it, up where the wood was bendy; he was shaking it like mad. Aidan couldn't get up as far as him.

—Hey! said Kevin.

Liam kept swinging the tree.

—Hey!

Liam stopped.

They didn't come down. We didn't go up.

—Why are you living with your auntie and not your da? Kevin said.

They said nothing.

—Why are yeh?

We left, across the gaelic pitch. I turned. I could hardly see them in the tree. They were waiting for us not to be there. I looked for stones. There weren't any.

—We know why!

I said it as well.

—We know why!

—Brendan Brendan look at me!

   I have got a hairy gee!

Mister O'Connell's name was Brendan.

—Brendan Brendan look at me!

   I have got a hairy gee!

—Mind you, I heard my da saying to my ma, —when was the last time we heard him howling at the moon?

Margaret was coming up from the shops. We were waiting, behind Kevin's hedge. We heard her steps; we could see the colour of her coat, bits of it through the hedge.

—Brendan Brendan look at me!

   I have got a hairy gee!

   Brendan Brendan look at me!

   I have got a hairy gee!

I wanted a drink of water. I didn't want it from the bathroom. I wanted it from the kitchen. It was dark on the landing after the night-light in the bedroom. I felt for the stairs.

I was down three steps before I heard them. People were talking, kind of shouting. I stopped. It was cold.

In the kitchen, that was where they were. Burglars. I'd get my da. He was in bed.

But the television was on.

I sat down for a bit. It was cold.

The television was on; that meant my ma and da weren't in bed. They were still downstairs. It wasn't burglars in the kitchen.

The kitchen door wasn't closed; the light from there was cutting across the stairs just below me. I couldn't make out what they were saying.

—Stop.

I only whispered it.

For a while I thought it was only Da, shouting in the way people did when they were trying not to, but sometimes forgot; a bit like screamed whispers.

My teeth chattered. I let them. I liked it when they did that.

But Ma was shouting as well. I could feel Da's voice but I could only hear hers. They were having another of their fights.

—What about you!?

She said that, the only thing I could hear properly.

I did it again.

—Stop.

There was a gap. It had worked; I'd forced them to stop. Da came out and went in to the television. I knew the weight of his steps and the time between them, then I saw him.

They didn't slam any doors: it was over.

I stayed there for ages.

I heard Ma doing things in the kitchen.

If your pony was healthy his skin was loose and flexible and if he was sick his skin was tight and hard. The television was

42

invented by John Logie Baird in 1926. He was from Scotland. The clouds that had rain in them were usually called nimbostratus. The capital of San Marino was San Marino. Jesse Owens won four gold medals in the 1936 Olympics and Hitler hated black men and the Olympics were in Berlin that year and Jesse Owens was a black man and Berlin was the capital of Germany. I knew all these things. I read them all. I read under the blankets with my torch, not only after I'd gone to bed; it was more exciting that way, like I was spying and might get caught.

I did my eccer in braille. It took ages, being careful not to rip the page with the needle. There were all little dots on the kitchen table when I was finished. I showed the braille to my da.

—What's this?

—Braille. Blind people's writing.

He closed his eyes and felt the bumps on the page.

—What does it say? he asked.

—It's my English homework, I told him. —Fifteen lines about your favourite pet.

—Is the teacher blind?

—No. I was just doing it. I did it properly as well.

Henno would have killed me if I'd brought in just the braille.

—You don't have a pet, said my da.

—We could make it up.

—What did you pick?

—Dog.

He held the page up and looked at the light through the holes. I'd done that already.

—Good man, he said.

He felt the bumps again. He closed his eyes.

—I can't tell the difference, he said. —Can you?

—No.

43

—When you don't have your sight your other senses take over; that's it, I'd say, is it?

—Yes. Braille was invented by Louis Braille in 1836.

—Is that right?

—Yes. He was blinded in a childhood accident and he was from France.

—And he named it after himself.

—Yes.

I tried. I tried to get my fingers to read. I knew what was on the page already. I got in under the blankets and I didn't turn on the torch. I touched the page lightly: just bumps, pimples. My favourite pet is a dog. That was how my fifteen lines started. But I couldn't read the braille. I couldn't separate the dots, where each letter started and ended.

I tried to be blind. I kept opening my eyes. I tied a blindfold around my head but I couldn't do a good knot and I didn't want to tell anyone what I was doing. I told myself that I'd put my finger on the bar of the electric heater for every time I opened my eyes, but I knew I wouldn't so I kept opening my eyes. I'd done that once, because Kevin told me to, put my finger on the bar of the heater. There was a striped mark for weeks after it and I kept smelling my finger burning.

The life expectancy of a mouse is eighteen months.

My ma screamed.

I couldn't move. I couldn't go and see.

She'd gone into the toilet and found a mouse running round and around inside the toilet bowl. Da was home. He flushed the toilet and the water went over the mouse's body because it was in close to the rim. He stuck his foot into the bowl and knocked the mouse into the water. I wanted to see now; I knew why she'd screamed. There was no room. The mouse was swimming and trying to get up the side and my da had to wait till the cistern filled up again.

44

—Oh Jesus, Jesus, said my ma. —Will it die, Paddy?

Da didn't answer. He was counting the seconds till the water stopped hissing into the cistern; I could see his lips.

—The life expectancy of a mouse is about eighteen months, I told them.

I'd just read it.

—Not in this house, said my da.

My ma nearly laughed; she patted my head.

—Can I see?

She got out of my way, then stopped.

—Let him, said my da.

The mouse would have been a good swimmer but he wasn't trying to swim properly. He was trying to run out of the water.

—Cheerio, said da, and he flushed the toilet.

—Can I keep him? I said.

I'd just thought of it. My favourite pet.

The mouse went round and further down into the water and he went backwards out of the bowl, down the pipe. Sinbad wanted to see.

—He'll come out at the seafront, I said.

Sinbad looked at the water.

—He'll be happier there, said my ma. —It's more natural.

—Can I get a mouse? I asked.

—No, said Da.

—For my birthday?

—No.

—Christmas?

—No.

—They frighten the reindeer, said Ma. —Come on now.

She was making us get out of the toilet. We were waiting for the mouse to come back up.

—What? said Da.

—Mice, said Ma. —They frighten the reindeer.

45

She nodded at Sinbad.

—That's right, said Da.

—Come on, lads, she said.

—I want to go, said Sinbad.

—The mouse'll get you, I told him.

—Number ones, said Sinbad. —Standing up; so there.

—He'll bite you in the mickey, I said.

Ma and Da were going down the stairs.

Sinbad stood too far back and he wet the seat and floor.

—Francis didn't lift the seat! I shouted.

—I did so.

He whacked the seat off the cistern.

—He only did it now, I said, —when I said it.

They didn't come back up. I kicked Sinbad when he was wiping the seat with his sleeve.

—If the world's moving why aren't we moving as well? said Kevin.

We were lying in the long grass on a flattened box, looking up. The grass was real wet. I knew the answer but I didn't say it. Kevin knew the answer; that was why he'd asked the question. I knew that. I could tell by his voice. I never answered Kevin's questions. I never rushed with an answer, in school or anywhere; I always gave him a chance to answer first.

The best story I ever read was about Father Damien and the lepers. Father Damien was this man and he was called Joseph de Veuster before he became a priest. He was born in 1840 in a place called Tremeloo in Belgium.

I needed some lepers.

When he was a small boy they all called him Jef and he was chubby. All the grown-ups drank dark Flemish beer.

46

Joseph wanted to become a priest but his father wouldn't let him. Then he did.

—How much do priests get paid? I asked.

—Too much, said my da.

—Shhhsh, Paddy, said my ma to my da. —They don't get paid anything, she told me.

—Why not?

—It's hard to – she started. —It's very complicated. They have a vocation.

—What's that?

Joseph joined a bunch of priests called the Congregation of the Sacred Hearts of Jesus and Mary. The priest that had started them up had had a life filled with narrow escapes and thrilling adventure during the French Revolution. He'd lived under the shadow of the guillotine itself. Joseph had to get a new name and he called himself Damien after a man called Damien who was a martyr when the Church was young. He was Brother Damien before he became Father Damien. He went to Hawaii. On the way there the captain of the ship played a trick on him. He got his telescope and he put a hair across the lens and he got Father Damien to look into it and he told him that it was the Equator. Father Damien believed him but that didn't make him an eejit because they didn't know about those kinds of things in those days. Father Damien had to make hosts for Holy Communion out of flour on the ship because they'd run out of paper hosts. He didn't get seasick. He found his sea legs nearly immediately.

Vienna roll was the best for making hosts, when it was fresh. You didn't have to wet it. Batch wasn't bad either but ordinary sliced bread was useless. It kept springing back up. It was hard to tear the hosts into perfect round shapes. I used a penny from my ma's purse. I told my ma I was taking it in case she saw me. I pressed the penny real hard into the flat bread and sometimes the shape came up with the penny. My hosts tasted nicer than the real ones. I left them on the windowsill for two days and they got hard like the real ones but they didn't taste nice any more. I wondered was it a sin for me to be making them. I didn't think so. One of the hosts on the windowsill went mouldy; that was a sin, letting that happen. I said one Hail Mary and four Our Fathers, because I preferred the Our Fathers to the Hail Mary and it was longer and better. I said them to myself in the shed in the dark.

—Corpus Christi.

—Amen, said Sinbad.

—Close your eyes, I said.

He did.

—Corpus Christi.

—Amen.

He lifted his head and stuck out his tongue. I gave him the mouldy one.

—How do the priests make hosts? I asked my ma.

—Flour, said my ma. —It's just bread until it's blessed.

—Not real bread.

—A different kind of bread, she said. —It's unleavened bread.

—What's that?

—I don't know.

I didn't believe her.

The real good part of the story started when Father Damien went to the leper colony. Molokai was the name of it. It was where all the lepers were put so they couldn't give it to anyone else. Father Damien knew what he was doing; he knew that he was going there forever. A strange expression burned on Father Damien's face when he told the bishop he wanted to go there. The bishop was pleased and edified by the bravery of his young missionary. The little church on Molokai was run-down and neglected but Father Damien fixed it up. He broke a branch from a tree and used it as a broom and began to sweep the floor of the tiny chapel. He put flowers in it. The lepers that were hanging around watching him just kept watching him for ages. He was a big healthy man and they were only lepers. After the first day the lepers still hadn't started to help him. When he went to bed he could hear the lepers moaning in the dark and the surf booming on the barren shore. Belgium had never seemed so far away. After a while the lepers started helping him. He became friends with them. They called him Kamiano.

—Are there any lepers in Ireland?

—No.

—Any?

—No.

Father Damien built a better church and houses and did loads of other things – he showed them all how to grow vegetables – and he knew all the time that he was going to catch the leprosy as well, but he didn't mind. His greatest happiness was to see his children, the boys and girls whom he had taken under his care. Each day he spent several hours with them.

Bits of the lepers fell off. That was what happened them. Did you hear about the leper cowboy? He threw his leg over his horse. Did you hear about the leper gambler? He threw in his hand.

One evening in December 1884 Father Damien put his aching feet into some water to ease the pain. He got red blisters all over his feet; the water was boiling but his feet were numb. He knew he had leprosy. —I can't bear to tell you but it's true, said the doctor sadly. But Father Damien didn't mind. —I have leprosy, he said. —Blessed be the Good God!

—Blessed be the Good God, I said.

My da started laughing.

—Where did you get that from? he said.

49

—I read it, I told him. —Father Damien said it.

—Which one's he?

—Father Damien and the lepers.

—Oh, that's right. He was a good man.

—Were there ever any lepers in Ireland?

—I don't think so.

—Why not?

—It only happens in hot places. I think.

—It's hot here sometimes, I said.

—Not that hot.

—Yes it is.

—Not hot enough, said my da. —It has to be very very hot.

—How much hotter than here?

—Fifteen degrees, said my da.

There was no cure for leprosy. He didn't tell his mother when he was writing to her. But the news got out. People sent money to Father Damien and he built another church with it. It was made of stone. The church is still standing and may be seen by travellers to Molokai today. Father Damien told his children that he was dying and that the nuns would take care of them from then on. They clung to his feet and said, —No, no, Kamiano! We want to stay as long as you are here. The nuns had to go back empty-handed.

—Do it again.

Sinbad grabbed my legs.

—No, no, Kam – Kam –

—Kamiano!

—I can't remember it.

—Kamiano.

—Can I not just say Patrick?

—No, I said. Do it again and you'd better get it right.

—I don't want to.

I gave him half a Chinese torture. He grabbed my legs.

50

—Lower down.

—How?

—Lower.

—You'll kick me.

—I won't. I will if you don't.

Sinbad grabbed me around the ankles. He held me tight so my feet were stuck.

—No, no, Kamiano! We want to stay as long you are here.

—Okay, my children, I said. —You can stay.

—Thanks very much, Kamiano, said Sinbad.

He wouldn't let go of my feet.

Father Damien died on Palm Sunday. The people sat on the ground beating their breasts in old Hawaiian fashion, swaying back and forth and wailing sadly. The leprosy had gone off him; there were no scabs or anything. He was a saint. I read it twice.

I needed lepers. Sinbad wasn't enough. He kept running away. He told our ma that I was making him be a leper and he didn't want to be one. So I needed lepers. I couldn't tell Kevin because he'd have ended up being Father Damien and I'd have been a leper. It was my story. I got the McCarthy twins and Willy Hancock. They were four, the three of them. They thought it was great being with a big boy, me. I made them come into our back garden. I told them what lepers were. They wanted to be lepers.

—Can lepers swim? said Willy Hancock.

—Yeah, I said.

—We can't swim, said one of the McCarthys.

—Lepers can swim, said Willy Hancock.

—They don't have to swim, I said. —You don't have to swim. You only have to pretend you're lepers. It's easy. You just have to be a bit sick and wobble a bit.

They wobbled.

—Can they laugh?

—Yeah, I said. —They only have to lie down sometimes so I can mop their brows and say prayers on them.

—I'm a leper!

—I'm a leper! Wobble wobble wobble!

—Wobble wobble leper!

—Wobble wobble leper!

—Our Father who art in heaven hallowed by thy name –

—Wobble wobble wobble!

—Shut up a sec –

—Wobble wobble wobble.

They had to go home for their dinners. I heard them through the hedge on the path to their houses.

—I'm a leper! Wobble wobble wobble!

—I have a vocation, I told my ma, just in case Missis McCarthy came to the door about the twins, or Missis Hancock.

She was still cooking the dinner and stopping Catherine from climbing into the press under the sink with the polish and brushes in it.

—What's that, Patrick?

—I have a vocation, I said.

She picked up Catherine.

—Has someone been talking to you? she said.

It wasn't what I'd expected.

—No, I said. —I want to be a missionary.

—Good boy, she said, but not the way I'd wanted. I wanted her to cry. I wanted my da to shake my hand. I told him when he got home from his work.

—I have a vocation, I said.

—No you don't, he said. —You're too young.

—I do, I said. —God has spoken to me.

It was all wrong.

He spoke to my ma.

—I told you, he said.

52

He sounded angry.

—Encouraging this rubbish, he said.

—I didn't encourage it, she said.

—Yes, you bloody did, he said.

She looked like she was making her mind up.

—You did!

He roared it.

She went out of the kitchen, beginning to run. She tried to undo the knot of her apron. He went after her. He looked different, like he'd been caught doing something. They left me alone. I didn't know what had happened. I didn't know what I'd done.

They came back. They didn't say anything.

Snails and slugs were gastropods; they had stomach feet. I poured salt on a slug. I could see the torture and agony. I picked him up with the trowel and gave him a decent burial. The real name for soccer was association football. Association football was played with a round ball on a rectangular pitch by two sides of eleven people. The object is to score goals, i.e. force the ball into the opponents' goal, which is formed by two upright posts upon which is mounted a crossbar. I learned this off by heart. I liked it. It didn't sound like rules; it sounded cheeky. The biggest score ever was Arbroath 36, Bon Accord o. Joe Payne scored the most goals, ten of them, for Luton in 1936. Geronimo was the last of the renegade Apaches.

I held up the ball. We were on Barrytown Grove. It had good high kerbs for hopping the ball. The ball was a burst one.

—The object, I said, —is to score goals, i.e. force the ball into the opponents' goal which is – is formed by two upright posts upon which is mounted a crossbar.

They were bursting out laughing.

—Say it again.

I did. I put on a posh accent. They laughed again.

—Ger-on-IMO!

He was the last of the renegade Apaches. The last of the renegades.

—You're a renegade, Mister Clarke.

Hennessey sometimes called us renegades before he hit us.

—What are you?

—A renegade, Sir.

—Correct.

—Renegade!

—Renegade renegade renegade!

I had a picture of Geronimo. He was kneeling on one knee. His left elbow was resting on his left knee. He had a rifle. He had a scarf around his neck and a shirt with spots on it that I didn't notice for ages until I was sticking the picture on my wall. He had a bracelet that looked like a watch on his right wrist. Maybe he'd robbed it. Maybe he'd cut someone's arm off to get it. The rifle looked homemade. The best part was his face. He was looking straight into the camera, straight through it. He wasn't frightened of it; he didn't think it would take his soul, like some of them did. His hair was black, parted in the middle, straight down to his shoulders; no feathers or messing. He looked very old, his face, but the rest of him was young.

—Da?

—What?

—What age are you?

—Thirty-three.

—Geronimo was fifty-four, I told him.

—What? he said. —Always?

He was fifty-four when the photograph was taken. He might have been older. He looked fierce and sad. His mouth was upside-down, like a cartoon sad face. His eyes were

54

watery and black. His nose was big. I wondered why he was sad. Maybe he knew what was going to happen to him. The part of his leg in the photograph was like a girl's, no hair or bumps. He was wearing boots. There were bushes around him. I put my fingers on the hair to cover it. His face was like an old woman's. A sad old woman. I lifted my fingers. He was Geronimo again. It was only a black-and-white photograph. I coloured in his shirt; blue. It took ages.

I saw another picture in a book. Of Geronimo with his warriors. They were in a big field. Geronimo was in the middle, in a jacket and a stripey scarf. He still looked old and young. His shoulders looked old. His legs looked young.

None of the pictures in books were like the Indians in the films. There was one of the Snake and Sioux Indians on the warpath. The main fella in the picture had a pony tail and the rest of his head was bald, and shiny like an apple. He was riding hunched down sideways on his horse so that the others couldn't fire their arrows at him. The horse's eye was looking down at him; the horse looked scared. It was a painting. I liked it. There was another great one of an Indian killing a buffalo. The buffalo had its head in under the horse; the Indian would have to kill it quick or the buffalo would turn the horse over. Something about the way the Indian was on the horse, with his back up and his arm stretched, ready, with his spear, made me know that he was going to win. Anyway, the picture was called The Last of the Buffalo. There were other Indians on the edge of the picture chasing after more buffalo. The field was covered in buffalo skulls and there were dead buffalos lying all around. I couldn't put this one on my wall because it was from a library book. I went to the library in Baldoyle. I went with my da. One room was the grown-ups' and there was another room for children.

He was always interfering. He'd come into our part of the

library after he'd changed his books and he'd start picking
books for me. He never put them back properly.

—I read this one when I was your age.

I didn't want to know that.

I could take two books. He looked at the covers.

—The American Indians.

He took out the tag and slipped it into my library card. He
was always doing that as well. He looked at the other one.

—Daniel Boone, Hero. Good man.

I read in the car. I could do it and not get sick if I didn't
look up. Daniel Boone was one of the greatest of American
pioneers. But, like many other pioneers, he was not much of
a hand at writing. He carved something on a tree after he'd
killed a bear.

—D. Boone killa bar on this tree 1773.

His writing was far worse than mine, than Sinbad's even.
I'd never have spelled Bear wrong. And anyway as well, what
was a grown-up doing writing stuff on trees?

—DANIEL BOONE WAS A MAN
    WAS A BI-IG MAN
    BUT THE BEAR WAS BIGGER
    AND HE RAN LIKE A NIGGER
    UP A TREE –

There was a picture of him and he looked like a spa. He
was stopping an Indian from getting his wife and his son with
a hatchet. The Indian had spiky hair and he was wearing pink
curtains around his middle and nothing else. He was looking
up at Daniel Boone like he'd just got a terrible fright. Daniel
Boone was holding his wrist and he had his other arm in a
lock. The Indian didn't even come up to Daniel Boone's
shoulders. Daniel Boone was dressed in a green jacket with a
white collar and stringy bits hanging off the sleeves. He had a
fur hat with a red bobbin. He looked like one of the women
in the cake shop in Raheny. His dog was barking. His wife

56

looked like she was annoyed about the noise they were making. Her dress had come off her shoulders and her hair was black and went down to her bum. The dog had a collar on with a name tag on it. In the middle of the wilderness. I didn't like the Daniel Boone on the television either. He was too nice.

—Fess Parker, said my da. —What sort of a name is that?

I liked the Indians. I liked their weapons. I made an Apache flop-head club. It was a marble, a gullier, in a sock, and I nailed it to a stick. I stuck a feather in the sock. It whirred when I spun it and the feather fell out. I hit the wall with it and a bit chipped off. I should have thrown away the other sock. My ma gave out when she found the one I didn't use, by itself.

—It can't have gone far, she said. —Look under your bed.

I went upstairs and I looked under the bed even though I knew that the sock wasn't there and my ma hadn't followed me up. I was by myself and I got down and looked. I climbed in under. I found a soldier. A German World War One one with a spiky helmet.

I read William. I read all of them. There were thirty-four of them. I owned eight of them. The others were in the library. William The Pirate was the best. I say! gasped William. I've never seen such a clever dog. I say! he gasped, he's splendid. Hi, Toby! Toby! Come here, old chap! Toby was nothing loth. He was a jolly, friendly little dog. He ran up to William and played with him and growled at him and pretended to bite him and rolled over and over.

—Can I've a dog for my birthday?

—No.

—Christmas?

—No.

—Both together?

—No.

—Christmas and my birthday?

—You want me to hit you, is that it?

—No.

I asked my ma. She said the same. But when I said two Christmases and birthdays she said, —I'll see.

That was good enough.

William's gang was the Outlaws; him, Ginger, Douglas and Henry. It was Ginger's turn to push the pram and he seized it with a new vigour.

—Vigour, I said.

—Vigour!

—Vigour vigour vigour!

For a day we called ourselves the Vigour Tribe. We got one of Sinbad's markers and did big Vs on our chests, for Vigour. It was cold. The marker tickled. Big black Vs. From our diddies to our tummy buttons.

—Vigour!

Kevin threw the cap of Sinbad's marker down a shore, an old one on Barrytown Road with goo at the bottom. We went into Tootsie's shop and showed her our chests.

—One two three –

—Vigour!

She didn't notice or say anything. We ran out of the shop. Kevin drew a big mickey on Kiernan's pillar. We ran. We came back for Kevin to draw the drops coming out of the mickey. We ran again.

—Vigour!

The Kiernans were only Mister and Missis Kiernan.

—Did their children die? I asked my ma.

—No, she said. —No. They had no children.

—Why didn't they?

—Oh, God knows, Patrick.

—That's stupid, I said.

They weren't old. They both went to work, in his car. She

drove it as well. We got into their back when they were at work. It was a corner house; it was easy. The wall was higher because of the corner so we could stay in there for ages and no one would see us. The biggest risk was climbing out and that was brilliant. It was great being second; first was too scary. Your ma could have been walking by with the pram. You weren't allowed to look first; that was the rule. You had to climb straight and slide over the wall without looking to see if there was anyone there. We were never caught. Missis Kiernan's knickers were on the line once. I took the pole away and the line dropped closer to us. We grabbed Aidan. We hadn't said anything but we knew. We made him, we shoved his face into the knickers. He sounded like he was being sick.

—Lucky they're not dirty ones.

I put the pole back. We took turns. We ran, jumped and headed the knickers. It was brilliant. We did it for ages. We didn't take them down off the line.

My ma saw the V when we were having our bath on Saturday after tea. Me and Sinbad were in together. She always gave us five minutes to splash. She saw the V. It was nearly faded. Sinbad had one as well.

—What are they? she asked.

—Vs, I said.

—What are they doing there? she asked.

—We just did them, I said.

She made the face-cloth real soapy. She held my shoulder while she rubbed the V off. It hurt.

I was in Mister Fitz's shop getting a half block of ice-cream. It was Sunday. Ripple ice-cream. I was to tell Mister Fitz to put it on my ma's list. That meant she'd pay him on Friday. He wrapped the ice-cream in the paper he wrapped Vienna rolls in. He folded it up. It was already wet.

—There now, he said.

—Thanks very much, I said.

Missis Kiernan was at the door; she was coming in, her shape was in the door. My face went hot. She was going to see my face and catch me. She'd know.

I got past her. She was going to stop me, going to grab my shoulder. There were people; they were talking on the path. They had newspapers and cartons of cream. They were going to see. Kevin's ma and da were there. And girls. She was going to catch me and shout.

I crossed the road and went home the wrong side. She knew. Someone had told her. She definitely knew. She was waiting. She'd followed me into the shop to see if I'd go red. She'd seen it. My face was still red; I could feel it. Her hair was longer than my ma's. It was fatter as well, thicker. Brown. She never said Hello. She never walked to the shops. They always drove and their house was only a bit down the road. He was the only grown man in Barrytown with locks, and he had a moustache as well.

I looked back. Safe; she wasn't following. I crossed back to our side. She was lovely. She was gorgeous. She was wearing jeans on a Sunday. Maybe she was waiting, for the right moment to catch me.

I whisked the ice-cream with my spoon till it was soft. I made mountains on it. The ripple was gone. All the ice-cream had gone pink. I always used a small spoon; it made it last longer. My face went hot again, thinking, not as bad though as earlier. I could hear my blood. I could see me going to the door and Missis Kiernan would be there; she'd want to see my ma and she'd tell her about what I'd done to her knickers, and my da. I could hear the steps. I waited for the bell.

If the bell didn't ring by the time I'd finished all the ice-cream she wouldn't be coming. But I couldn't rush it. I had to eat it the slow way I always did, always the last one to finish. I was allowed to lick the bowl. The bell didn't ring at all. I felt like I'd done something; my mission had been accomplished. I waited till my face felt normal again. It was very quiet. I was the only one left at the table with them. I didn't look at them when I asked.

—Are you allowed to wear jeans on a Sunday?

—No, said my da.

—It depends, said my ma. —Not till after mass anyway.

—No, said my da.

My ma looked at him with a face, like the look she had when she caught us doing something; sadder, though.

—He doesn't have any jeans, she said. —He's just asking.

My da said nothing. My ma said nothing.

My ma read books. Mostly at night. She licked her finger when she was coming to the end of her page, then she turned the page; she pulled the corner up with her wet finger. In the mornings I found her book marker, a bit of newspaper, in the book and I counted back the number of pages she'd read the night before. The record was forty-two.

There was a smell of church off the desks in our school. When I folded my arms and put my head in the hollow, when Henno told us to go asleep, I could smell the same smell as you got off the seats in the church. I loved it. It was spicy and like the ground under a tree. I licked the desk but it just tasted horrible.

Ian McEvoy really went to sleep one day when Henno told us all to go to sleep. Henno was having a chat with Mister Arnold at the door and he told us to fold our arms and go to sleep. That was what always happened when Henno was talking to anyone or reading the paper. Mister Arnold had big locks that nearly met under his chin. He was on the Late Late Show once, singing a song and playing the guitar with another man and two ladies. I was allowed to stay up and watch him. One of the ladies played the guitar as well. She and Mister Arnold were on the outside and the other two were in the middle. They all had the same kind of shirts on but the men had cravats and the ladies didn't.

—He should stick to the day job, said my da.

My ma told him to shush.

James O'Keefe's foot tapped the seat of my desk. I shifted my arms so I could lift my head, and looked back at him quickly.

—Gee, he said. —Pass it on.

His head went back into his arms.

I slipped down in my seat so I could reach the seat of Ian McEvoy's desk. I tapped it. He didn't move. I did it again. I slipped down further and my foot went past the seat and I hit his leg. He didn't turn. I sat up properly again and waited, and turned to James O'Keefe.

—McEvoy's gone asleep.

James O'Keefe bit his jumper to stop himself from laughing. Someone in the class was in big trouble, and it wasn't him.

We all waited. We shushed each other so we wouldn't wake Ian McEvoy, even though we weren't making any noise anyway.

Henno closed the door.

—Sit up now.

We did, quickly; we sat up straight. We looked at Hennessey, to see when he'd see Ian.

We were doing spellings, English ones. Henno had his book out on the desk. He put all our scores and marks into the book and added them up on Fridays, and made us change our places. The best marks sat in the desks along the windows and the worst were put down the back beside the coats. I was usually in the middle somewhere, sometimes near the front. The ones at the back got the hardest spellings; instead of asking them, say, eleven threes, he'd ask them eleven elevens

62

or eleven twelves. If you got put into the last row after the marks were added up it was very hard to get out again, and you were never sent on messages.

—Mediterranean.

—M.e.d. –

—The easy part; continue.

—i.t. –

—Go on.

He was going to get it wrong; it was Liam. He usually sat behind me or in the row beside me nearer the coats, but he'd got ten out of ten in sums on Thursday so he was sitting in front of me, in front of Ian McEvoy. I only got six out of ten in the sums test because Richard Shiels wouldn't let me have a look in his copy, but I gave him a dead leg later for it.

—t.e.r. —— a. –

—Wrong. You're a worm. What are you?

—A worm, Sir.

—Correct, said Henno. —Urr-wronggg! he said when he was marking Liam's mistake into the book.

He didn't only make us change our places on Fridays; he biffed us as well. It gave him an appetite for his dinner, he told us. It gave his appetite an edge, and he needed that because he didn't like fish as a rule. One biff for every mistake. With the leather he soaked in vinegar during the summer holidays.

Kevin was next, then Ian McEvoy.

—M.e.d., said Kevin. —i.t.e.r.r.a.n –

—Yes?

—i.a.n.

—Urr-wrong! —— Mister McEvoy.

Ian McEvoy was still fast asleep. Kevin sat in the same desk as him and he told us later that Ian McEvoy was smiling in his sleep.

—Dreaming about a molly, said James O'Keefe.

Henno stood up and stared over Liam at Ian McEvoy.

—He's gone asleep, Sir, said Kevin. —Will I wake him up?

—No, said Henno.

Henno put his finger to his lips; we were to be quiet.

We giggled and shushed. Henno walked carefully down to Ian McEvoy's side of the desk; we watched him. He didn't look like he was joking.

—Mis-ter McEvoy!

It wasn't funny; we couldn't laugh. I felt the rush of air when Henno's hand swept through and smacked Ian McEvoy's neck. Ian McEvoy shot up and gasped. He groaned. I couldn't see him. I could see the side of Kevin's face. It was white; his bottom lip was out further than his top one.

Hennessey warned us about being sick on Fridays. If we weren't in school on Friday for our punishment he'd get us on Monday, no excuses.

All the desks smelt the same, in all the rooms. Sometimes the wood was lighter because the desk was near a window where the sun could get at it. They weren't the old-fashioned desks where the top was a lid on hinges that you lifted and there was a place for your books under it. The top was screwed down on our desks; there was a shelf in under it for books and bags. There was a hollow for your pens and a hole for the inkwell. You could roll your pen down the desk. We did it for a dare cos Henno hated the noise when he heard it.

James O'Keefe drank the ink.

When we had to stand up, when we were told to, we had to lift the seat back and we weren't allowed to make noise doing it. When there was a knock at the door, if it was a master coming in or Mister Finnucane, the headmaster, or Father Moloney, we had to stand up.

—*Dia duit,** we said.

* Hello / God be with you.

Henno just raised his hand like he was holding something on his palm and we all said it together.

There were two boys in each desk. When a boy in front of you got up to go to the blackboard or the *leithreas** you could see a red mark from the seat across the back of his legs.

I had to go down to my parents. Sinbad kept crying, bawling over and over like a train. He wouldn't stop.

—I'll burst you if you don't.

I didn't know how they hadn't heard it. The hall light was off. They were supposed to leave it on. I got to the bottom of the stairs. The lino at the hall door was freezing. I checked: Sinbad was still whining.

I loved getting him into trouble. This way was best. I could pretend I was helping.

They were watching a cowboy film. Da wasn't pretending to read the paper.

—Francis is crying.

Ma looked at Da.

—He won't stop.

They looked, and Ma stood up. It took her ages to get up straight.

—He's been doing it all night.

—Go on back up, Patrick; come on.

I went up ahead of her. I waited at the beginning of the real dark to make sure she was coming after me. I stood beside Sinbad's bed.

—Ma's coming, I told him.

It would have been better if it had been Da. She wasn't going to do anything to him. She'd talk to him, that was all, maybe hug him. I wasn't disappointed though. I didn't want to get him now. I was cold.

* Toilet.

65

—She's coming, I told him again.

I'd rescued him.

He made his whining go a bit louder, and Ma pushed the door open. I got into bed. There was still some of the warmth left from earlier.

Da wouldn't have done anything either; the same as Ma, he'd have done.

—Ah, what's wrong, Francis?

She didn't say it like What's wrong *this time*.

—I've a pain in my legs, Sinbad told her.

His rhythm was breaking down: she'd come.

—What sort of a pain?

—A bad one.

—In both your legs?

—Yeah.

—Two pains.

—Yeah.

She was rubbing his face, not his legs.

—Like the last time.

—Yeah.

—That's terrible; you poor thing.

Sinbad got a whimper out.

—That's you growing up, you know, she told him. —You'll be very tall.

I never got pains in my legs.

—Very tall. That'll be great, won't it? Great for robbing apples.

That was brilliant. We laughed.

—Is it going now? she asked him.

—I think so.

—Good. —— Tall and handsome. Very handsome. Lady-killers. Both of you.

When I opened my eyes again she was still there. Sinbad was asleep; I could hear him.

*

We all baled into the hall; threepence each to Mister Arnold and we were through. All the front seats were taken by the little kids from high babies and low babies and the other classes under us. It didn't matter cos when they turned the lights off we'd get up on our seats; it was better at the back. Sinbad was in there with his class, wearing his new glasses. One of the eyes was blacked, like Missis Byrne's on our road. Da said it was to give the other one a chance to catch up because it was lazy. We'd got Golly Bars on the way home from the place in town where Sinbad had got the glasses. We came home in the train. Sinbad told Ma that when he was a man he was going to get the first five pounds he ever earned and bring it in the train and pull the emergency cord and pay the fine.

—What job, Francis?

—Farmer, he told her.

—Farmers don't go in the train, I said.

—Why don't they? said Ma. —Of course they do.

Sinbad's glasses had wire bits that went right around the back of his ears and made them stick out, to stop him from losing them, but he lost them anyway.

Some Fridays we didn't have proper school after the little break; we went to the pictures instead, in the hall. We were warned on Thursdays to bring in threepence to get in, but Aidan and Liam forgot their threepences once and they still got in; they just had to wait till everyone else had gone in. We said that it was because Mister O'Connell didn't have sixpence to give them – I thought it up – but they brought in the money on Monday. Aidan cried when we kept saying it.

Henno was in charge of the projector. He thought he was great. He stood beside it like it was a Spitfire or something. The projector was on a table at the back of the hall, in the middle between the rows of seats. For a dare when the lights were turned off, we crawled out into the aisle and got up a bit and made shapes with our hands in the path of light that the projector made; the shape – usually a dog barking – would go up on the screen on the stage at the top of the hall. That was the easy part. The hard bit was getting back to your seat before they turned the lights back on. Everyone would try to stop you, to keep you trapped in the aisle. They'd kick you and stand on your hands when you were crawling under the seats. It was brilliant.

—Take out your English copies, said Henno.

We waited.

—*Anois.**

We took them out. All my copies were covered in wallpaper that our Auntie Muriel had left over when she was doing her bathroom and she gave my da about ten rolls of it.

—She must have thought she was going to be papering the Taj Mahal, he said.

—Ssh, said Ma.

I'd used a plastic stencil for the names. Patrick Clarke. Mister Hennessey. English. Keep Out.

—These rows, here and here, said Henno. —Bring your copies with you. *Seasaígí suas.***

When we got to the hall we gave our copies to Henno and he put them under the front legs of the projector so the picture would hit the screen bang on.

The teachers stood at the side and went Shh all through the films. They leaned against the wall in twos and threes and smoked, some of them. Only Miss Watkins patrolled around but she never caught anyone cos we would see her head on the screen when she was coming up the aisle.

—Get out of the way!

—Get out of the way!

If it was a sunny day outside we could see hardly anything

* Now.   ** Stand up.

68

on the screen because the curtains on the windows weren't thick enough. We cheered when a cloud got in the way of the sun and we cheered when the sun came back out. Sometimes we just heard the film. But it was easy to tell what was happening.

It always started with two or three Woody Woodpeckers. I could do Woody Woodpecker's voice.

—Stop that! a teacher would say.

—Shhh!

But they gave up early. By the time Woody Woodpecker was finished and The Three Stooges came on most of the teachers weren't in the hall any more, just Henno and Mister Arnold and Miss Watkins. My Woody Woodpecker hurt the back of my throat but it was worth it.

—I know that's you, Patrick Clarke.

We could see Miss Watkins squinting in at us but she couldn't see anything.

—Do it again.

I waited till she was looking straight at us, then I did it.

—WAA-CAH-CAH-CAH-CEHHH-CUH –

—Patrick Clarke!

—It wasn't me, Miss.

—It was the bird in the picture, Miss.

—Your head's in the way, Miss.

—Hey; you can see Miss's nits in the light!

She went down to Henno at the projector but he wouldn't stop it for her.

—WAA-CAH-CAH-CAH-CEHHH-CUH –

I loved The Three Stooges as well. Sometimes it was Laurel and Hardy but I preferred The Three Stooges. Some of the fellas called them The Three Stoogies but I knew it was Stooges because my da told me. We could never tell what the story was about in their films; there was too much noise and, anyway, all they ever did was beat each other up. Larry and

Moe and Curly, that was their names. Kevin poked my eyes the way the Stooges did it – we were in the field behind the shops, all of us – and I couldn't see for ages. I didn't know about that at first because of the pain; I couldn't open my eyes. It was like all the headaches I used to get; it was like the headaches you got when you ate ice-cream too fast; it was like being hit with a soft branch across the eyes. I had my hands covering my eyes and I wouldn't take them down. I was shaking the way my sister, Catherine, did when she'd been crying and bawling for ages. I didn't want to do it.

I didn't know I was screaming. They told me later. It had scared them, I could tell. The next time I got hurt, when I cut my shoulder on a nail on a goalpost, I screamed then as well. But, because I'd decided to do it, I thought it sounded stupid. I stopped and rolled on the ground, in the wet. My da went down to Kevin's house when he came home from work and Ma told him what had happened. I watched him from their bedroom window. When he came back he said nothing. Kevin didn't know what had happened between my da and his da. He'd expected to be killed, especially when he saw the shape of my da through the hall door glass. But nothing happened him. His da did nothing, and didn't even say anything to him. I told my da this when he was having his tea the day after; he didn't look surprised or anything.

I had two bloodshot eyes and one black one.

The best thing about The Three Stooges was that there were no breaks. For the main film Hennessey had to change the reel and spin back the old one. The picture would go white with little coloured explosions and the sound would go; we'd hear the film clacking around, hitting against the empty spool. It took ages to get going again.

They turned on the lights so Henno could see what he was doing. We got down off the seats in time. We played chicken; first down was a spa.

Once, during the main film, Fluke Cassidy took one of his epileptic fits and no one noticed. It was The Vikings. The sun was covered by the clouds outside so we saw the whole film. Fluke fell off his chair, but that happened all the time. It was a great film, easily the best I'd ever seen. We stamped the floor to make Henno hurry up when the first reel finished. Then we saw Fluke.

—Sir! Luke Cassidy's having a fit.

We all got far away from him in case we got the blame for it.

Fluke had stopped shaking – he'd knocked over three chairs and Mister Arnold had put his jacket over him.

—Maybe they won't finish the film, said Liam.

—Why won't they?

—Cos of Fluke.

Mister Arnold called for coats.

—Coats, lads; come on.

—Let's look, said Kevin.

We went up two rows, and in, so we could get a proper look at Fluke. He only looked like he was asleep. He was whiter then normal.

—Give him room, lads.

Henno was with Mister Arnold now. They'd put four coats over Fluke. If they put one over his head that meant he was dead.

—Someone to go to Mister Finnucane.

Mister Finnucane was the headmaster.

—Sir!

—Sir!

—Sir, me!

—You. Henno chose Ian McEvoy. —Report what happened to Mister Finnucane. What happened?

—Luke Cassidy took a fit, Sir.

—Correct.

71

—D'you want us to carry him, Sir?

—OH YOU'RE ALL VERY QUIET IN THE BACK –
YOU'RE ALL VERY QUIET –

—Shut! – Up! —— Sit —— Down – .

—That's my place – !

—Shut! —— Up!

We were all sitting down. I turned to Kevin.

—Not a squeak, Mister Clarke, said Henno. —Face the screen. All of you.

Kevin's little brother, Simon, put his hand up. He was way up at the front.

—Yes; you with your hand up.

—Malachy O'Leary's after going toilet.

—Sit down.

—Number twos.

—Sit! —— Down!

The music in The Vikings was the best thing about it; it was brilliant. Any time there was a Viking boat coming home a fella on a cliff would see it and he'd blow the music through a huge horn and everyone would come out of their huts and run down to meet the boat. Whenever there was a battle they played the same music. It was brilliant; you remembered it for ever. In the end one of the main fellas was killed – I wasn't sure which one – and they put him in his boat and covered him in wood; they set fire to it and pushed the boat out. I started humming the music, slower; I knew it was going to happen in the film. And it did.

I killed a rat with a hurley. It was a fluke. I just swung the hurley. I didn't know for definite that the rat was going to be coming my way. I hoped he wouldn't. It was great though, the full feeling when the hurley smacked the rat's side and lifted him way up; perfect.

I whooped.

72

—D'yeh see that?

It was perfect. The rat lay there in the muck, twitching; there was stuff coming out of his mouth.

—Champi-on! Champi-on! Champi-on!

We crept up to him but I wanted to get there before the rest so I crept fast. He was still twitching.

—He's still twitching.

—He isn't. That's his nerves.

—The nerves die after the rest of him.

—Did you see the way I got him?

—I was waiting for him, said Kevin. —I'd've got him.

—I got him.

—What'll we do with him? said Edward Swanwick.

—Have a funeral.

—Yeahhh!

Edward Swanwick hadn't seen The Vikings; he didn't go to our school.

We were in Donnelly's yard, behind the barn. We'd have to smuggle the rat out.

—Why?

—It's their rat.

Questions like that spoiled everything.

Uncle Eddie was in front of the house raking the gravel. Missis Donnelly was in the kitchen. Kevin went to the side of the barn and threw a stone in the hedge – a decoy – and looked.

—She's washing trousers.

—Uncle Eddie's dirtied his pants.

—Uncle Eddie did a gick and Mister Donnelly put it on his cabbages.

Two routes were blocked. We had to escape over the back wall, the way we'd got in.

No one had picked up the rat yet.

Sinbad was poking the stuff with his spear, the stuff that had come out of the rat's mouth.

—Pick him up, I told him, and I knew he wouldn't.

But he did. By the tail. He held him up and he let him twirl slowly.

—Give us him, said Liam, but he didn't put his hand out or try to take the rat off Sinbad.

He wasn't that big of a rat; his tail made him look bigger when he was on the ground but not the way Sinbad was holding him. I stood near Sinbad; he was my brother and he was holding a dead rat in his hand.

The tide was going out. That was good; the plank wouldn't keep coming back in. Sinbad had cleaned the rat. He'd put him on the ground under the pump at the cottages and he'd pumped four loads down on top of him. He wrapped the rat in his jumper with just his head showing.

Kevin was holding the end of the plank, trying to stop it from bobbing.

I started.

—Hail Mary, full of grace, the Lord is with thee –

It sounded great, five voices together and the wind. Kevin picked the plank out of the water; there was a wave coming.

—now and at the hour of our death amen.

I was the priest because I was useless with matches. My job was done. Edward Swanwick sat on the wet steps and held the plank for Kevin. Kevin turned his back to the sea and the wind and lit the match. He turned and saved the flame by the shield of his hand. I loved the way he could do that.

The flame lasted long enough. It was like a Christmas pudding for a while; I could see the fire but it wasn't doing anything to the rat. I could smell the paraffin. They pushed the plank out, not too strong like a battleship; we didn't want the fire to go out. The rat stayed on the plank. The fire was still going but the rat wasn't changing.

We all made trumpets out of our hands. Edward Swanwick
as well even though he didn't know what was happening.
—Now.
We all did The Vikings music.
—DUH DEEH DUH –
   DUH DEEEH DUH –
   DUH DEEEH DUH DUH – DUH DUH –
                        DUH DUH DUHHH –
The flame lasted long enough for us to do it twice.

I had a book on top of my head. I had to get up the stairs
without it falling off. If it fell off I would die. It was a
hardback book, heavy, the best kind for carrying on your
head. I couldn't remember which one it was. I knew all the
books in the house. I knew their shapes and smells. I knew
what pages would open if I held them with the spine on the
ground and let the sides drop. I knew all the books but I
couldn't remember the name of the one on my head. I'd find
out when I got to the top, touched my bedroom door and got
back down again. Then I could take it off my head – I'd bring
my head forward slowly and let it slide off and I'd catch it –
and see what it was. I could have seen the corner of the cover
if I'd looked up very carefully; I could have got the name
from the colour of the corner. But it was too dangerous. I
had a mission to complete. Steady was better than too slow.
If I went too slow I'd go all unsteady and I'd think I'd never
make it and the book would fall off. Death. There was a
bomb in the book. Steady was best, steps one two; no rush.
Rushing was as bad as too slow. You panicked towards the
end. Like Catherine walking across the living room. She
walked fine for four or five steps, then you could see her face
change because she saw that it was ages to go to the other
side; her smile became a stretch, she knew she wouldn't make
it, she tried to get there quicker, she fell. She knew she was

75

going to; her face got ready for it. She cried. Steady. Nearly at the top. The point of no return. Napoleon Solo. When you got to the top you had to get used to not having any more steps to go up; it was nearly like falling over.

The toilet door opened.

My da came out with his paper. He looked at me and past me.

He spoke.

—Monkey see, monkey do.

He was looking down, past me.

I turned my head. The book fell. I caught it. Our Man In Havana. Sinbad was on the stairs behind me with a book on his head. Ivanhoe. My book slid out of its cover and dropped onto the floor. I was dead.

Liam broke his teeth playing Grand National. It was no one's fault except his own. They were his second teeth, the ones he was supposed to have for the rest of his life. He split his lip as well.

—His lip's gone!

That was what it looked like when it happened. The blood and the way he was holding his hand up to his mouth made it look like his whole mouth had been cut off. All that stood out was one big front tooth that was made pink by blood. The pink gathered into red at the bottom of the tooth and fell off, into what was behind his hand.

His eyes looked mad. At first – when he came out of the hedge – they'd just looked like he'd been in the dark and the light had been turned on, but they'd changed; mad, scared and sticking out, pushing out over his eyelids.

Then he started howling.

His mouth didn't move, or his hand. The noise was just there. The eyes told me that it was his.

—Oh mammy – !

—Listen to him.

It was like someone doing a ghost but they weren't any good at it; they were trying to scare us but we knew; we didn't even start being scared. But this was scary; this was terrible. This was Liam right in front of us, not behind a curtain. He was making this noise but he wasn't pretending. His eyes said that; he couldn't do anything else.

If it had been ordinary, an ordinary accident, we'd have run; we'd have run before we were given the blame for it just because we were there. That always happened. A fella kicked a ball and it broke a window and ten fellas got the blame for it.

—I'm holding you all responsible.

That was what Missis Quigley'd said when Kevin had smashed her toilet window. She'd shouted over her high side wall at us. She couldn't see us but she knew who we were.

—I know who you are.

Mister Quigley was dead and Missis Quigley wasn't that old, so she must have done something to him; that was what everyone thought. We decided that she'd ground up a wine glass and put the powder in his omelette – I'd seen that in Hitchcock Presents and it made a lot of sense. Kevin told his da about it and his da said that she'd just bored Mister Quigley to death, but we stuck to our version; it was better. That didn't make us scared of her, though. She hated it when we sat on her wall. She knocked on her window to make us go, not always from the same window, sometimes upstairs, sometimes downstairs.

—That's just to let us think she isn't in the front room looking out all the time.

We weren't scared of her.

—She can't make us eat anything.

That was the only way she could get us, by poisoning us. She didn't know any other way. She wasn't small and wrinkly enough to be frightening. She was bigger than my ma. Big women – not big, fat ones – big women were normal. Little ones were dangerous; little women and big men.

She had no children.

—She ate them.

—No, she didn't!

That was going too far.

Kevin's brother knew why.

—Mister Quigley couldn't get his mickey to go hard.

We never went over the wall. I told my parents this when Missis Quigley complained to them about me. She'd never done anything before. They did their usual, made me stay in my bedroom till they were good and ready to deal with me. I hated it; it worked. They made me stay in there for hours. I had all my stuff in the room with me, my books and my cars and stuff, but I couldn't concentrate on the sentences in the books and it was stupid to be playing with my Dinkies when I was about to be hammered by my da – it was Saturday. I didn't want to be on the floor playing when he came in; I didn't want him to get the wrong idea. I wanted to look right. I wanted it to look like I'd already learnt my lesson. It was getting dark but I didn't go near the light switch. It was too near the door. I sat on the bed in the corner made by the walls. I shivered. I let my teeth chatter. My jaws went sore.

—Explain yourself.

It was a terrible question, a trap; everything I'd say was wrong.

—Explain yourself I said.

—I didn't do any –

—I'll decide that, said my da. —Go on.

—I didn't do anything.

—You must have.

—I didn't, I said.

There was a gap. He stared at my left eye, then my right one.

—I didn't, I said. —Honest.

—Then why did Missis Quigley come all the way down here –

It was only five doors.

—to complain about you?

—I don't know; it wasn't me.

—What wasn't you?

—What she said.

—What did she say?

—I don't know. I didn't do anything, I swear, Dad. Dad. Cross my heart and hope to die. Look.

I crossed my heart. I did it all the time; nothing ever happened and I was usually lying.

I wasn't lying this time, though. I hadn't done anything. It was Kevin who broke her window.

—She must have had a reason, said my da.

Things were going well. He wasn't in the right mood, when he wanted to hit me. He was being fair.

—She prob'ly thinks I did something, I said.

—But you didn't.

—Yeah.

—You say.

—Yeah.

—Say Yes.

—Yes.

That was the only thing my ma said. Say yes.

—I only –

I wasn't sure if this was right – wise – but it was too late to stop; I could tell from his face. My ma sat up when I started speaking and looked at my da. I thought about changing, and telling him about Missis Quigley poisoning Mister Quigley, but I didn't. My da wasn't like that; he didn't believe things.

—I only sat on the wall, I said.

He could have hit me then. He spoke.

—Well, don't sit on her wall. Again. Okay?

—Yeah.

—Yes, said my ma.

—Yes.

Nothing else; that was it. He looked around for something to do, to get away. He plugged in the record player. His back was turned; I could go. An innocent man. Wrongly convicted. Trained birds while I was in jail and became an expert on them.

Liam's howling stuck us to the grass; we couldn't move. I couldn't touch him or run away. The howl went into me; I was part of it. I was helpless. I couldn't even fall.

He was dying.

He had to be.

Somebody had to come.

The hedge he fell out of wasn't Missis Quigley's. It had nothing to do with Missis Quigley. It was the only really big hedge on our road. Liam and Aidan's was bigger and branchier but they didn't live on our road; they lived off it. This one grew quicker than the others, and it had smaller leaves that weren't as shiny or as green as normal. The leaves were nearly not green at all; the backs of them were grey. Most of the hedges weren't that big; the houses weren't old enough. Only this hedge; it was the last jump, we kept it till last.

The hedge was in the Hanleys' front garden. It was their hedge. It was Mister Hanley's. He did everything in the garden. They had a pond in their back, but with nothing in it. There used to be goldfish but they froze to death.

—He just left them in there till they rotted.

I didn't believe that.

—Floating.

I didn't believe it. Mister Hanley was always in his garden,

80

picking up things, bits of leaf, slugs – he picked them up with his hand; I saw him. His bare hands. He was always digging, leaning in near the wall. I saw a hand when I was going to the shops, Mister Hanley's hand, on the wall, holding himself up as he dug; only his hand. I tried to get past before he stood up, but I couldn't run – I could only walk fast. I wasn't trying not to let him see me; I wasn't scared of him; I just did it. He didn't know I was doing it. I once saw him lying down in the front garden, on his back. His feet were in the flower bed. I waited to see if he was dead; then I was afraid someone was looking at me through the window. When I came back Mister Hanley was gone. He didn't have a job.

—Why not?

—He's retired, said my ma.

—Why is he?

That was why he had the best garden in Barrytown and that was why invading the Hanleys' garden was the biggest dare of all. And that was why the Grand National ended there. Over the hedge, up, through the gate, the winner. Liam hadn't been winning.

In a way, winning was easiest. The winner was the first out onto the path. Mister Hanley couldn't get you there, or his sons, Billy and Laurence. It was the ones that came over the hedge last that were in the biggest danger. Mister Hanley just gave out and spits flew out of his mouth; there was always white stuff in the corners. A lot of old people had mouths like that. Billy Hanley and especially Laurence Hanley killed you if they got you.

—It's about time those two slobs went and got married or something.

—Who'd have them?

Laurence Hanley was fat but he was fast. He grabbed us by the hair. He was the only person I knew who did that. It was weird, a man grabbing people by the hair. He did it

81

because he was fat and he couldn't fight properly. He was evil as well. His fingers were stiff and like daggers, much worse than a punch. Four stabs on the side of your chest, while he was holding you up straight with your hair.

—Get out of our garden.

One more for good measure, then he let go.

—Now —— stay out!

Sometimes he kicked but he couldn't get his leg up far. He sweated through his trousers.

There were ten fences in the Grand National. All the walls of the front gardens were the same height, the exact same, but the hedges and the trees made them different. And the gardens between the fences, we had to charge across them; pushing was allowed in the gardens, but not pulling or tripping. It was mad; it was brilliant. We started in Ian McEvoy's garden, a straight line for us. There was no handicapping; no one was allowed to start in front of the rest. No one would have wanted it anyway, because you needed a good run at the first wall and no one was going to stand in the next garden alone, waiting for the race to start. It was Byrne's. Missis Byrne had a black lens in her glasses. Specky Three Eyes she was called, but that was the only funny thing about her.

It always took ages for the straight line to get really straight. There was always a bit of shoving; it was allowed, as long as the elbows didn't go up too far, over the neck.

—They're under starter's orders – , said Aidan.

We crept forward. Anyone caught behind the group when the race started could never win and would probably be the one caught by Laurence Hanley.

—They're off!

Aidan didn't do any more commentating after that.

The first fence was easy. McEvoy's wall into Byrne's. There was no hedge. You just had to make sure that you had enough room to swing your legs. Some of us could swing right over without our legs touching the top of the wall – I could – but you needed loads of space for that. Across Byrne's. Screaming and shouting. That was part of it. Trying to get the ones at the back caught. Off the grass, over the flower bed, across the path, over the wall – a hedge. Jump up on the wall, grip the hedge, stand up straight, jump over, down. Danger, danger. Murphy's. Loads of flowers. Kick some of them. Around the car. Hedge before the wall. Foot on the bumper, jump. Land on the hedge, roll. Our house. Around the car, no hedge, over the wall. No more screaming; no breath for it. Neck itchy from the hedge. Two more big hedges.

Once, Mister McLoughlin had been cutting the grass when we all came over the hedge, and he nearly had a heart attack.

Up onto Hanley's wall, hold the hedge. Legs straight; it was harder now, really tired. Jump the hedge, roll, up and out their gate.

Winner.

I looked over their heads.

—I MARRIED A WIFE – OH THEN – OH THEN –

I MARRIED A WIFE – OH THEN –

My auntie and my uncle and my four cousins were looking at me. They were sitting on the couch, and two of the cousins on the floor.

—I MARRIED A WIFE –

SHE'S THE PLAGUE OF MY LIFE –

I liked singing. Sometimes I didn't wait to be asked.

—OH I WISH I WAS SINGLE AGAIN-NNN –

We were in my auntie and uncle's house, in Cabra, but I didn't know where that was really. It was Sinbad's Holy Communion. One of my cousins wanted to see his prayer book but Sinbad wouldn't let go of it. I sang louder.

—I MARRIED ANOTHER – OH THEN – OH THEN –

My mother was getting ready to clap. Sinbad would get the money off my uncle; his hand was looking around in his pocket. I could see him. He straightened his leg so he could get his hand to the coins at the bottom.

My auntie had a hankie up her sleeve; I could see the bulge where it was. We had two more auntie's and uncle's houses to go to. Then we were going to the pictures.

—I MARRIED ANOTHER –
  AND SHE'S WORSER THAN THE OTHER –
  AND I WISH I WAS SINGLE AGAIN-NNN –

They all clapped. My uncle gave Sinbad two shillings, and we went.

When Indians died – Red ones – they went to the happy hunting ground. Vikings went to Valhalla when they died or they got killed. We went to heaven, unless we went to hell. You went to hell if you had a mortal sin on your soul when you died, even if you were on your way to confession when the lorry hit you. Before you got into heaven you usually had to go to Purgatory for a bit, to get rid of the sins on your soul, usually for a few million years. Purgatory was like hell but it didn't go on forever.

—There's a back door, lads.

It was about a million years for every venial sin, depending on the sin and if you'd done it before and promised that you wouldn't do it again. Telling lies to your parents, cursing, taking the Lord's name in vain – they were all a million years.

—Jesus.
—A million.
—Jesus.
—Two million.
—Jesus.
—Three million.

—Jesus.

Robbing stuff out of shops was worse; magazines were more serious than sweets. Four million years for Football Monthly, two million for Goal and Football Weekly. If you made a good confession right before you died you didn't have to go to Purgatory at all; you went straight up to heaven.

—Even if the fella killed loads of people?

—Even.

It wasn't fair.

—Ah, now; the same rules for everybody.

Heaven was supposed to be a great place but nobody knew much about it. There were many mansions.

—One each?

—Yes.

—Do you have to live by yourself?

Father Moloney didn't answer quickly enough.

—Can your ma not live with you?

—She can, of course.

Father Moloney came into our class on the first Wednesday of every month. For a chat. We liked him. He was nice. He had a limp and a brother in a showband.

—What happens to her mansion, Father?

Father Moloney raised his hands to hold our questions back. He laughed a lot and we didn't know why.

—In heaven, lads, he said, and waited. —In heaven you can live wherever and with whoever you like.

James O'Keefe was worried.

—Father, what if your ma doesn't want to live with you?

Father Moloney roared laughing but it wasn't funny, not really.

—Then you can go and live with her; it's quite simple.

—What if she doesn't want you to?

—She will want you to, said Father Moloney.

—She mightn't, said James O'Keefe. —If you're a messer.

—Ah there, you see, said Father Moloney. —There's your answer. There are no messers in heaven.

The weather was always nice in heaven and it was all grass, and it was always day, never night. But that was all I knew about it. My Granda Clarke was up there.

—Are you sure? I asked my ma.

—Yes, she said.

—Positive?

—Yes.

—Is he out of Purgatory already?

—Yes. He didn't have to go there because he made a good confession.

—He was lucky, wasn't he?

—Yes.

I was glad.

My sister was up there as well, the one that died; Angela. She died before she came out of my ma but they'd had time to baptise her, she said; otherwise she'd have ended up in Limbo.

—Are you sure the water hit her before she died? I asked my ma.

—Yes.

—Positive.

—Yes.

I wondered how she managed, a not-even-an-hour-old baby, by herself.

—Granda Clarke looks after her, said my ma.

—Till you go up?

—Yes.

Limbo was for babies that hadn't been baptised and pets. It was nice, like heaven, only God wasn't there. Jesus visited there sometimes, and Mary his mother as well. They had a caravan there. Cats and dogs and babies and guinea pigs and goldfish. Animals that weren't pets didn't go anywhere. They

86

just rotted and mixed in with the soil and made it better. They didn't have souls. Pets did. There were no animals in heaven, only horses and zebras and small monkeys.

I was singing again. My da was teaching me a new one.
   —I WENT DOWN TO THE RIVER
     TO WATCH THE FISH SWIM BY-YY –
I didn't like it.
   —BUT I GOT TO THE RIVER –
     SO LONESOME I WANTED TO DIE-EE-IE – OH LORD –
I couldn't get the DIE-EE-IE bit properly; I couldn't get my voice to go up and down the way Hank Williams on the record did.
I liked the next bit though.
   —THEN I JUMPED INTO THE RIVER
     BUT THE DOGGONE RIVER WAS DRY-YY –
   —Not bad, said my da.
It was Sunday, the afternoon, and he was bored. That was when he always taught me a new song. He came searching for me. The first time it had been Brian O'Linn. There was no record, just the words in a book called Irish Street Ballads. I followed Da's finger and we sang the words together.
   —BRIAN O'LINN – HIS WIFE AND WIFE'S MOTHER –
     THEY ALL LAY DOWN IN THE BED TOGETHER –
     THE SHEETS THEY WERE OLD AND THE BLANKETS WERE THIN –
     LIE CLOSE TO THE WAW-ALL SAYS BRIAN O'LINN –
It was all like that, funny and easy. I sang it in school and Miss Watkins stopped me after the verse about Brian O'Linn going a-courting because she thought it was going to get dirtier. It didn't but she didn't believe me.

I sang the last verse in the yard during the little break at eleven o'clock.

—It's not dirty, I warned them.

—Sing it anyway; go on.

—Okay, but –

—BRIAN O'LINN – HIS WIFE AND WIFE'S MOTHER –

They laughed.

—It's not –

—Shut up and keep singing.

—WERE ALL GOING HOME O'ER THE BRIDGE TOGETHER –

THE BRIDGE IT BROKE DOWN AND THEY ALL TUMBLED IN –

WE'LL GO HOME BE THE WATER SAYS BRIAN O'LINN –

—That's stupid, said Kevin.

—I know, I said. —I told you.

I didn't think it was stupid at all.

Henno came over and broke us all up because he thought there was a fight. He grabbed me and said that he knew I was one of the ringleaders and he was keeping an eye on me and then he let me go. He didn't have our class yet – that was the year after – so he didn't know me.

—You mind yourself, sonny, he said.

—SHE'S A LONG-HONG GOH-HON –

I couldn't do it; I didn't even know what Hank Williams was singing.

Da hit me.

On the shoulder; I was looking at him, about to tell him that I didn't want to sing this one; it was too hard. It was funny; I knew he was going to wallop me from the look on his face a few seconds before he did it. Then he looked as if he'd changed his mind, like he'd controlled himself, and then

I heard the thump and felt it, as if he'd forgotten to tell his hand not to keep going towards me.

He hadn't lifted the needle.

—A MAN NEEDS A WOMAN THAT HE CAN LEAN ON –

BUT MY LEANING POST IS DONE LE-HEFT AND GONE

I rubbed my shoulder through my jumper and shirt and vest; it was like it was expanding and shrinking, filling and shrinking. It wasn't that sore.

I didn't cry.

—Come on, said Da.

He lifted the needle this time, and we started again.

—I WENT DOWN TO THE RIVER

TO WATCH THE FISH SWIM BY-YY –

He put his hand on my shoulder, the other one. I wanted to squirm it away but after a while I didn't mind.

The record player was a red box. He'd carried it home from work one day. You could pile six records in it, over the turntable. We only had three; The Black and White Minstrels, South Pacific and Hank Williams The King of Country Music. When he brought the record player home we only had one, South Pacific. He played it all Friday night and all the weekend. He tried to make me learn I'm Gonna Wash That Man Right Out of My Hair but my ma stopped him. She said if I ever sang that in school or outside they'd have to sell the house and move somewhere else.

It played 33s and 45s and 78s. 33s were L.P.s like the three we had. Kevin smuggled his brother's record, I'm A Believer by The Monkees, out of his house. It was a 45. But my da wouldn't let us play it. He said there was a scratch on it; he didn't even look at it. He wasn't even using the record player. It was his. It was in the same room as the television. When he was playing it the television stayed off. He once put on the Black and White Minstrels at the same time they were on the television and he turned the television sound down but it didn't work. The singer's mouth, the black fella that sang the serious songs, was opening and shutting when the record was over and the needle was about to go up, but it didn't. It kept going over the scratch. Da had to lift it.

—Were you messing with this? he said to me.

—No.

—You then; were you?

—No, said Sinbad.

—Somebody was, he said.

—They didn't touch it, said my ma.

My face burned when I was waiting for something else to happen, for him to say something back to her.

Once, he put on Hank Williams during The News. It was brilliant; it was like Charles Mitchell was singing NOW YOU'RE LOOKING AT A MAN THAT'S GETTING KIND O' MAD, I'VE HAD A LOT O' LUCK BUT IT'S ALL BEEN BAD. We all roared. Me and Sinbad were let stay up half an hour later.

When we got the car, a Cortina like Henno's, a black one, Da drove it up and down the road, learning how to drive it, teaching himself. He wouldn't let us into it.

—Not yet, he said.

He went up to the seafront. We followed him; we could keep up with him. He couldn't turn it to go back down to the house. He saw us looking and called us over. I thought he was going to kill us. There were seven of us. We all baled in the back and we reversed all the way back to the house. Da sang the Batman music; he was mad sometimes, brilliant mad. Aidan had a bleeding nose when we got out. He was whinging. Da got down on his knees and held Aidan's

90

shoulders. He wiped his nose with his hankie and got him to blow into it, and told him he'd have great crack picking the dried blood out of his nose when he went to bed later and Aidan started laughing.

They all went down to the field behind the shops to find the big boys' hut and wreck it but I didn't go; I wanted to stay with Da. I sat beside him up and down the road. We went to Raheny. When he was turning he went right over the road and brushed the ditch.

—Stupid place to put a ditch, he said.

A fella honked at him.

—Bloody eejit, said my da, and he honked back when the fella was gone.

We came back to Barrytown along the main road and Da put the foot down. We rolled down our windows. I stuck my elbow out but he wouldn't let me. He parked outside on the verge two gates down from our house.

—That'll do us, he said.

Sinbad was in the back.

We went on a picnic the next day. It was raining but we went anyway; me and Sinbad in the back, my ma beside my da with Catherine on her knee. Deirdre wasn't born yet then. My ma's belly was all round, filling up with her. We went to Dollymount.

—Why not the mountains? I wanted to know.

—Stay quiet, Patrick, said my ma.

Da was getting ready to go from Barrytown Road onto the main road. We could have walked to Dollymount. We could see the island from where we were in the car. Da made it across and right. The Cortina jerked a bit and made a noise like when you pressed your lips together and blew. And something scraped when we went right in to the kerb.

—What's that sound from?

—Shhh, said Ma.

She wasn't enjoying herself; I could tell. She needed a decent day out.

—There's the mountains, I said.

I got between her seat and his seat and pointed out the mountains to them, across the bay, not that far.

—Look.

—Sit down!

Sinbad was on the floor.

—There's forests there.

—Stay quiet, Patrick.

—Sit down, you bloody eejit.

Dollymount was only a mile away. Maybe a bit more, but not much. You had to cross over to the island on a wooden bridge; the rest was boring.

—The toilet, said Sinbad.

—Jesus Christ!

—Pat, my ma said to my da.

—If we go to the mountains, I said, —he can go behind one of the trees.

—I'll swing you from one of the trees if you don't sit down out of my light!

—Your father's nervous –

—I'm not!

He was.

—I just want a bit of peace.

—The mountains are very peaceful.

Sinbad said that. The two of them laughed, Ma and Da in the front, especially Da.

We got there, Dollymount, but he had to drive past the bridge twice before he could slow down enough to turn onto it and not miss it and drive through the sea wall. It was still raining. He parked the car facing the sea. The tide was way out so we couldn't see it. Anyway, with the engine off the wipers weren't working. The best thing about it was the noise

of the rain on the roof. Ma had an idea; we could go home
and have the picnic there.

—No, said Da.

He held the wheel.

—We're here now, he said, —so –

He tapped the wheel.

Ma got the straw bag up from between her feet and dished
out the picnic.

—Don't get crumbs and muck all over the place, Da said.

He was talking to me and Sinbad.

We had to eat the sandwiches; there was no place to hide
them. They were nice; egg. They'd gone real flat; there were
no holes left in the bread. We had a can of Fanta between us,
me and Sinbad. Ma wouldn't let us open it. She had the
opener. She hooked it under the rim of the can and pressed
once for the triangular hole for drinking out of and again, for
the hole on the other side for the air to go into. After a few
slugs each I could feel little bits of food in the Fanta; I could
feel them when I was swallowing. The Fanta was warm.

Ma and Da said nothing. They had a flask with tea in it.
There was the cup off the top of the flask and a real cup that
Ma had wrapped in toilet paper. She held out the cups for Da
to hold so she could pour but he didn't take them off her. He
was looking straight in front of him at the rain milling down
the windscreen. She didn't say anything. She put one cup
down and filled it, over Catherine's head. She held it out; Da
took it. It was the big cup, the one off the flask. He sipped it,
then he said Thanks, like he didn't mean it.

—Can we get out?

—No.

—Why not?

—No.

—It's too wet, said Ma. —You'd catch your death out in
that.

93

Sinbad put his hand under his arm and slammed his arm shut. It made a fart noise. Margaret, Mister O'Connell's girlfriend, had taught us how to do it. Sinbad did it again.

—Once more – , said Da.

He didn't turn around.

—See what happens.

Sinbad put his hand under his arm again. I held his arm up so he couldn't slam it; I'd get the blame. He smiled at me trying to stop him. He never used to smile at all. Even when Da was taking photographs of us, Sinbad wouldn't smile. We had to stand side by side in front of our ma – it was always the same – and Da would walk away and turn around and look at us through the camera – it was one of those box ones; my ma bought it with her first wages before she got married, before she met my da – and he'd tell us to move a bit and then he'd take ages looking down into the camera and then up at us, and then he'd notice that Sinbad wasn't smiling.

—Smile now, he'd say, to all of us first.

Smiling was easy.

—Francis, he'd say, sounding ordinary.

—Head up; come on.

Ma would put her hand on Sinbad's shoulder and still try to hold one of the babies.

—God damn it; the sun's gone behind a cloud.

But Sinbad kept his head down. And Da lost his temper. All the photographs were the same, me and Ma smiling like mad and Sinbad looking down at the ground. We held the smile for so long, they weren't really smiles any more. When Ma swapped so Da could be in the photograph Da looked like he was really smiling and Sinbad's face disappeared completely he was looking down so much.

There were no photographs this day.

Ma had the biscuits wrapped in tinfoil for each of us. That way we didn't have to share and there were no fights. I could

94

tell from the shape of the foil what biscuits were inside; four Mariettas, two together like a sandwich with butter in the middle, and the square shape at the bottom was a Polo. I'd keep the Polo till last.

Ma said something to Da. I didn't hear it. I could tell by the look on the side of her face, she was waiting for him to answer. But it was more than that, her face.

You got the Mariettas and you squeezed them together and the butter came out the holes. We called them botty bickies sometimes, because of the way the butter came out, but Ma wouldn't let us call them that.

I took the Fanta off Sinbad. He let me. It was empty, and it shouldn't have been.

I looked at Ma again. She was still looking at Da. Catherine had one of Ma's fingers in her mouth and she was biting real hard – she had a few teeth – but Ma didn't do anything about it.

Sinbad was eating his biscuits the way he always did, and I did as well. He was nibbling all around the edge till he went all the way round and the Mariettas were the same shape again, only smaller. He licked where the butter had come out of the holes. When he got to the end of his first lap he stopped. I grabbed the hand the biscuit sandwich was in and I squashed his hand in my hands and made him smash the biscuits into crumbs that were too small to rescue. That was for drinking all the Fanta.

Ma was getting out of the car. It was awkward because of Catherine. I thought we were all getting out, that it had stopped raining.

But it hadn't. It was lashing.

Something had happened; something.

Ma left the door open; it closed back a bit but it was still open. Me and Sinbad waited for Da to move, to see what we were supposed to do. He leaned over and grabbed the passenger door handle and pulled the door shut. He grunted when he was straightening up.

Sinbad was licking his hand.

—Where's Ma gone to? I asked.

Da sighed, and turned a bit so I could see some of the side of his face. Then he didn't say anything. He was looking in the windshield mirror at us. I couldn't see his eyes. Sinbad had his head down, the way he used to. I rubbed the wet off the inside of the window beside me. I hadn't been going to touch it until we got home. I couldn't see anything, miles of the sand but not Ma. I was on the wrong side, behind Da.

—Has she gone for 99s?

I rubbed the window again.

The door clicked open. Ma got in, ducking her head, making sure that Catherine wasn't bashed against anything. Her hair was stuck down on her. She didn't have anything; she hadn't got us anything.

—It was too wet for Cathy, she said after a while, to Da.

He started the car.

—You're getting very tall, she said.

She was trying to get the zip of my trousers to close.

—You'll soon be the same size as your daddy.

I wanted that, to be the same size as my da. My name was the same as his one. I'd waited till he'd gone to work before I'd shown her that the zip wouldn't shut properly. He'd have shut it. I hoped she wouldn't be able to do it. I hated the trousers. They were yellow corduroy. One of my cousins had owned them first. They'd never been mine.

She hitched them up. She tried to hold the two sides together so the zip would go up. I didn't cheat. I even sucked in my belly.

—No, she said. —No use.

She let go of the trousers.

96

—They're finished, she said. —You're growing too fast, Patrick.

She didn't mean it.

—We'll have to use a safety pin, she said.

She saw my face.

—Just for today.

They were checking the B.C.G., that was what everyone said. Henno hadn't told us anything. He'd just said that we were to queue up and the first two in the queue were always to have their jumpers and shirts and vests off ready when the door opened or there'd be trouble. Only two had gone in and they hadn't come back out yet. He was supposed to be looking after us but he wasn't. He'd gone off, upstairs to the teachers' room for a cup of tea.

—I'll hear any noise, he said. —Don't worry.

He stamped his foot on the wooden floor. The noise bounced down the corridor. It took ages to die.

—There, he said. —Whispering is impossible in this school. I'll hear every little thing.

Then he went.

We heard him at the top of the stairs. He'd stopped.

Ian McEvoy made sure that the wall was guarding him, then he stamped his foot the way Henno had. The laughing was great, waiting to hear Henno coming back down. He didn't. We all stamped our feet. It must have been his shoes though; we couldn't get the same noise. But that was all we did; we didn't shout or mess.

They were checking the B.C.G. marks.

What'll they do if you don't have all of them?

You were supposed to have three of them.

—They'll give you more.

There was a triangle of them up on your left arm. The skin was funny in the little circles.

—It means you have polio.

—It does not!

—It means you can get polio.

—You don't have to have it.

David Geraghty, the fella in our class with polio, was in the queue behind us.

—Hey Geraghty, I said. —Did you get your B.C.G.?

—Yeah, he said.

—Then how did you get your polio? Fluke Cassidy asked him.

The queue broke a bit and crowded around David Geraghty.

—I don't know, he said. —I don't remember.

—Were you born with it?

David Geraghty looked like he was going to start crying. The queue straightened up again; we all tried to get as far away from him as we could. The first two still hadn't come out.

—You can get polio from drinking water from out of the toilet.

The door opened. The two fellas came out. Brian Sheridan and James O'Keefe. They were dressed again. They didn't look pale or scared or anything. There were no tear tracks. The two other fellas went in.

—What did they do to yeh?

—Nothing.

They didn't know what they were to do now. They couldn't go back to the classroom because there was no one there and Henno would kill them if they went in on their own. I took my jumper off and dropped it on the floor.

—What did they do?

—Nothing, said Brian Sheridan. —They just looked.

He looked different now. His face had gone stiff. He was

98

messing with his shoe. I stopped taking my shirt off. Kevin grabbed Brian Sheridan.

—Lay off!

—What did they do? Tell us!

—They looked at me.

His face was real red now and he wasn't really trying to get away from Kevin; he was trying not to let Kevin or the rest of us see his face properly. He'd start crying, for definite.

The other fella, James O'Keefe, wasn't blushing.

—They looked at our mickeys, he said.

I could hear the rubber knobs on the bottom of David Geraghty's crutches squeaking on the floor. James O'Keefe looked right down the queue. He knew he had power. He knew it wouldn't last long. I was freezing. James O'Keefe's face was dead serious. He had us.

—Let go o' me!

Kevin let go of Brian Sheridan.

—Why?

James O'Keefe didn't answer that one. It wasn't good enough.

—Why did they?

—Just look?

—Yeah, said James O'Keefe. —She bent down and only had a look. Me. She touched his.

—She didn't! said Brian Sheridan. —She didn't.

He was nearly crying again.

—She did so, said James O'Keefe. —You're a liar, Sherro.

—She didn't.

—She used an ice-pop stick, said James O'Keefe.

We were all shouting now. To get James O'Keefe to hurry up.

—Not her fingers!

Brian Sheridan yelled it. It was important; his face told us that.

—Not her fingers! Not her hand.

He calmed down after that but his face was still red and very white. Kevin grabbed James O'Keefe. I got my jumper round his neck to choke him. We had to know what she did with the ice-pop stick. We were nearly next.

—Tell us!

I choked James O'Keefe a bit.

—O'Keefe, tell us! Go on.

I loosened the jumper. There was a burn mark on his neck. We weren't messing.

—She lifted his mickey up with an ice-pop stick.

He turned to me.

—I'm going to get you, he said.

He didn't say it to Kevin, only to me.

—Why? said Ian McEvoy.

—To see the back of it, said James O'Keefe.

—Why?

—Don't know.

—To make sure it was normal, maybe.

—Is it? I asked Brian Sheridan.

—Yeah!

—Prove it.

The door opened. The two others came out.

—Did she touch yeh with the ice-pop stick? Did she?

—No. She only looked. Didn't she?

—Yeah.

—How come you? Kevin asked Brian Sheridan.

Brian Sheridan was crying again.

—She only looked, he said.

We left him alone. I took my shirt off, and my vest. We were next. Then I wondered.

—Why are we to take our stuff off?

James O'Keefe answered.

—They do other things as well.

—What other things?

The two in front of us were very slow. The nurse had to put her hands on their elbows to get them into the room. She closed the door.

—Is that the one? I asked James O'Keefe.

—Yeah, he said.

She was the one with the ice-pop stick. The one down on her knees staring at our mickeys. She didn't look that way. She looked nice. She'd been smiling when she grabbed the two in front of us. Her hair was up in a big bun with some down the side between her eyes and her ears. She wasn't wearing a cap. She was young.

—Dirty wagon, said David Geraghty.

We broke ourselves laughing, because it was funny and because David Geraghty had said it.

—Does your mickey have polio? Kevin asked him.

Kevin didn't get what he'd expected.

—Yeah, said David Geraghty. —She won't touch it.

Then we remembered.

—What other things?

Brian Sheridan told us. The blotches were gone off his face. He looked normal.

—He listens to your back with a stethoscope, he said. —And your front.

—It's freezing, said James O'Keefe.

—Yeah, said Brian Sheridan.

—Yeah, said one of the others that had just come out. —It's the worst bit.

—Did he check your B.C.G.?

—Yeah.

—Told yeh.

I checked mine again. All the marks were there, the three of them. They were very clear, like the top of a coconut. I looked at Kevin's. His were there as well.

—Any needles? someone asked.

—No, said Brian Sheridan.

—Not us anyway, said James O'Keefe. —Maybe some of youse.

—Shut up, O'Keefe.

David Geraghty spoke again.

—Did they do anything with your bum?

The laughs exploded. I laughed louder than I had to. We all did. We were scared and we'd made David Geraghty nearly cry. It was the first time David Geraghty had been funny out loud, in front of everybody. I liked him.

The two came out. They were smiling. The door was open for us. It was our turn, me and Kevin. I went first. I had to. I was pushed.

—Ask her for a choc-ice, said David Geraghty.

I laughed later. Not then though.

She was waiting. I stopped looking when she looked at me.

—Trousers and underpants, lads, she said.

I only remembered the safety pin on the top of my zip, only now. My ma had put it there. My face burned. I turned a bit, away from Kevin. I got it into my pocket. I turned back and I whistled to get rid of the heat in my face. Kevin's underpants were dirty. Down the middle, a straight brown line that got lighter on the outside. I didn't look at my own. I just let them fall. I didn't look anywhere. Not down. Not at Kevin. Not at the doctor at the desk. I waited. I waited for the feel of the stick. She was in front of me. I could tell. I didn't look. I couldn't feel my mickey there. There was no feeling there at all. When the ice-pop stick went under I'd scream. And dirty myself. She was still there. Bent down looking at it. Staring. Maybe rubbing her chin. Making her mind up. There was a cobweb in the corner over the doctor, a big dry one. There was a thread of it swinging. There was a breeze up there. She was making her mind up. If it was bad enough to lift to see the other side. If I didn't look she wouldn't do it. I was looking for the spider. If she did it I'd be finished forever. The most amazing thing about spiders was the way they made their webs. I'd never be normal again –

—Righto, she said. —Off you go, over to Doctor McKenna.

No touch. No stick. I nearly forgot to pull up my underpants and trousers. I took the first step. I pulled them up. Between my bum was wet. It didn't matter now. No stick. Three B.C.G. marks.

—Did she touch yours? Kevin asked me.

At the door, going out. He whispered.

—No, I said.

It felt brilliant.

—Me neither, he said.

I didn't tell him about his underpants.

Under the table was a fort. With the six chairs tucked under it there was still plenty of room; it was better that way, more secret. I'd sit in there for hours. This was the good table in the living room, the one that never got used, except at Christmas. I didn't have to bend my head. The roof of the table was just above me. I liked it like that. It made me concentrate on the floor and feet. I saw things. Balls of fluff, held together and made round by hair, floated on the lino. The lino had tiny cracks that got bigger if you pressed them. The sun was full of dust, huge chunks of it. It made me want to stop breathing. But I loved watching it. It swayed like snow. When my da was standing up he stood perfectly still. His feet clung to the ground. They only moved when he was going somewhere. My ma's feet were different. They didn't settle. They couldn't make their minds up. I fell asleep in there; I used to. It was always cool in there, never cold, and warm when I wanted it to be. The lino was nice on my face. The air wasn't alive like outside, beyond the table; it was safe. It had a smell I liked. My da's socks had diamonds on them. I woke up once and there was a blanket on top of me. I wanted to stay there forever. I was near the window. I could hear the birds outside. My da's legs were crossed. He was humming. The smell from the kitchen was lovely; I wasn't hungry, I didn't need it. Stew. It was Thursday. It must have been. My ma was humming as well. The same song as my da. It wasn't a proper song, just a hum with a few notes in it. It didn't sound like they knew they were humming the same thing. The notes had just crept into one of their heads, my da's probably. My ma did most of the humming. I stretched till my foot pushed a chair leg, and curled up again. The blanket had sand in it, from a picnic.

That was before my mother had Cathy and Deirdre. Sinbad couldn't walk then; I remembered. He slid along the lino on his bum. I couldn't do it any more. I could get under the table but my head pressed the top when I sat straight and I couldn't sit still; it hurt, my legs ached. I was afraid I'd be caught. I tried it a few times but it was stupid.

Most of us could stand up straight in the pipe. Only Liam and Ian McEvoy had to bend a bit so they wouldn't bash their heads. They thought they were great because of it. Liam knocked his head off the top of the pipe on purpose. We got down into the trench; it was real deep, like in a war. The men that were digging it – we waited till they'd gone home – had wooden ladders to get in and out. They locked them in their hut. We used planks. We lowered the plank into the trench and ran down along it. It was better than a ladder. You ran into the far wall of the trench and shouldered it and got away fast before the next fella came down the plank.

The trench was right outside our gate for a while, for a week about; it seemed like ages because it was coming up to

Easter and the days were getting longer and the workmen still stopped at half-five even though there was loads of bright left. It was a huge water pipe, to bring water to all the new estates being built along the road as far as Santry and for all the factories as well, or to bring dirty water away from the houses and factories; we weren't sure which.

—It's for sewerage, said Liam.

—What's sewerage?

—Gick, I said.

I knew what the word meant. Our drain was blocked once and my da had to open the square manhole below the toilet window and climb into it and prod at the pipe down there with a coat hanger. I asked him what the manhole was for, and the pipes, and he said Sewerage when he was telling me, before he roared at me to go away.

—He'd love you to help him, said my ma.

I was still crying but I had it under control.

—It's dirty, Patrick.

—He-he's standing in it, I said.

—He has to. To fix it.

—He shouted at me.

—It's dirty work. Messy.

Later, Da let me put the cover back on the manhole. The smell was terrible. He made me laugh. He pretended he'd dirtied his trousers and that that was the smell.

—Toilet paper as well, I said.

We were standing in the trench. Liam's wellington was caught in the muck. His foot had come out. Sinbad was up at the side of the trench. He wouldn't come down.

—And hair, I said.

—Hair isn't sewerage, said Kevin.

—It is so, I said. —It gets stuck in the pipes.

My da blamed my ma because her hair was the longest. A big ball of it had blocked the pipe.

—My hair isn't falling out, she said.

—And mine is, is that what you mean?

She smiled.

The pipes were cement. There were pyramids of them at the top of the road for ages before they started digging the trenches. Our part of Barrytown Road, where the houses were, was straight but all the rest of it, after the houses, was windy and crooked, with hedges high enough to stop you from seeing the fields. The county council had stopped trimming the hedges because they were going to be dug up. So the road was getting narrower. The pipes were going to join in a straight line and the new road over them was going to be straight as well. We'd gone down the pipe, a bit further every evening after the men had gone home. It was outside the shops the first time, then outside McEvoys', outside our house, further down the road every day. The ripped-up hedges lying on their sides looked the same as they did when they were upright; they were wide and full. My mother thought that they were going to put them back.

Running through the pipe was the most frightening brilliant thing I'd ever done. I was the first to do it for a dare, run all the way down, from outside my house down to the seafront, in the pitch black after a few steps. The dark was only broken once all the way by an open manhole over a cement platform built into the pipe; the rest of the way was back to dark, total black. You judged by the sound of your breath and feet – you could tell when you were swerving up the side of the pipe – until the dot of light at the end that got bigger and brighter, out the end of the pipe, roaring into the light, hands up, the winner.

You ran as fast as you could, faster than you normally could, but the others were always there at the end waiting.

Kevin didn't come out.

We laughed.

—Keva – Keva – Keva – Keva –

Liam did the gang whistle; he was the best at it. I wasn't able to do it. When I put the four fingers in my mouth there was no room for my tongue. The back of my throat went dry and I nearly got sick.

Kevin was still in there. We began to drop the muck we'd been going to belt at him; Kevin was in there with the blood pumping out of him. I jumped into the trench. The muck was hard and dry at this end.

—Come on! I yelled up at the rest.

I knew they wouldn't follow me; that was why I'd said it. I was going to rescue Kevin alone; it was great. I went into the pipe. I looked back, like an astronaut getting into his space-ship. I didn't wave. The others were beginning to climb into the trench. They'd never follow me in, not until it was too late.

I saw Kevin immediately. I couldn't see him from the entrance, but now I could. He wasn't far in. He was sitting down. He stood up. I didn't shout back that I'd found him, or anything. This was me and Kevin together. The two of us went deeper into the pipe so the others wouldn't see us. I wasn't disappointed that Kevin wasn't injured. This was better.

I didn't like the idea of sitting down in the absolute dark but I did it, the two of us. We made sure we were touching, right beside each other. I could see Kevin's shape, his head moving. I could see him stretching his legs. I was happy. I could have gone asleep. I was afraid to whisper, to ruin it. We could hear the others shouting, miles away. I knew what we'd do. We'd wait here till the shouting stopped, then we'd come out of the pipe before they told our parents or grown-ups. They knew we weren't hurt or anything; they'd do it to get us into trouble, pretending they were saving us.

I wanted to talk now. It was cold. It was darker even though my eyes were comfortable.

Kevin let off a fart. We beat the air with our hands. He tried to get my mouth, to cover it, to stop me from laughing. He was laughing. We were fighting now, just shoving, trying to stop one another from shoving back. We'd be caught soon; the others would hear us and come in. These were the last moments. Me and Kevin.

Next thing, he pruned me.

Pruning was banned in our school. The headmaster, Mister Finnucane, had seen James O'Keefe doing it to Albert Genocci when he was looking out his window at the weather, deciding whether to call us in or let us stay out. He'd been shocked, he said, when he went round to all the classes about it; he'd been shocked to see a boy doing that to another boy. He was sure that the boy who had done it hadn't meant to seriously hurt the other boy; he certainly hoped that the boy hadn't meant to hurt the other boy. But –

He let it hang there for a while.

This was great. James O'Keefe was in bigger trouble than he'd ever been in before, than any of us had ever been in. He had James O'Keefe standing up. He kept his head down even though Mister Finnucane kept telling him to hold his head up.

—Always hold your heads high, boys. You're men.

I didn't know for certain if I'd heard it when he said it the first time; Pruning.

—what I believe is being called pruning.

That was how he said it. It was like a big hole fell open in front of me – in front of all of us, I could tell from the faces – when Mister Finnucane said that. What else was he going to say? The last time he'd talked to us it was about someone robbing his big ink bottle from where he kept it outside his door. Now he was going to talk about pruning. The shock made me forget to breathe.

—Come on, James, now, he said. —Hold your head up, like I said.

Albert Genocci wasn't in our class. He was in the thicks' class. His brother, Patrick Genocci, was in our class.

—I know you're only playing when you do it, said Mister Finnucane.

Henno was standing behind him. He was blushing as well. He'd been out in the yard looking after us; he should have seen what was happening. There was no escape; James O'Keefe was dead.

—only having a bit of fun. But it's not funny. Not funny at all. Doing what I saw being done this morning could cause serious injury.

Ah; was that all?

—That part of the body is very delicate.

We knew that.

—You could ruin a boy's life for the rest of his – life. All for a joke.

The big hole in front of us was filling up. He wasn't going to say anything wrong or funny. He wasn't going to say Balls or Mickey or Testicles. It was disappointing, only it had stopped another history test – the life of the Fianna – and now he was going to kill James O'Keefe.

—Sit down, James.

I couldn't believe it. Neither could James O'Keefe or anybody.

—Sit down.

James O'Keefe got half-way between sitting down and standing up. It was a trick; it had to be.

—I don't want to see it happening again, said Mister Finnucane.

That was all.

Henno'd get him when Mister Finnucane was gone. But he
didn't. We went straight back to the test.

There was no proper road outside our house for months, up
as far as the summer holidays. Da had to park the car down
at the shops. Missis Kilmartin, the woman from the shop
who spied on the shoplifters, knocked at our door: there was
no room for the H.B. man in his lorry to make his delivery
because of Da's car and Kevin's da's car and three others.
Missis Kilmartin was angry. It was the first time I'd ever
really seen an angry woman. It wasn't a bloody car-park, she
said; she paid her rates. She was squinting. That was because
she was never out in the daylight; she was always behind the
one-way glass door. Ma was stuck; Da was at work – he
went in the train – and she couldn't drive. Missis Kilmartin
put her hand out.
—The keys.
—I don't have them. I –
—For Christ's sake!
She slammed the gate. She grabbed it so she could slam it.
When I'd opened the door she'd said, —Your mother.
I'd thought I was in for it. I'd been framed. She'd seen me
buying something and she thought I was robbing it. The way
I'd picked it up, it had looked like I was going to rob it.
I never robbed from that shop.
You only went to jail if you robbed more than ten shillings
worth of stuff, at one time. People my age and Kevin's didn't
go to jail when they were caught. They were sent to a home.
You went to Artane if you were caught twice. They shaved
your head there.
We had to stop running through the pipe; it was too far. It
had gone up past my house, out of Barrytown. We took over
the manholes. They stuck out of the ground, like small
buildings. They'd become level with the ground when they

were surrounded by cement; they'd become just parts of the path. We got Aidan and shoved him down the hole. He had to stay down there on the platform and we lobbed muck in. He could hide because the platform down there was much wider than the hole. If we lobbed the muck low it went through the hole at an angle and hit the platform walls and maybe Aidan. We surrounded him. If it had been me I'd have got down to the pipe and charged down to the next hole and climbed out before the others found out what I was doing. And I'd have pelted them and have used stones as well. Aidan was crying. We looked at Liam because he was his brother. Liam kept throwing the muck into the hole so, so did we.

The new road was straight now, all the way. The edges of Donnelly's fields were chopped off and you could see all the farm because the hedges were gone; it was like Catherine's dolls' house with the door opened. You could see all the being-built houses on the other side of the fields. The farm was being surrounded. The cows were gone, to the new farm. Big lorries took them. The smell was a laugh. One of the cows skidded on the ramp getting up into the lorry. Donnelly hit it with his stick. Uncle Eddie was behind him. He had a stick as well. He hit the cow when Donnelly did. We could see the cows all packed in the lorries, trying to get their noses out between the bars.

Uncle Eddie went in one of the lorries beside the driver. He had his elbow sticking out the window. We waved at him, and cheered when the lorry full of cows went through the knocked-down gates of the farmhouse and turned left onto the new road. It was like Uncle Eddie was going away.

I saw him later, running down to the shops before they shut to get the Evening Press for Donnelly.

The old railway bridge wasn't big enough any more for the road to get under it. They built a new one, made of huge slabs of concrete, right beside the old one. The road dipped down under the bridge so that big traffic, lorries and buses, could get under it. They cut away the land beside the road so the road could go further down. More concrete slabs stopped the cut-away land from falling onto the road. They said that two men were killed doing this work but we never saw anything. They were killed when some of Donnelly's field fell on them, after it had been raining and the ground was loose and soggy. They drowned in muck.

I had a dream sometimes that made me wake up. I was eating something. It was dry and gritty and I couldn't get it wet. It hurt my teeth; I couldn't close my mouth and I wanted to shout for help and I couldn't. And I woke up and my mouth was all dry, from being open. I wondered had I been shouting; I hoped I hadn't but I wanted my ma to come in and ask me was I alright and sit on the bed.

They didn't blow up the old bridge. We thought they'd have to, but they didn't.

—If they blew it up they'd blow up the new one as well, said Liam.

—No, they wouldn't; that's stupid.

—They would so.

—How would they?

—The explosion.

—They have different explosions for different things, Ian McEvoy told him.

—How do you know, Fatso?

That was Kevin. Ian McEvoy wasn't all that fat. He just had little diddies, like a woman's. He never swam now, after we'd seen him.

—I just do, said Ian McEvoy. —They're able to control the explosion.

We weren't interested any more.

The old bridge was gone. They just knocked it down; took away the rocks and rubble in lorries. I missed it. It had been a great place for hiding under and shouting. It only fitted one car at a time. Da kept his hand on the horn right through it. The new bridge whistled when it was windy, but that was all.

He let us look in the window, but no further. Only a few got into the house. He pushed the couch away from the window so we could see it properly, his Scalextric. Alan Baxter was the only one in Barrytown that had it. He was a Protestant, a proddy, and he was older than us. He was the same age as Kevin's brother. He went to secondary school and he played cricket; he had a real bat and the yokes for your legs. When they played rounders, the bigger boys, behind the shops, when he played he kept taking his jumper off and putting it back on again but he wasn't any better of a player than the others. When he was fielding he put his hands on his knees and bent forward. He was a sap. But he had Scalextric.

It wasn't as good as the ads, a track the same shape as a train-set track – two tracks joined together like an eight – and the cars never went too far without jamming. But it was brilliant. The controls looked great and easy. The blue car was much better than the red one. Terence Long had the red one; Alan Baxter had the blue. Our breathing and hand-prints were messing up the window. Terence Long – he was six foot one and still only fourteen – kept having to straighten up the red car; when it started a corner it got stuck. A few times it beat the corner and kept going. But the blue one was way ahead. Kevin's brother picked up the red one and looked under it but Alan Baxter made him put it back. They were the only ones in the living room, Alan Baxter, Terence Long and Kevin's brother. The rest of us – we were all much younger – had to watch outside. The worst was when it was dark. It really felt outside then. Kevin got in once, because of his brother. But I didn't. I was the oldest in my family; I had nobody to get me through the door. They didn't let Kevin do anything. They just let him watch.

Kevin's brother got into big trouble once. His name was Martin. He was five years older than us and what he did was, he went to the toilet down a bit of hosepipe through Missis Kilmartin's car window and he got caught because Terence Long blabbed to his ma because he'd been the one holding the hose and he was afraid he'd get blamed for going to the toilet as well. Terence Long's ma told Kevin and Martin's ma.

—Terence Long Terence Long —

Has a mickey three foot long —

He tried to get Kevin's brother and them to call him Terry or Ter but everybody still called him Terence, especially his ma.

—Terence Long Terence Long —

Wears no socks —

What a pong —

He wore sandals in the summer, big ones like priests', and no socks. Kevin's da killed Martin and he made him wash Missis Kilmartin's car seat with everyone watching. He was crying. Missis Kilmartin didn't come out. She sent Eric out with the car keys. He was her son and he was mental.

Martin smoked and he was leaving school after the Inter. He drank Coca-Cola with aspirins in it and got sick. He mitched all the time, all day down at the seafront even in the winter. He was an altar boy. But he got thrown out for painting white stripes on his black runners. He got Sinbad — him and Terence Long and even Alan Baxter — and they painted the other lens of his glasses black. They made him walk home wearing the glasses, right up to our house, with a stick they'd painted white. Ma did nothing about it; she sang to Sinbad while he was crying —

—I TOLD MY BROTHER SEAMUS

– and when he was finished she went into the garage and got a bottle of spirits and started to clean his lens and she showed him how to do it. I said I'd help him but he wouldn't let me. Da laughed; he was home late and Sinbad was in bed, but I wasn't. He laughed. So did I. He said that Sinbad would be doing things like that when he was Kevin's brother's age. Then he got annoyed because the plate covering the plate that his dinner was on was stuck because the gravy had hardened to it in the cooker. Ma sent me to bed.

Martin wore longers in the summer. He always had his hands in his pockets. He had a comb. I thought he was brilliant. Kevin did too but he hated him as well.

He got Missis Kilmartin back. He gave Eric Kilmartin a box in the face and Eric couldn't tell who'd done it cos he couldn't talk properly; he could only make noises.

Martin and them built huts. We did too, from the stuff we got off the building sites – it was one of the first things we did when the summer was coming – but theirs were better, miles better than our ones. There was a field behind the newest of our type of houses – not the one behind the shops – and that was where most of the huts got built. It was full of hills like dunes, only made of muck instead of sand. It used to be part of a farm but that was years before. The wreck of the farmhouse was at the edge of the field. The walls weren't bricks; they were made of light brown mud full of gravel and bigger stones. They were dead easy to demolish. I found a piece of cup in the nettles against the wall. I took it home and I washed it. I showed it to my da and he said it was probably worth a fortune but he wouldn't buy it off me. He told me to put it in a safe place. It had flowers on it, two full ones and a half one. I lost it.

This field looked like they had started to get it ready for building on but they'd stopped. There was a wide trench, wider than a lane, down the middle and other trenches grown over. Some of the fields hadn't been touched. Da said that the building had been stopped because they'd had to wait till the mains pipes were down and finished, with water in them.

I ran through the untouched part of the field – for no reason, just running – and the grass was great, up to way over my knees. I had to lift my legs out of it, like in water. It was the type of grass that could cut you sometimes. It had tops like wheat. I brought loads of it home to my ma once but she said you couldn't make bread out of it. I said she could but she said you couldn't, you just couldn't, it was a pity. My feet made swoosh noises going through the grass and then there was another noise, one in front of me. And the grass moved. I stopped, and a long bird flew out of the grass. And stayed low, flew out in front of me. I could feel its wings beating. It was a pheasant. I turned back.

Kevin's brother built his huts in the hills. They dug long holes; they got lends of their das' spades. Terence Long had his own one; he got it for his birthday. They divided the hole into segments, rooms. They covered the hole with planks. They sometimes got hay out of Donnelly's barn. That was the basement.

When I came out of a hut my hair was full of clay and muck. I could make my hair stand up.

The rest of the hut was made of mostly sods. Wherever you went in Barrytown you found places where sods had been cut out, even in front gardens; patches of bare earth, all straight lined. Kevin's brother was able to get the spade through the grass into the earth with no effort. I loved the watery crunch of the blade going through the mesh of roots. Terence Long stood up on the spade and rocked, and got down and moved the spade and did it again. They piled the sods like thin bricks and pushed them down. They became a solid wall but they could be pushed over easily. But if you did that you got killed;

Kevin's brother always found out who'd done it. There were more walls inside the main walls, rooms again, planks on top, and a plastic sheet and more sods for the roof. From not too far away the hut was like a square hillock. It didn't look built, not until you were up to it.

Worms came out of the sods.

We made booby traps all around our hut. We buried open paint cans and hid them with grass. If your foot went through the grass into the can usually nothing happened except you fell over. But if you were running your leg could be broken. It was easy to imagine. We buried one with the paint still in it but no one stood in it. We got a milk bottle and broke it. We put the biggest bits of glass standing up in a can right in front of the hut door.

—What if one of us puts our foot in it?

The traps were supposed to be for the enemy.

—We won't, said Kevin. —We know where it is, stupid.

—Liam doesn't.

Liam was at his auntie's.

—Liam's not in our gang.

I hadn't known that – Liam had been playing with us the day before – but I didn't say anything.

We sharpened sticks and stuck them in the ground pointing out towards where the enemy would be sneaking up from. We kept the sticks low. If the enemy was creeping along he'd get a pointy stick in the face.

Ian McEvoy ran into a trip wire and he had to go to hospital for stitches.

—His foot was hanging off him.

It was real wire, not string like we usually used. We didn't know who'd set it up. It was tied between two trees in the field behind the shops. There was no hut near it. We didn't build huts in that field; it was too flat. They'd been playing relievio, Ian McEvoy and them, in front of the shops and when Kilmartin's hall door opened Ian McEvoy had thought that it was Missis Kilmartin going to yell at them to go away and he'd run into the field and the trip wire. The wire was a mystery.

—Fellas from the Corpo houses did it.

There were six new families living in the first row of finished Corporation houses. Their gardens were full of hardened half-bags of cement and smashed bricks. Some of the children were the same age as us but that didn't mean that they could hang around with us.

—Slum scum.

My ma hit me when I said that. She never hit me usually but she did then. She smacked behind my head.

—Never say that again.

—I didn't make it up, I told her.

—Just never say it again, she said. —It's a terrible thing to say.

I didn't even know what it really meant. I knew that the slums were in town.

The road with the six Corporation houses wasn't joined to any other road. It ended just before the first house. There was a turn-off for the new road off our road, just past the beginning of Donnelly's first field, but it only went in a few feet, then stopped. Our pitch was on the bit of field between the two roads. We only had one goal. We used jumpers at the other end for the other goal. We usually played three-and-in. You only needed one goal. It was easy to score, especially on the left side cos there was a hill there and you could get the ball way over the keeper's head, but it was always crowded. There were no teams in three-and-in; it was every man for himself. Twenty players meant twenty teams. Sometimes there were more than twenty players. There were only ever three or four of us really playing, trying to score goals. The rest, mostly little kids smaller than Sinbad, just ran around after the ball but never tried to get it; they just followed it, laughing, especially when they all had to turn back the way they'd come. Elbowing and pushing kids out of the way was allowed. When I had the ball I'd go so there were some kids between me and the nearest real player, Kevin or Liam or Ian McEvoy or one of them. The kids would run beside me, so no one could get at me, like in a film I saw where John Wayne got away from the baddies by riding in the middle of a stampede, low down, hanging on to the side of his horse. Then when he was safe he hooshed himself back up properly into the saddle and looked back to where he'd just come from and grinned and rode on. The only thing about three-and-in, the only bad thing, was that when you won, when you'd scored three goals, you had to go in goal. I was a better player than Kevin but I stopped trying after two goals. I hated being in goal. Aidan was the best player, way easily – he was a brilliant dribbler – but he was still picked last or second-last when we were playing five-a-side; no one wanted him. He was the only one who played for a real club, Raheny Under Elevens, even though he wasn't even nine.

—Your uncle's the manager.

—He isn't, said Liam.

—What is he?

—He isn't anything. He just watches.

Aidan had a blue jersey with a real number, a stitched one, on it; number 11.

—I'm a winger, he said.

—So what?

It was a real heavy jersey, a real jersey. He didn't tuck it in. You couldn't see his nicks.

He was good in goal as well.

Five-a-side games never finished. The team playing into the jumper goal end were always winning.

—Charlton to Best —— Great goal!

—It wasn't a goal! It went over the jumper, it hit the bar.

—It hit the inside of the jumper.

—Yeah; in-off.

—No way.

—Yeah way.

—I'm not playing then.

—Good.

Sometimes we played when we were eating our lunch. I'd scored two goals already. I hit an easy shot for Ian McEvoy to save. He put his sandwich down on the jumper and the ball bounced past him. I'd scored; I'd won. I was in goal now.

—You did that on purpose.

I pushed Ian McEvoy.

—I did not, you.

He pushed me back.

—You just wanted to get out of goal.

I didn't push him this time. I was thinking of kicking him.

—He should stay in goal for that, I said.

—No way.

—You have to try and save them.

—I'll go in.

It was one of the boys from the Corporation houses. He was standing behind the jumpers goal.

—I'll go in, I said.

He was younger than me, and smaller. Safe smaller; he'd never be able to kill me, even if he was a brilliant fighter.

I pushed him away from the goal.

—This is our field, I said.

I'd pushed him hard. He was by himself. He was surprised. He nearly fell over. He slid on the wet grass.

I could tell: he didn't know whether to go away or stay. He didn't want to turn his back; he was afraid something would happen him if he did. And he couldn't go; I'd pushed him and he'd be a coward.

—This is our field, I said again.

I kicked him.

My ma warned us about the mangle, to stay away from it, not to mess with it. The rolls were hard but only rubber. I scratched a mark on the bottom one with the breadknife. I loved it in the kitchen – the steam and the heat – when my ma was putting the sheets through the mangle, and my da's shirts. The sheets were shiny with huge wet bubbles and my ma put a corner up to the mangle and turned the handle and the sheet rose out of the water like a whale being caught. The water ran down the sheet and the bubbles were crushed as the sheet was pulled through the rolls and came out flat, looking like material again, the shininess all gone. Another sheet, the rubber creaked and groaned, then the rest slid through easily. She wouldn't let me help. She only let me stand behind the washing machine and guide the sheet into the red basin. The sheet was warm and kind of solid and hard. My fingers were safe on that side. The smaller clothes came through and I caught them and put them on top of the sheets. The basin was full. She had to empty the machine now and fill it again for the nappies. The steam in the kitchen was what I really liked, and the wet on the walls.

We needed ice-pop sticks for it; the tar in the road was bubbling. It was the first time this year, so we'd no sticks ready. There was me and Kevin, and Liam and Aidan – just the four of us because Ian McEvoy wasn't coming out. He had pains in his legs. Great spurts of growing pain, his ma said when we'd called for him, around the back. We never went to the front doors, unless it was for knick-knacking at night. The front porches on my side of the road were always nice and cool, especially on hot days. The sun never got in there. Our porch had great corners of dust: Dinkies bounced over the grit and sometimes crashed. There were three small round holes under the door, for air for under the floorboards, to stop them from rotting. If one of your soldiers fell in one of the holes you could never get him back and the mice got in that way. The ice-pop sticks were for bursting the bubbles; they were definitely the best. You could manage the bubble with an ice-pop stick, flatten it, get all the air in one part, that kind of thing.

Great spurts of growing pain. Ian McEvoy was strapped to the bed. He had a bit of leather in his mouth to stop him from screaming, like John Wayne getting a bullet out of his leg. They poured whiskey over the hole in his leg. I poured whiskey on Sinbad's scab, just a tiny drop. He was squirming before I even did it so I couldn't tell if it was really sore or not, as sore as John Wayne made it look, or if it cured it.

Kevin and me took one side, Liam and Aidan the other one. We had the shops side; there'd be loads more sticks. Sinbad wasn't with us either. He was sick again. If he wasn't better by the night my ma was going to get the doctor. She always believed we were sick when the holidays were on. It was the Easter holidays. The sky was all blue. It was Good Friday.

The roads were cement, all the roads round our way, the parts that hadn't been dug up. The roads were cement and the tar went between the slabs of cement. It was hard and you didn't notice it for most of the time but when it softened and bubbled it was great. The top was old and grey looking, like an elephant's skin around its eyes, but under that, when you got your ice-pop stick in, there was new tar, black and soft, a bit like toffee that had been in your mouth. You burst the bubble and the clean soft tar was under there; the top was gone off the bubble – it was a volcano. Pebbles went in; they died screaming.

—No no, please – ! – don't – ! Aaaaaaaahaaah——

Bees if we could get them. We shook the jar to make sure that the bee was stunned, nearly dead, then turned it over before it could wake up. We aimed for it to fall on the new tar hole. We pushed it closer with the ice-pop stick. We shoved it down a bit so it stuck to the tar. We watched. It was hard to tell the pain. The bee made no noise, no buzz or anything. We broke it in half and buried it in the tar. I always left a bit showing, as an example to others. Sometimes the bee got away. It wasn't dopey enough when we turned over the jar. It flew off before it hit the ground properly. It didn't matter. We didn't try to stop it. Bees could kill you; they didn't want to, only if they had no choice. Not like wasps. Wasps got you on purpose. A fella in Raheny swallowed a bee by accident and it stung him in the throat and he died. He choked. He was running with his mouth open and the bee flew in. When he was dying he opened his mouth to say his last words and the bee flew out. That was how they knew. We put flowers and leaves in the jars to make the bees feel more at home. We had nothing against them. They made honey.

I had seven sticks now and Kevin had six. Liam and Aidan were way ahead of us because they didn't have the shops and we wouldn't let them cross the road to our side. We'd batter them if they tried. Chinese torture. Whoever ended up with the smallest number of sticks was going to have to eat a lump of tar. It was going to be Aidan. We'd make sure he swallowed it. We'd let him eat a clean bit. I got another stick, a real clean one. Kevin ran to the next one, and I saw one and ran and grabbed it before he did and he got two while I was getting that one. It was a race now. Next it would be a fight. A mess one. I bent over to pick one out of the gutter – we were past the shops – and Kevin shoved me. I went flying but I had the stick; I laughed. Out onto the road.

—Stop messing.

He went for a stick; it was my turn. I didn't shove him too hard. I let him get a hold of the stick first. We both saw one, and ran. I was faster; he tripped me. I hadn't planned for it. I was going to fall. I couldn't control it, I was too fast. My knees, my palms, chin. The skin was off them. My knuckles where I'd been holding the sticks. I still held them. I sat up. There was dirt in the redness of my palm. Spots of blood were getting bigger. Becoming drops.

I put the sticks in my pocket. The pain was starting.

An earwig flew into my mouth once. I was charging, it was in front of me – then gone. There was a taste, that was all. I swallowed. It was far back, too far to cough out. My eyes went watery but it wasn't crying. It was in the school yard. There was still a horrible taste. Like petrol. I went to the toilet and got my head under the tap. I drank for ages. I wanted the taste to go and I wanted to drown the earwig. It had gone down whole. Straight down.

I didn't tell anyone.

This fella went to Africa on his holidays –

—You don't go to Africa on your holidays.

—Shut up.

When he was in Africa he had a salad for his tea and when he came back from his holidays he started getting pains in his stomach and they brought him into Jervis Street because he was screaming in agony – they brought him in in a taxi – and the doctor couldn't tell what was wrong with him and the boy couldn't say anything because he couldn't stop screaming because of the pain, so they did an operation on him and they found lizards inside him, in his stomach, twenty of them; they'd made a nest. They were eating the stomach out of him.

—You're still to eat your lettuce, said my ma.

—He died, I told her. —The boy did.

—Eat it up; go on. It's washed.

—So was the stuff he ate.

—That's just rubbish someone told you, she said. —You shouldn't listen to it.

I hoped I'd die. I hoped I'd just last till my da got home, then I'd tell him what had happened and I'd die.

The lizards were in a jar in Jervis Street, in a fridge, for them all to look at when they were training to be doctors. They were all in one jar. Floating in liquid for keeping them fresh.

There was tar in my trousers, the knees.

—Not again.

That was what my ma was going to say. It was what she always said.

She did say it.

—Ah, Patrick, not again; for God's sake.

She made me take them off. She made me take them off in the kitchen. She wouldn't let me go upstairs. She pointed at my legs and clicked her fingers. I took them off.

—Your shoes first, she said. —Hang on a minute.

She checked that there was no tar on the soles.

—There isn't any, I told her. —I checked them.

She made me lift my other foot. My trousers were halfway down. She slapped the side of my leg and opened and closed and opened her hand. I put my foot into it. She looked at the sole.

—I told you, I said.

She let go of my leg. She always said nothing when she was being annoyed. She clicked and pointed.

Confucius he say, go to bed with itchy hole, wake up in morning with smelly finger.

He made his hand open and close like a beak, the fingers stiff, right into her face.

—Nag nag nag.

She looked around and then at him.

—Paddy, she said.

—The minute I get in the door.

—Paddy –

I knew what Paddy meant, what she meant the way she'd said Paddy. So did Sinbad. So did Catherine, the way she stared up at my ma and then, sometimes, my da.

He stopped. He took two deep breaths. He sat down. He looked at us, like he used to know us, then properly.

—How was school?

Sinbad laughed, and made himself laugh more.

I knew why.

—Great, said Sinbad.

I knew why Sinbad had laughed but he was too late. He thought it was over. Da sitting down, asking us how school was – that meant the fight was over.

He'd learn.

—Why was it great? said Da.

That wasn't a fair question. He'd said it to catch out Sinbad, like he was in the fight as well.

—It just was, I said.

—Well? Da said to Sinbad.

—A fella got sick in his class, I said.

Sinbad looked at me.

—Is that right? said Da.

—Yeah, I said.

Da looked at Sinbad.

Sinbad stopped looking at me.

—Yeah, he said.

Da changed. It had worked. His foot was bouncing at the end of his crossed leg; that was the sign. I'd won. I'd saved Sinbad.

—What fella?

126

I'd beaten Da. It had been easy.

—Fergus Sweeney, I said.

Sinbad looked at me again. Fergus Sweeney wasn't in his class.

Da loved these kind of stories.

—Poor Fergus, said Da. —How did he get sick?

Sinbad was ready.

—It came out of his mouth, he said.

—Is that right? said Da. —Janey mack.

He thought he was smart, making a mock of us: we were doing it to him.

—Lumps, said Sinbad

—Lumps, said Da.

—Yellow bits, I said.

—All over his copy, said Da.

—Yeah, said Sinbad.

—All over his eccer, said Da.

—Yeah, said Sinbad.

—And the fella's beside him, I said.

—Yeah, said Sinbad.

We were all in a circle. Kevin was the only one outside it. We had a fire. We had to look into the fire. It wasn't dark yet. We had to hold hands. That meant that we had to lean forward nearly into the fire. My eyes were burning. It was forbidden to rub them. This was the third time we'd done it.

It was my turn.

—Banjaxed.

—Banjaxed! we all went; no laughing.

—Banjaxed banjaxed banjaxed!

We'd started this bit the second time, the chanting. It was better, more organised than what we'd had before, just shouting and Indian calls. Especially when it wasn't even dark.

Liam was next to me, on my left. The ground was damp. Kevin tapped Liam's shoulder with his poker. It was Liam's turn.

—Trellis.

—Trellis!

—Trellis trellis trellis!

We were in the field behind the shops, in away from the road. We hadn't as many places any more. Our territory was getting smaller. In the story Henno had read to us that afternoon, a stupid mystery one, there'd been a woman at the trellis pruning her roses. Then she died and the story was about finding out who did it. We didn't care though. We just waited for Henno to say Pruning again. He didn't, but Trellis was in every second sentence. None of us knew what Trellis was.

—Bucko.

—Bucko!

—Bucko bucko bucko!

—Ignoramus.

—Ignoramus!

—Ignoramus ignoramus ignoramus!

I could never guess what word was going to be next. I always tried; I looked at all the faces in the class when a new word or a good one got said. Liam and Kevin and Ian McEvoy were the same, doing what I was doing, storing the words.

It was my turn again.

—Substandard.

—Substandard!

—Substandard substandard substandard!

That part was over now. My eyes were killing me. The wind was blowing it all my way, the smoke, last week's ashes as well. It would be good later though; I loved picking dry stuff out of my hair.

The names part was next. The real ceremony. Kevin walked around behind us. We weren't allowed to look. I could only go by his voice and his feet in the grass if he stepped off the muck fire circle. I heard a swish from near. It was the poker. It was great and terrible, not knowing. The excitement was brilliant when we remembered it later.

—I am Zentoga, said Kevin.

Swish.

Behind me.

—I am Zentoga, the high priest of the great god, Ciúnas.*

Swish.

Over the other side. I had to keep my eyes shut. I hoped I'd be first but I was glad that Kevin was over there.

—Ciúnas the Great gives all his people names! The word was made flesh.

Swish.

—Aaah!

He'd got Aidan, right across the back.

—Shite! said Aidan.

—From henceforth thou will be called Shite, said Kevin.
—Ciúnas the Mighty has spoken.

—Shite! we shouted.

We were a safe bit away from the shops.

—The word made flesh!

Swish.

Close.

Ian McEvoy.

—Tits!

Beside me; I felt the pain through him to me.

—From henceforth thou will be called Tits. Ciúnas the Mighty has spoken.

—Tits!

* Silence.

129

It had to be a bad word. That was the rule. If it wasn't bad enough you got another belt of the poker.

—The word was made flesh!

—Diddies!

My turn was coming up. My head was in my lap. My hands were wet and kept slipping out of Liam and Ian McEvoy's grips. Someone was crying. More than one.

His voice was behind me.

—The word was made flesh!

—Aaah!

Liam.

Again. Swish. The second thump sounded worse; it sounded unfair and shocking.

—That wasn't a word, said Liam, out of a gasp.

Kevin had hit him again because he hadn't said a bad word the first time. Liam's agony and protest made his voice shimmer.

—The followers of Ciúnas feel no pain, said Kevin.

Liam was crying.

—The followers of Ciúnas do not *cry*! said Kevin.

He was going to hit him again. I could feel it, the poker going back. But Liam's hand slid out of mine. He was standing up.

—I don't care, he said. —It's stupid.

Kevin was going to hit him anyway. But Liam got in too close. I watched. We all watched. I rubbed my face. It felt stretched and raw.

—A curse on your family, Kevin said to Liam, but he let Liam get past him.

Smiffy O'Rourke had walked out the week before after Kevin had hit his back five times because Bloody wasn't a bad enough word and Smiffy O'Rourke wouldn't say anything worse. Missis O'Rourke had gone to the Guards about it – that was what Kevin'd said – but she'd had no evidence, only

Smiffy's back. We'd laughed then, when we'd watched Smiffy running away like he was ducking bullets because he couldn't straighten his back. No one laughed now though. Liam walked away towards the gap in the new wire fence. It was getting dark now. Liam walked carefully. We could hear him snuffling. I wanted to go with him.

—Ciúnas the Mighty killed your mother!

Kevin had both arms stretched up. I looked over at Aidan; she was his mother as well. He stayed where he was. He was looking at the fire. I watched. He stayed that way. I'd take my punishment now, for the same reason that Aidan was staying. It was good being in the circle, better than where Liam was going.

I was next. There were two others left but I'd be next. I knew it: Kevin was going to take it out on me. We joined the circle again. It was even tighter now without Liam. If I'd pulled quickly someone would have been tipped into the fire. We nudged in closer on our bums.

It took him ages. I heard him over the other side. It was dark now. I could hear the wind. I had to close my eyes again. My legs were hot, too close to the fire. He'd gone; I couldn't place him. I listened. He was nowhere.

—The word was made flesh!

My back was ripped. The bones exploded.

—— Fuck!

—From henceforth thou will be called Fuck.

It was over.

—Ciúnas the Mighty has spoken!

I'd done it.

—Fuck!

The best word. It wasn't as loud as it should have been. They were afraid. They pillowed the shout. I didn't though. I'd paid for it. He'd hit me right on one of the knobs of my spine. I couldn't straighten. I couldn't relax yet. It was over though. I'd made it. I unclenched my eyes.

—The word was made flesh!

I enjoyed the crunch of someone else's pain.

Fuck was the best word. The most dangerous word. You couldn't whisper it.

—Gee!

Fuck was always too loud, too late to stop it, it burst in the air above you and fell slowly right over your head. There was total silence, nothing but Fuck floating down. For a few seconds you were dead, waiting for Henno to look up and see Fuck landing on top of you. They were thrilling seconds — when he didn't look up. It was the word you couldn't say anywhere. It wouldn't come out unless you pushed it. It made you feel caught and grabbed the minute you said it. When it escaped it was like an electric laugh, a soundless gasp followed by the kind of laughing that only forbidden things could make, an inside tickle that became a brilliant pain, bashing at your mouth to be let out. It was agony. We didn't waste it.

—The word was made flesh!

Swish.

The forbidden word. I'd shouted it.

—From henceforth thou will be called Mickey.

The last one.

—Ciúnas the Mighty has spoken!

—Mickey!

It was all over now, we could get up from the fire; till next week. I straightened my back. It had been worth it. I was the real hero, not Liam.

—Ciúnas the Mighty will give you all new names next Friday, said Kevin.

But no one was really listening. He was just Kevin again. I was hungry. Fish on a Friday. We were supposed to use our names all week but we could never remember who was Gee and who was Shite. I was Fuck though. They all remembered that.

There wasn't another Friday. We were all sick of being hit on the back with a poker by Kevin. He wouldn't take his turn. He had to be the high priest all the time. Ciúnas had said, he said. It would have gone on longer if we'd all had a go with the poker, probably forever. But Kevin wouldn't allow it and it was his poker. I still called him Zentoga after the others had stopped but even I was happy when it didn't happen the next Friday. Kevin went off by himself and I went with him and pretended that I'd been up for him. We went to the seafront. We threw stones at the sea.

I ran out into the garden. The house wasn't big enough. I couldn't stay still. I did two laps; I must have gone real fast because I was back in the living room in time to see the action replay. I had to stay standing up.

George Best –

George Best –

George Best had just scored in the European Cup Final. I watched him running away, back to the centre circle; he was grinning but he didn't look that surprised.

My da put his arm around my shoulders. He'd stood up to do it.

—Wonderful, he said.

He supported United as well, not as much as me though.

—Bloody wonderful.

Pat Crerand, Frank McLintock and George Best were up in the air. The ball was nearly on top of Frank McLintock's head but it was hard to say who'd headed it. Probably George Best, because his fringe was flying out like he'd just swung his head to meet the ball and the ball looked like it was going away from him, not towards him. Frank McLintock looked like he was smiling and Pat Crerand looked like he was bawling crying but George Best looked just right, like he'd headed the ball and he was watching it going towards the net. He was ready to land.

There were hundreds of pictures in the book but I kept going back to this one, the first one. Crerand and McLintock looked like they were jumping in the air but George Best looked like he was standing, except for his hair. His legs were straight and a bit apart, like at ease in the army. It was as if they'd cut out a photograph of George Best and stuck it onto another one of McLintock and Crerand and the thousands of little heads and black coats in the stand behind them. There was no effort on his face. His mouth was only a little bit open. His hands were closed but not clenched. His neck looked relaxed, not like Frank McLintock's; it looked like there were pieces of rope growing under the skin.

There was something else I'd just found out. There was an Introduction on page eleven, beside the page with the George Best photograph. I read it, and then the last bit, the last paragraph, again.

—When I was first shown the manuscript of this book, I was especially pleased to see how the records and statistics had been integrated with the general narrative –

I didn't really know what that meant but it didn't matter.

—The book certainly represents the happiest marriage of education and entertainment I can ever recall. You will enjoy it.

And under all that was George Best's autograph.

George Best had signed my book.

My da hadn't said anything about the autograph. He'd just given it to me and said Happy Birthday and kissed me. He'd left me to find it for myself.

George Best.

Not Georgie. I never called him Georgie. I hated it when I heard people calling him Georgie.

George Best.

His jersey was outside his nicks in the photograph. The other two had theirs tucked in. No one I knew tucked theirs in, even the ones that said that George Best was useless; they all wore their jerseys outside.

I brought the book in to my da to let him know I'd found the autograph and it was brilliant, easily the best thing I'd ever got for a present. It was called A Pictorial History of Soccer. It was huge, much fatter than an annual, real heavy. It was a grown-up's sort of book. There were pictures, but loads of writing too; small writing. I was going to read all of it.

—I found it, I told him.

My finger was in the book, where George Best's autograph was.

My da was sitting in his chair.

—Did you? he said. —Good man. What?

—What?

—What did you find?

—The autograph, I told him.

He was messing.

—Let's see it, he said.

I put the book and opened it on his knees.

—There.

My da rubbed his finger across the autograph.

George Best had great handwriting. It slanted to the right; it was long and the holes were narrow. There was a dead-straight line under the name, joining the G and the B, all the way to the T at the end and a bit further. It finished with a swerve, like a diagram of a shot going past a wall.

—Was he in the shop? I asked my da.

—Who?

—George Best, I said.

Worry began a ball in my stomach but he answered too quickly for it to grow.

—Yes, he said.

—Was he?

—Yes.

—Was he; really?

—I said he was, didn't I?

That was all I needed, for certain. He didn't get annoyed when he said it, just calm like he'd said everything else, looking right at me.

—What was he like?

I wasn't trying to catch him out. He knew that.

—Exactly like you'd expect, he said.

—In his gear?

That was exactly what I'd have expected. I didn't know how else George Best would have dressed. I'd seen a colour picture of him once in a green Northern Ireland jersey, not his usual red one, and it had shocked me.

—No, said Da. —He——, a tracksuit.

—What did he say?

—Just –

—Why didn't you ask him to put my name on it?

I pointed to George Best's name.

—As well.

—He was very busy, said my da.

—Was there a huge queue?

—A huge one.

That was good; that was right and proper.

—Was he in the shop just for the day only? I asked.

—That's right, said my da. —He had to go back to Manchester.

—For training, I told him.

—That's right.

A year after that I knew that it wasn't George Best's real autograph at all; it was only printing and my da was a liar.

The front room was not for going into. It was the drawing room. Nobody else had a drawing room although all the houses were the same, all the houses before the Corporation ones. Our drawing room was Kevin's ma's and da's living room, and Ian McEvoy's television room. Ours was the drawing room because my ma said it was.

—What does it mean? I asked her.

I'd known it was the drawing room since I could remember but today the name seemed funny for the first time. We were outside. Whenever there was even a bit of blue in the sky my ma opened the back door and brought the whole house out. She thought about the answer but with a nice look on her face. The babies were asleep. Sinbad was putting grass in a jar.

—The good room, she said.

—Does Drawing mean Good?

—Yes, she said. —Only when you put it with Room.

That was fair enough; I understood.

—Why don't we call it just the good room? I asked. —People prob'ly think we draw in it, or paint pictures.

—No, they don't.

—They might, I said.

I wasn't just saying it for the sake of saying it, like I said some things.

—Especially if they're stupid, I said.

—They'd want to be very stupid.

—There's lots of stupid people, I told her. —There's a whole class of them in our school.

—Stop that, she said.

—A class in every year, I said.

137

—That's not nice, she said. —Stop it.

—Why not just the good room? I said.

—It doesn't sound right, she said.

That made no sense: it sounded exactly right. We were never allowed into that room so it would stay good.

—Why doesn't it? I asked.

—It sounds cheap, she said.

She started smiling.

—It —— I don't know —— Drawing room is a nicer name than good room. It sounds nicer. Unusual.

—Are unusual names nice?

—Yes.

—Then why am I called Patrick?

She laughed but only for a little bit. She smiled at me, I think to make sure that I knew she wasn't laughing at me.

—Because your daddy's called Patrick, she said.

I liked that, being called after my da.

—There are five Patricks in our class, I said.

—Is that right?

—Patrick Clarke. That's me. Patrick O'Neill. Patrick Redmond. Patrick Genocci. Patrick Flynn.

—That's a lot, she said. —It's a nice name. Very dignified.

—Three of them are called Paddy, I told her. —One Pat and one Patrick.

—Is that right? she said. —Which are you?

I stopped for a minute.

—Paddy, I said.

She didn't mind. I was Patrick at home.

—Which one's Patrick? she asked.

—Patrick Genocci.

—His grandad's from Italy, she said.

—I know, I said. —But he's never gone there, Patrick Genocci.

—He will sometime.

—When he's big, I said. —I'm going to Africa.

—Are you? Why?

—I just am, I said. —I have my reasons.

—To convert the black babies?

—No.

I didn't care about the black babies; I was supposed to feel sorry for them, because they were pagans and because they were hungry, but I didn't care. They frightened me, the idea of them, all of them, millions of them, with stick-out bellies and grown-up eyes.

—Why then? she asked.

—To see the animals, I said.

—That'll be nice, she said.

—Not to stay, I said.

She wasn't to give my bed away.

—What animals? she said.

—All of them.

—Especially.

—Zebras and monkeys.

—Would you like to be a vet?

—No.

—Why not?

—There's no zebras and monkeys in Ireland.

—Why do you like zebras?

—I just do.

—They're nice.

—Yeah.

—We'll go to the zoo again; would you like that?

—No.

Phoenix Park was brilliant – the Hollow and the deers; I wanted to go back there again. The bus, where you could see over the wall into the park when you were upstairs. We went there on my Holy Communion after we were finished with my aunties and uncles; on buses all morning, before my da got his car. But not the zoo, I didn't want to go there.

—Why not? said my ma.

—The smell, I said.

It wasn't just the smell. It was more than the smell; it was what the smell had meant, the smell of the animals and the fur on the wire. I'd liked it then, the animals. Pets' Corner – the rabbits – the shop; I'd loads of money – they'd made me buy sweets for Sinbad, Refreshers. But I remembered the smell and I couldn't remember the animals much. Wallabies, little kangaroos that didn't hop. Monkeys' fingers gripping the wire.

I was going to explain it to my ma, I wanted to; I was going to try. She remembered the smell; I could tell by her smile and the way she stopped it from getting too big because I hadn't said it for a joke. I was going to tell her.

Then Sinbad came over and ruined it.

—What are fish-fingers made of?

—Fish.

—What kind of fish?

—All kinds.

—Cod, said my ma. —White fish.

—Why do they –

—No more questions till you're finished.

That was my da.

—Everything on the plate, he said. —Then you can ask your questions.

There were twenty-seven dogs in Barrytown, our part, and fifteen of them had had their tails docked.

—Docked off.

—There's no Off. Docked, by itself.

They got their tails docked to stop them from falling over.

When they wagged their tails they couldn't balance properly and they fell over, so they had to have most of their tails cut off.

—Only when they're pups.

—Yeah.

They only fell over when they were pups.

—Why don't they wait? said Sinbad.

—Thick, I said, though I didn't know what he meant.

—Who? Liam said to Sinbad.

—The vet, said Sinbad.

—For what?

—They only fall over when they're puppies, said Sinbad.

—Why do they cut their tails just for that? They're only puppies for a little while.

—Puppies, I said. —Listen to him. They're pups, right.

He made sense though. None of us knew why. Liam shrugged.

—They just do.

—It must be good for them. Vets are like doctors.

The McEvoys had a Jack Russell. His name was Benson.

—That's a thick name for a dog.

Ian McEvoy said it was his but it was really his ma's. Benson was older than Ian McEvoy.

—They don't dock the ones with long legs, I said.

Benson hardly had any legs. His belly touched the grass. It was easy to catch him. The only problem was having to wait till Missis McEvoy had gone to the shops.

—She likes him, Ian McEvoy told us. —She prefers him to me.

He was stronger than he looked. I could feel his muscles trying to get away. We only wanted to have a look at his tail. I held his back half. He tried to get his mouth back to my hand.

Kevin kicked him.

—Watch it.

Ian McEvoy was worried; if his ma caught us. So worried, he pushed Kevin away.

Kevin let him get away with it.

All we wanted to do was look at his tail, that was all. It was sticking up in the air. It was the healthiest-looking part of Benson. Dogs were supposed to wag their tails when they were happy but Benson definitely wasn't happy and his tail was wagging like mad.

My da wouldn't let us have a dog. He had his reasons, he said. My ma agreed with him.

Kevin held Benson where I'd been holding him and I grabbed his tail to stop it. The tail was a bone, a hairy bone, no fleshiness at all. I closed my fist and the tail wasn't there. We laughed. Benson yelped, like he was joining in. I fisted just my top two fingers so we could see the top of his tail. I made sure that my free fingers didn't touch his bum. It was hard for them not to, the way I was holding him, but I made sure that they didn't rub across his hole.

Ma always sent us to wash our hands before our dinner. Only before our dinner, never before our breakfast or our tea. I sometimes didn't bother; I just went up the stairs, turned the tap on and off, and came back down.

I pushed the hair out of the way. It was white and bristly. Benson tried to charge away in front of me. He hadn't a hope. Me touching his tail hair made him panic; we could feel it in him. Now we could see the butt of his tail. It didn't look like it had been cut – his hair kept springing back – it looked normal, like it was supposed to be that way. There was nothing else to do.

We were disappointed.

—No marks there.

—Press your finger down on it.

We didn't want to let him go yet. We'd expected more, scars or redness or something; bone.

Ian McEvoy was really worried now. He thought we were going to do something to Benson because his tail hadn't been worth looking at.

—My ma's coming; I think she's coming.

—She's not.

—Chicken.

We were definitely going to do something now.

—One –

—Two——

—Three!

We got our hands away and, just when Benson thought he was free, we kicked him, me and Kevin; hollow thumps, one boot each, nearly together on each side. Benson staggered when he was getting away. I thought he was going to fall over on his side; a terror screamed through me, up through me. Blood would come out of his mouth, he'd pant, and stop. But he stayed on his legs and straightened and ran to the side of the house, to the front.

—Why can't we? I asked my da.

—Will you feed it? he said.

—Yeah, I said.

—Will you pay for his food?

—Yeah.

—With what?

—Money.

—What money?

—My money, I said. —My pocket money, I said before he could get anything in.

—Mine as well, said Sinbad.

I'd take Sinbad's money but it was still going to be my dog. I got sixpence on Sundays and Sinbad got threepence. We were getting more after our next birthdays.

—Okay, said my da.

I could tell: he didn't mean Okay you can have a dog; he meant Okay I'll get you some other way.

—They cost nothing, I told him. —You just have to go down to the cats and dogs' home and pick one and they give him to you.

—The dirt, he said.

—We'll make him wipe his paws, I said.

—Not that dirt.

—We'll wash him; I will.

—His number twos, said my da.

He stared. He had us.

—We'll bring him for walks and he'll be able –

—Stop, said my da.

He didn't say it like he was angry; he just said it.

—Listen, he said. —We can't have a dog –

We.

—and I'll tell you why not and that'll be the end of it and you're not to go pestering your mammy. Catherine's asthma.

He waited a bit.

—The dog hair, he said. —She couldn't cope with it.

I hardly knew Catherine; I didn't really know her. She was my sister but she was only a baby, a bit bigger. I never spoke to her. She was useless; she slept a lot. Her cheeks were huge. She walked around showing us what was in her potty; she thought it was great.

—Look!

She followed me.

—Pat'ick! Look!

She had asthma. I didn't know what asthma was, only that she had it and it was noisy and it worried my ma. Catherine had been in the hospital twice because of it, never in an ambulance though. I didn't know why dog hairs had anything to do with her asthma. He was just using it as an excuse for

144

not getting a dog, my da; he just didn't want one. He was just saying about Catherine's asthma because he knew that we couldn't say anything about it. We'd never complain to our ma about Catherine's asthma.

Sinbad spoke. I jumped.

—We can get a dog with no hair.

My da started laughing. He thought it was a great joke. He messed up our hair – Sinbad started smiling – and that killed it. We'd never get a dog.

Marrowfat peas sat in the gravy and soaked it up into themselves. I ate them one at a time. I loved them. I loved the hard feel of their skin, and the inside soft and messy and watery.

They came in a net in the packet, with a big white tablet as well. They had to be soaked in water, starting on Saturday night. I did it, slid them into the bowl of water. My ma stopped me from putting my tongue on the tablet.

—No, love.

—What's it for? I asked.

—To keep them fresh, she said. —And to soften them.

Sunday peas.

My da spoke.

—Where was Moses when the lights went out?

I answered.

—Under the bed looking for matches.

—Good man, he said.

I didn't understand it but it made me laugh.

Sinbad and me knocked on their bedroom door. I did the knocking.

—What?

—Is it morning yet?

145

—Morning not to get up.

That meant we had to go back to our bedroom.

It was hard to tell in the summer when you woke up and it was bright.

Our territory was getting smaller. The fields were patches among the different houses and bits left over where the roads didn't meet properly. They'd become dumps for all the waste stuff, bits of wood and brick and solidified bags of cement and milk bottles. They were good for exploring but bad for running in.

I heard the crack, felt it through my foot and I knew there was going to be pain before it came. I had time and control to decide where to fall. I fell onto a clean piece of grass and rolled. My cry of pain was good. The pain was real though, and rising. I'd hit a scaffolding joint hidden in the grass. The pain grew quickly. The whimper surprised me. My foot was wet. My shoe was full of blood. It was like water, creamier. It was warm and cold. My sock was wringing.

They were all standing around me. Liam had found the scaffolding joint. He held it in front of my face. I could tell it was heavy, the way he was holding it. It was big and impressive. There'd be loads of blood.

—What is it? said Sinbad.

—A scaffold thing.

—Thick eejit.

I wanted to take my shoe off. I held the heel and groaned. They watched. I pulled slowly, slowly. I thought about getting Kevin to pull it off, like in a film. But it would have hurt. It didn't feel as wet in there now, just warm. And sore. Still sore. Enough for a limp. I lifted my foot out. No blood. The sock was down at the back, under the heel. I took it off, hoping. They watched. I groaned again and took the sock away. They gasped and yeuched.

146

It was brilliant. The toenail had come off my big toe. It looked cruel. It was real. It was painful. I lifted the nail a little bit. They all looked. I sucked in breath.

—Aaah ——!

I tried to put the nail into its proper position but it really hurt. The sock wasn't going to go back on. They'd all seen it. I wanted to go home now.

Liam carried my shoe. I leaned on Kevin all the way home. Sinbad ran ahead.

—She'll put your foot in Dettol, said Aidan.

—Shut up, you, I said.

There were no farms left. Our pitch was gone, first sliced in half for pipes, then made into eight houses. The field behind the shops was still ours and we went there more often. Over at the Corporation houses, that end, wasn't ours any more. There was another tribe there now, tougher than us, though none of us said it. Our territory was being taken from us but we were fighting back. We played Indians and Cowboys now, not Cowboys and Indians.

—Ger-on-IMO!

We built a wigwam in the field behind the shops. Liam and Aidan's da called it an igloo by mistake. He came into the field to look at us building it. He was walking back from the shops.

—That's a grand igloo, boys, he said.

—It's a wigwam, I said.

—It's a tepee, said Kevin.

Liam and Aidan said nothing. They wanted their da to go away.

—Oh, that's right, said Mister O'Connell.

He had a net bag for his messages. He took a brown bag out of it. I knew what was in it.

—D'yis want a biscuit, boys?

We queued up. We let Liam and Aidan go first. He was their da.

—Did you see his handbag? said Kevin when Mister O'Connell was gone.

—It wasn't a handbag, said Aidan.

—It was so, said Kevin.

No one joined in.

There were fields past the Corporation houses but they were too far away now. Past the Corporation houses. Somewhere else.

We'd done the compass points in school the day we got the summer holidays.

—Which way am I pointing —— NOW.

—East.

—One of you at a time. —— YOU.

—East, Sir.

—Just to make sure you didn't say that just because Mister Bradshaw got there before you. —— NOW.

—West, Sir.

The Corporation houses were west. The seafront was east. Raheny was south. The north was interesting.

—The last frontier, said my da.

First there were more new houses. There was no one in them yet because they'd all flooded before they were finished. Past the houses was the field with the hills, the one that had been dug up and stopped and grown over, where we built our huts. And over the hills was Bayside.

Bayside wasn't finished yet but it wasn't the building sites we were after this time. It was the shape of the place. It was mad. The roads were crooked. The garages weren't in the proper place. They were in blocks away from the houses. Down a path, into a yard, a fort made of garages. The place made no sense. We went there to get lost.

—It's a labyrinth.

148

—Labyrinth!

—Labyrinth labyrinth labyrinth!

We charged through on our bikes. Bikes became important, our horses. We galloped through the garage yards and made it to the other side. I tied a rope to the handlebars and hitched my bike to a pole whenever I got off it. We parked our bikes on verges so they could graze. The rope got caught between the spokes of the front wheel; I went over the handlebars, straight over. It was over before I knew. The bike was on top of me. I was alone. I was okay. I wasn't even cut. We charged into the garages –

—Woo wooo wooo wooo wooo wooo wooo!

and the garages captured our noise and made it bigger and grown-up. We escaped out the other end, out onto the street and back for a second attack.

We got material from our houses and made headbands. Mine was a tartan one, with a seagull's feather. We took off our jumpers and shirts and vests. James O'Keefe took off his trousers and rode through Bayside in his underpants. His skin was stuck to the saddle when he was getting off, from the sweat; you could hear the skin clinging to the plastic. We threw his trousers onto the roof of a garage, and his shirt and his vest. We put his jumper down a shore.

The garage roofs were easy to get up onto. We climbed up on our saddles and onto the roofs when we'd conquered the forts.

—Woo wooo wooo wooo wooo wooo wooo!

A woman looked out of a bedroom window and made a face and moved her hands, telling us to get down. We did the first time. We got on our bikes and hightailed it out of Bayside. She'd called the police; her husband was a Guard; she was a witch. I got straight from the roof onto the bike without touching the ground. I pushed off from the wall.

149

There was a wobble but then I was gone. I circled the garages to make sure that the others had time to escape.

I'd got the bike for Christmas, two Christmases before. I woke up. I thought I did. The bedroom door was closing. The bike was leaning against the end of my bed. I was confused. And afraid. The door clicked shut. I stayed in the bed. I heard no steps outside in the hall. I didn't try to ride the bike for months after. We didn't need them. We were better on foot through the fields and sites. I didn't like it. I didn't know who'd given it to me. It should never have been in my bedroom. It was a Raleigh, a gold one. It was the right size for me and I didn't like that either. I wanted a grown-up one, with straight handlebars and brakes that fit properly into my hands with the bars, like Kevin had. My brakes stuck down under the bars. I had to gather them into my hands. When I held the bar and the brake together the bike stopped; I couldn't do it. The only thing I did like was a Manchester United sticker that was in my stocking when I woke up again in the morning. I stuck it on the bar under the saddle.

We didn't need bikes then. We walked; we ran. We ran away. That was the best, running away. We shouted at watchmen, we threw stones at windows, we played knick-knack – and ran away. We owned Barrytown, the whole lot of it. It went on forever. It was a country.

Bayside was for bikes.

I couldn't cycle it. I could get my leg over the saddle and onto the pedal and push but that was all. I couldn't go; I couldn't stay up. I didn't know how. I was doing everything right. I ran the bike, got onto it and fell over. I was frightened. I knew I was going to fall before I started. I gave up. I put the bike in the shed. My da got angry. I didn't care.

—Santy got you that bike, he said. —The least you can do is learn how to cycle the bloody thing.

I said nothing.

—It comes natural, he said. —It's as natural as walking.
I could walk.
I asked him to show me.
—About time, he said.
I got up on the bike; he held the back of the saddle and I pedalled. Up the garden. Down the garden. He thought I was enjoying it; I hated it. I knew: he let go: I fell over.
—Keep pedalling keep pedalling keep pedalling –
I fell over. I got off the bike. I wasn't really falling. I was putting my left foot down. That made him more annoyed.
—You're not trying.
He pulled the bike away from me.
—Come on; get up.
I couldn't. He had the bike. He realised this. He gave it back. I got up. He held the back. He said nothing. I pedalled. We went down the garden. I went faster. I stayed up; he was still holding. I looked back. He wasn't there. I fell over. But I'd done it; I'd gone a bit without him. I could do it. I didn't need him now. I didn't want him.
He was gone anyway. Back into the house.
—You'll be grand now, he said.
He was just lazy.
I stayed on. I turned at the top of the garden instead of getting off and turning the bike and getting back on. I stayed on. Around the garden three times. Nearly into the hedge. I stayed on.
We ruled Bayside. We camped up on the garage roofs. We lit a fire. We could see in all directions. We were ready for any attack. There were boys in Bayside but they were mostly smaller and saps. The ones our age were saps too. We got one of the small ones; we held him hostage. We made him climb up on the saddle, onto the roof. We surrounded him. We held him over the side of the roof. We kicked him. I gave him a dead leg.

—If we get attacked you're dead, Kevin told him.

We held him for ten minutes. We made him jump off the roof. He landed the right way. Nothing ever happened. No one came after us.

Bayside was great for knick-knacking. In the night. There were no walls or hedges, no real gardens. A straight row of bells. It was easy. There was a path or a lane at the end of each row. Escaping was nothing. The really great bit was doubling back and doing it all over again. Our record was seventeen. Seventeen times we rang the five bells in the row and escaped. One of the houses didn't have a bell so I knocked on the glass. We were dizzy by the time we'd finished. We did it in a relay. Me first, then Kevin, Liam, Aidan, me again. The thrill was coming round to start again, not knowing if there'd be a door open waiting to catch you.

—Maybe they're all out.

—No way, said Kevin. —They're all in.

—How?

—They are, I said. —I saw them.

It was getting cold. I put my shirt and jumper back on.

—Is it morning yet?

—Morning not to get up.

I was good at waiting for the scab to be ready. I never rushed. I waited until I was sure it was hollow, sure that the crust had lifted off my knee. It came off neat and tidy and there was no blood underneath, just a red mark; that was the knee being fixed. Scabs were made by things in your blood called corpuscles. There were thirty-five billion corpuscles in your blood. They made the scabs to stop you from bleeding to death.

I was the same way with sticky eyes. I let them stay sticky and they got hard. In the mornings this happened sometimes.

One eye was sticky where I'd had my head on the pillow. My ma said a draught caused it. I turned on my back. I concentrated on the eye; I kept it shut. Sleepy eyes, my ma called them. She'd cleared them out with the facecloth when I'd shown her them the first time, both of them sticky. I didn't tell her any more. I kept them for myself. I waited. When my ma shouted up at us to hurry up for our breakfast I got up and got dressed. I tested the eye. I pulled the lids as if I was going to open them. They were nice and stuck, and dry. I finished dressing. I sat on the bed and touched the eye carefully, around the outside and the corners. The outside corner first, I scooped the crust away on the top of my finger and looked. There was never as much on the finger as it felt there'd be, only a tiny bit of flake. They'd pop open and I could feel the air on my eyeball. Then I'd rub the eye and it was normal again. There was nothing when I looked in the mirror in the bathroom. Just two eyes the same.

Sinbad didn't notice the way I did. There had to be shouts and screams and big gaps between them before he knew anything. When it was quiet it was fine; that was the way he thought. He wouldn't agree with me, even when I got him on the ground.

I was alone, the only one who knew. I knew better than they did. They were in it: all I could do was watch. I paid more attention than they did, because they kept saying the same things over and over.

—I do not.
—You do.
—I do not.
——You do, I'm afraid.

I waited for one of them to say something different, wanting it – they'd go forward again and it would end for a while. Their fights were like a train that kept getting stuck at the corner tracks and you had to lean over and push it or straighten it. Only now, all I could do was listen and wish. I didn't pray; there were no prayers for this. The Our Father didn't fit, or the Hail Mary. But I rocked the same way I sometimes did when I was saying prayers. Backwards and forwards, the rhythm of the prayer. Grace Before Meals was the fastest, probably because we were all starving just before lunch, just after the bell.

I rocked.

—Stop stop stop stop –

On the stairs. On the step outside the back door. In bed. Sitting beside my da. At the table in the kitchen.

—I hate them this way.

—They're the same as last Sunday.

Da only had a fry on Sunday mornings. We had a sausage each and black pudding if we wanted it, as well as what we always had. At least an hour before mass.

—Gollop it down now, Ma warned me, —or you won't be able to go up for communion.

I looked at the clock. There were nine minutes before half-eleven and we were going to half-twelve mass. I divided my sausage in nine.

—I told you before, I hate them runny.

—They were runny last week.

—I hate them this way; I won't –

I rocked.

—Do you need to go to the toilet?

—No.

—What's wrong with you then?

—Nothing.

—Well, stop squirming there like a half-wit. Eat your breakfast.

He said nothing else. He ate everything, the runny egg as well. I liked them runny. He got it all up with about half a slice of bread. I could never do that properly. The egg just ran ahead in front of the bread when I did it. He cleaned his plate. He didn't say anything. He knew I was watching; he'd caught me rocking and he knew why.

He said the tea was nice.

He was still chewing at half-eleven. I watched for the minute hand to click, up past the six; I watched him. I heard the click from behind the clock. He didn't swallow for thirty-six seconds after that.

I kept it to myself. If he went up for communion I'd see what happened. I knew and God knew.

I loved twirling the dial on the radio. I turned it on and put it on its back on the kitchen table. I was never allowed to bring it out of the kitchen. I got the dial and turned it as much as my wrist would let me, as quick as I could. I loved the high-pitched scratch and then the voice and the scratching again, different, and a voice, maybe a woman; I wouldn't stop to find out. Around and back, around and back; music and bloops, voices, nothing. There was dirt in the lines of the plastic front, where the sound came out, like the dirt under your nails, and in the letters of the gold BUSH stuck on the bottom corner. My ma listened to The Kennedys of Castle-ross. I stayed in the kitchen with her when it was on during the holidays, but I didn't listen to it. I sat on a chair and waited till it was over and watched her listening.

I opened the box of Persil and sprinkled some of it on the sea. Nothing happened really; it just spotted the water and disappeared. I did it again. I couldn't think of anything else to do with it.

—Give us it, said Kevin.

I did.

He grabbed Edward Swanwick. We grabbed him as well

when we saw what he was doing. Edward Swanwick wasn't really a friend of ours. He was on the edge. I'd never called for him. I'd never been in his kitchen. At Halloween, when we knocked at his house, they never gave us sweets or money – always fruit. And Missis Swanwick warned us to eat it.

—What did she mean?

—It's none of her business what we do with it, said Liam.

We got Edward Swanwick onto the ground and tried to get his mouth open. It was easy; there were ways of doing it. Keeping it open was the problem. Kevin started pouring the Persil onto his face; Liam held Edward Swanwick's head by the ears so he couldn't get his face away; I held his nose and pinched his diddy. Some of the Persil got in. Edward Swanwick was gagging and shuddering, trying to shake us off. It was in his eyes as well. The box was empty. Kevin shoved it up Edward Swanwick's jumper and we let him up. He didn't say anything. He couldn't; if he didn't pretend he'd enjoyed himself he was gone, out of the gang. He got sick; not much, mostly the Persil.

That was the type of thing we robbed, mostly. Sweets were hard, up at the counter, hard to get at because of the glass and the women. They guarded the sweets because they thought that no one would be bothered robbing the other stuff. They didn't understand. They didn't understand that robbing had nothing to do with what we wanted; it was the dare, the terror, the getting away with it.

It was always women. There were about six shops between Raheny and Baldoyle that we raided. There were no supermarkets yet, just grocers and shops that sold everything. Once, when we were out on a walk, Ma asked for the Evening Press, four Choc-pops, a packet of Lyons Green Label and a mouse trap and the woman was able to get them all without stretching. I was a bit nervous: I'd robbed a box of Shredded Wheat out of there a few days before and I was afraid she'd recognise me. I minded the pram while my ma talked to her, about the weather and the new houses.

We only robbed when the weather was nice. We never robbed in Barrytown. That would have been stupid. There was Missis Kilmartin's one-way glass, but that wasn't all; the people in the shops were friends with our parents. They'd all got married and moved to Barrytown at the same time. They were all pioneers, my da said. I didn't know what he meant but he liked saying it; he loved going down to the shops and meeting and talking to the owners, except Missis Kilmartin. He told me that Mister Kilmartin was locked up in the attic.

—Don't listen to him, said my ma. —He's in the British Navy.

—In a ship?

—I think so.

—Anywhere except at home, said my da.

He'd just fixed the wonky kitchen chair so he was feeling a bit proud of himself; you could tell by the way he kept sitting on it and looking down at the legs and trying to rock it.

—That's grand now, he said. —Isn't it?

—Smashing, said my ma.

The grocer in Barrytown was a man, a nice one, Mister Fitzpatrick. He gave you more broken biscuits than you were entitled to. He was huge. He leaned over you. I remembered when I was small, he stepped over me. We'd never have robbed off Mister Fitz. He'd have known what we were up to, and everyone loved him. Our parents would have killed us. Missis Fitz sat on a chair in the front door when the weather was nice, like an ad for the shop. She was lovely looking. They had a daughter, Naomi; she was in secondary school. She was as nice looking as her mother. She worked in the shop on Saturdays, after school; filled the cardboard boxes, the weekend orders for all the houses in Barrytown. Kevin's brother did the deliveries on a colossal black bike with a basket in the front. He got seven and six for it. He said Naomi could open bottles of Fanta with her gee. I wanted to kill him when he said that. I wanted to save Naomi.

Get the biggest box. It was Kevin's idea. It was great. Whoever got the thing in the biggest box out of the shop, he won. It had to be a full box; that was one of the first rules, after Liam came out of a shop with an empty one, a huge one that had had boxes of Cornflakes inside it. You couldn't do this in any shop. You had to be careful. Most of the shops had their own specialities, although the women behind the counter didn't know this. The one in Raheny was great for robbing magazines; the comics were up on the counter, too near the noses of the three ancient women that patrolled the counter. The magazines, though, were much easier. The women were saps: they thought that we wouldn't be interested in women's magazines and knitting magazines, so they put them on a rack right beside the door so they'd look nice in the window. Another thing, they served grown-ups first, always. I waited for the right moment. I was outside, tying my lace. A woman went in; the three old women dashed to serve her and I leaned in and grabbed five Women's Weeklys. I brought them down the lane beside the new library and we tore them up. I once got a Football Monthly out of the window rack. I couldn't believe it when I saw it there. They must have run out of room on the counter. I thought for a sec that they might have put it there as bait. I thought about it; I looked around. I took it. There was another shop that invited you to rob their biscuits. It was in Baldoyle. The tins of biscuits – the loose ones – were on a ledge that ran along the counter, just under it. You could fill your pockets while the woman counted your aniseed balls. One box had Milk-choc Goldgrain in it, the only chocolate ones. We'd queue up in front of that box, waiting our turn. She thought we were being polite. It was dark in the shop; she must never have seen the crumbs.

For boxes, we went to Tootsie's.

—A quarter of jelly babies, Tootsie; all boys.

Tootsie was in charge of this big manky shop up a bit from where we swam at the seafront. The windows were wasps' graveyards; they dried and cracked in the sun. We added some. We collected them, and bees, in jars, watched them dying and milling each other, then went up to Tootsie's and poured them all over the stuff in the window when Tootsie wasn't looking. We'd have done it even if she was looking; she looked at you and didn't see anything; it took ages for her face to catch up. Tootsie didn't own the shop. She minded it for someone. She did everything in slow motion, everything. Sometimes there was even an action replay; she'd pick up something again, dead slow-ow-owly, to check the price again. She wrote the price of everything on a paper bag, real neat; she used a ruler to do the line under the numbers. Then she did the sum, but she stopped and started again all the way, like she was climbing down a ladder with wobbly rungs. That was when you could have walked out of the shop with anything. We robbed her steps, the ones she used for the top shelves. I took one end and Kevin took the other. The woman Tootsie was serving wasn't from our place. We didn't know her. We made it look like we were helping Tootsie, kept our faces serious. We threw the steps into the sea. It made a good noise but not much of a splash. We stood on them when the tide was half-in to make it look like we were walking on the water. You could ask Tootsie anything.

—D'you sell cars, Tootsie?

—No.

She thought about it first.

—Why not?

She just looked.

—D'you sell rhinoceroses, Tootsie?

—No.

You could see the track-marks of Tootsie's fingers in the cream in the cakes on the tray on the fridge behind the counter. The cream was yellow, the tracks hard and permanent. The fridge was small and fat, for ice-pops and blocks of ice-cream. I crept behind the counter and pulled out the plug.

There was a bakery in Raheny guarded by two women. It had the best smell of any shop. It wasn't bread; it wasn't a rushing smell, like steam surrounding you. It was quieter, part of the air, not warm and smothering and upsetting. The smell made me feel good. The cakes were on shelves inside the all-glass counter, not stacks of them, a few of each on plates two feet apart down the shelves; small cakes, not huge things exploding with cream. The cakes were bright, hard in a nice way – biscuits that were too good to be called biscuits. Like cakes in a fairy tale; you could have built things out of them. I didn't know where the baking got done. There was a door at the back but the women always closed it when they were coming and going, never together – there was always one of them behind the counter, knitting. They both knitted. They might have been having a race. They were very fast. We couldn't go in there to look around; we couldn't pretend we were looking for something. There was just the counter, and the shelves under it. We looked in the window. Sometimes I'd have enough money for a cake. They weren't as nice as they looked. And I'd have to share. You had to hold the cake so that most of it was behind your fingers, safe, so the others could only get a small bite.

We got caught.

My ma saw us and she blabbed to my da. She was out on a walk with the girls and she saw us grabbing a pile of Woman's Ways. I saw her before I went down the lane. I pretended I didn't. My legs weren't there for a few seconds; my stomach felt empty and full; I had to stop a moan from getting out. What was she doing in Raheny? She never went to Raheny. It was miles from Barrytown. I had to go to the toilet, immediately. The others kept watch. I'd told them about my ma. They were in trouble too. I wiped myself with Sinbad's hankie. He wanted to run after Ma; he was crying. Kevin gave him a Chinese torture. He looked over at me to make sure it was alright. But Sinbad was crying already; he didn't seem to notice the pain, so Kevin stopped. We looked at my gick. It was like a plastic one, perfect. None of them jeered at me when they saw it.

There was only one way out of the lane, back the way we'd run in. I hated my ma. She'd be waiting behind the wall, waiting. She'd smack me, and give me Sinbad's share as well, in front of the others.

Kevin had done it. I'd only been with him.

I tested it.

I was still in trouble.

Ian McEvoy went out onto the path first. I could tell from his face that my ma wasn't there. We cheered and ran out onto the path. She hadn't seen us.

She'd seen us.

She hadn't seen us. She'd have come after us and made us bring the Woman's Ways back and say Sorry to the women. She'd been too far away to recognise us. She hadn't seen what we'd done, just us running away. We hadn't been running away, we'd only been running – having a chase. We'd paid for the Woman's Ways; they were old ones and the women had said that we could take them, they'd asked us to. She'd been too far away. I looked like two of my cousins. I took my jumper off. I'd hide it and go into the house in just my shirt. It couldn't have been me if it had been a boy in a blue jumper like mine cos I wasn't wearing it. She'd been looking at Cathy in the pram. She'd been too busy.

She'd seen us.

She told my da and I got killed. He didn't give me a chance to deny it. It was just as well. I would have denied it and I'd have got into even bigger trouble. He used his belt. He didn't wear a belt. He kept it just for this. The back of my legs. The outside of my hand that was trying to cover my legs. The arm that he held onto was sore for days after. Round in a circle in the living room. Trying to get well in front of the sweep of the belt so it wouldn't hurt as much. I should have done it the other way, backed into the belt, given him less room to swing. Everyone else in the house was crying, not just me. The whistle of the belt; he was trying to get in a good shot. Messing, playing with me, that was what he was doing. Then he stopped. I kept moving, jerking ahead; I didn't know he'd stopped for good. He let go of my arm, and I noticed the pain there. Up where it joined the shoulder, it was very sore there. I was heading into uncontrollable sobs. I didn't want that; I didn't enjoy it any more. I held my breath. It was over. It was over. Nothing more would happen. It had been worth it.

He was sweating.

—Go up to your room now. Go on.

He didn't sound as hard as he'd wanted to.

I looked at my ma. She was white. Her lips had disappeared. It served her right.

Sinbad was already up there. He'd only got a few belts; it had all been my fault. He was lying face-down on his bed. He was crying. When he saw it was me he slowed down.

—Look.

I showed him the backs of my legs.

—Show me yours.

He didn't have half as many marks. I didn't say anything. He could see for himself; some of them should have been his. I could see that that was what he was thinking, and that was enough for me.

—He's a big bastard, I said. —Isn't he?

—Yeah.

—He's a big bastard, I said again.

—He's a big bastard, said Sinbad.

We got under our blankets and had a war. I liked the dark under the blankets. You could get rid of it easily when you wanted to. And it was nice the way the blankets pressed me down; I could feel it in my head. It was warm. Light came in. The blanket had been lifted up. It was Sinbad. He climbed in.

Our venetian blinds were different colours. One day – it was raining – I realised that there was a pattern. The bottom one was yellow, the one next was light blue, then pink, then red. Then yellow again. The top one was blue. The frame at the top was white. So was the cord. I lay on the floor with my feet towards the window and counted the slats, faster and faster.

There were lots of venetian blinds in Barrytown but we were the only ones I knew that had them in the back of the house as well as the front. Me and Kevin went around all the houses and there were seventeen blinds in the front windows that were crooked. There were fifty-four houses in Barrytown, not counting the new Corporation ones and the other ones that were just finished and had no one in them yet. We went around again; eleven of the seventeen were crooked on the left side. The blinds came down to the window ledge on the right but were stuck about five slats up on the left. Worst was the Kellys' with ten slats. We could see Missis Kelly in the front room doing nothing. O'Connell's weren't only crooked, they were buckled; not Mister O'Connell's bedroom ones upstairs – they were perfect, and closed – the front-room ones, the room we played in. Only twenty houses didn't have blinds.

—Useless.

Kevin's house had coloured ones as well.

—Multi-coloured are best.

—Yeah.

My ma filled the bath with water when she was washing them. She only ever did it once. I wanted to help but there wasn't room; I wanted to make sure that she put them back in the right order. She pulled the cord out of all the holes in the slats and put each slat in the bath, one at a time. I looked at a new washed yellow one and a dirty yellow one while she was feeding the babies; I put them beside each other. They were different colours now. I pulled my finger through the dirt; the new yellow was underneath it.

I asked her not to wash one of each colour.

—Will you not? I asked again.

—Why?

She always stopped and listened; she always wanted to know.

—Just —

I couldn't explain it; it was kind of a secret.

—To compare.

—But they're filthy dirty, love.

I knew when I was going to bed that I'd never lie on the floor and look up at the colours again. She came in to turn off the light. She put her hand on my forehead and hair. Her hand smelt of water and the dirt behind the fridge. I got my head from under her hand; I shifted to the corner.

—Is it because of the blinds?

—No.

—What is it?

—I'm hot.

—D'you want one of the blankets off?

—No.

She spent ages tucking me in; I wanted her to go but I didn't as well.

Sinbad was asleep. He'd once got his head caught in the bars of his cot and he'd cried all night, till daylight when I saw him. That was years ago. He slept in a bed now. My Uncle Raymond had brought it on the roof of his car. The mattress was wet because it had started raining when he was half-way between his house and our house. We said it was because of all our cousins' wee-wees, me and Sinbad. We didn't know till two days later, when the mattress was dry, that it was Sinbad's bed. Then Uncle Frank took Sinbad's cot away on the roof of his car.

—They were dirty, Patrick, she said. —You have to wash things when they're dirty. Specially with babies. D'you understand?

If I said Yes that would mean more than I just understood. I said nothing, the way Sinbad always did.

—Patrick?

I said nothing.

—Have you any tickles?

I tried like mad not to laugh.

Aidan was the commentator. He was brilliant at it. We had to tell him our names before the match. We were playing across the road. Our pitch was gone. The gates on each side were the goals. There were eight of us, just right, four a side. Whoever had the ball when a car was coming got a throw-in when the car had gone. If you decided to risk it but the driver blasted the horn before you took your shot the goal was disallowed, if it was a goal. You couldn't use the kerb for shielding the ball. Anything higher than the top of the pillar was over the bar.

I had to fight for George Best.

Kevin didn't follow Manchester United. He followed Leeds. He'd once followed United but then he'd changed because of his brother; his brother followed Leeds.

It was Kevin's turn to pick.

—Eddie Gray, he said.

No one else wanted to be Eddie Gray. Ian McEvoy followed
Leeds as well but he was always Johnny Giles. Kevin was sick
once, and Ian McEvoy picked Eddie Gray.

—Why not Johnny Giles?

—Just——

I'd caught him.

Four of us followed Manchester United. All of us wanted
to be George Best. We always made Sinbad be Nobby Stiles
so he stopped following United and started following Liverpool, although he didn't really follow anyone. For a while I
nearly changed to Leeds as well, but I couldn't. They'd have
said that it was just because of Kevin but, mostly, it was
because of George Best.

What we did was, Kevin got four ice-pop sticks and broke
one of them and each United supporter picked a stick and
whoever got the broken stick got to choose first.

Aidan picked the small stick.

—Bobby Charlton, he said.

He picked Bobby Charlton because he knew what would
happen to him if he picked George Best. I'd do him. There
was no ref. You could do what you wanted, even tackle one
of your own team. I could beat Aidan. He was a good fighter
but he didn't like it. He always let you up before you
surrendered properly; then you could get him back.

Kevin threw away one of the big sticks. I picked the small
one this time.

—George Best.

Liam was Denis Law. If he'd picked the small stick he'd
have been George Best. I wouldn't have stopped him. He was
different. I'd never had a fight with him. There was something; he'd have won. He wasn't that much bigger. There was
something. It hadn't always been like that. He'd been very

166

small once. He wasn't that big now. His eyes. There was no shine on them. When the brothers were together, standing beside each other, it was easy to see them the way we saw them; little, jokes, sad, nice. They were our friends because we hated them; it was good to have them around. I was cleaner than them, brainier than them. I was better than them. Separate, it was different. Aidan got smaller, unfinished looking. Liam became dangerous. They looked the same together. They were nothing alike when you met one of them alone. That nearly never happened. They weren't twins. Liam was older than Aidan. They both followed United.

—It's cheaper, said Ian McEvoy when they weren't there.

—The game's about to commence, said Aidan.

Me, Aidan, Ian McEvoy and Sinbad versus Kevin, Liam, Edward Swanwick and James O'Keefe. We were given a two-goal lead because we had Sinbad. He was much smaller than everyone else. Teams with Sinbad in them usually won. We all thought it was because of the automatic two-goal lead but it wasn't. (The score in one match was seventy-three, sixty-seven.) It was because Sinbad was a good player. But none of us knew this; he was a twirp; we were stuck with him because he was my little brother. He was a brilliant dribbler. I didn't know until Mister O'Keefe, James O'Keefe's da, told me.

—He has the perfect centre of gravity for a soccer player, said Mister O'Keefe.

I looked at Sinbad. He was just my little brother. I hated him. He never wiped his nose. He cried. He wet the bed. He got away with not eating his dinner. He had to wear specs with one black lens. He ran to get the ball. No one else did that. They all waited for it to come to them. He went through them all, no bother. He was brilliant. He wasn't selfish like most fellas who could dribble. It was weird, looking at him.

167

It was great, and I wanted to kill him. You couldn't be proud of your little brother.

We were two-nil up before we started.

—The captains shake hands.

I shook hands with Kevin. We squeezed real hard. We were Northern Ireland. Kevin was Scotland. Bobby Charlton was playing for Northern Ireland because he was on his holidays there.

—Scotland to kick off.

These games were fast. It was nothing like being on grass. The road wasn't wide. We were packed in together. The gates were closed. The smack of the ball against the gate was a goal. Goalkeepers scored about half the goals. We tried to change the rules but the goalkeepers objected; they wouldn't go in goal if they weren't allowed score goals. The useless players went in goal but we still needed them. Once, James O'Keefe, the worst player of us all, kicked out from goal. He scored a goal but the ball whacked off the gate and back across the road, into his own goal. He'd scored a goal and an O.G. with the one shot.

—My word, said the commentator. —Extraordinary.

Scotland kicked off.

—Denis Law taps to Eddie Gray –

I got a foot in; the ball hit the gate.

—Yessss!

—My word, said the commentator. —A goal by Best. One-nil to Northern Ireland.

—Hey! I reminded him. —Sinbad's goals.

—Three-nil to Northern Ireland. What a start. What can Scotland do now?

Scotland scored three.

It made you dizzy. The ball bombed over the road, and over. It was a bit burst. It hurt when it got you in the leg.

—I can't recall a game quite as exciting as this one, said the commentator. —My word.

He'd just scored a goal.

It always slowed down after a while. If it hadn't we'd never have played it. It would have been just stupid. Your feet got sore blemming a burst ball.

—Seventeen, sixteen to Northern Ireland.

—It's seventeen-all!

—It isn't. I've been counting.

—What is it? Kevin asked Edward Swanwick.

—Seventeen-all.

—There, said Kevin.

—He's on your team, I said. —He's just saying it cos you said it.

—He's on your team, he said.

He was pointing at the commentator.

—Really, the referee will have to take control of the situation.

—Shut up, you.

—I'm supposed to talk. It's my job.

—Shut up; your da's an alco.

This always happened as well.

—Okay, I said. —Seventeen-all. We'll win anyway.

—We'll see about that.

Kevin turned to his team.

—Come on! Wake up! Wake up!

Liam and Aidan never did anything when we said things about their da.

The game had slowed down. Aidan didn't commentate for a while. It was getting dark. The game ended at teatime. If James O'Keefe was late for his tea his ma gave it to the cat. That was what she'd shouted one day when he'd been hiding behind a hedge when she'd called him in.

—James O'Keefe! I'm going to give your fish-fingers to the cat!

He went in. He said later that he'd been hiding cos he thought they'd be having mince and turnips for their tea, not fish-fingers. But he was always lying. He was the biggest liar in Barrytown.

Twenty-seven, twenty-three; we were winning again.

—My word, said Aidan. —Roger Hunt is posing problems for the Scotland defence.

Roger Hunt was Sinbad. They couldn't cope with him. It was because he was small and he was able to hide the ball behind himself. Kevin was good at sliding tackles but we were playing on the road so Sinbad was safe. It was much easier to foul someone the same size as you. Another thing about Sinbad, he didn't score the goals himself. He passed the ball to someone who couldn't miss – mostly me – and they all marked me instead of Sinbad because I was scoring the goals. I'd scored twenty-one of our goals. Seven hat-tricks.

—Why are they called hat-tricks?

—Cos you get given a hat if you score one.

If you played for Ireland you got a cap. It was like a school cap or a cub's cap, with a badge on it. England caps had a thing on the top of them, like the cord on my da's dressing gown. You'd never have worn one if you got one. You were supposed to put them in one of those presses with glass doors and people could look at them when they came to your house, and your medals. When I was sick I was let wear my da's dressing gown.

Mister O'Keefe invented Barrytown United. I liked Mister O'Keefe. His first name was Tommy and he let us call him that. It was weird at first. James O'Keefe didn't call him Tommy and none of us called him Tommy either when Missis O'Keefe was around but that wasn't because Tommy told us not to. We just didn't. James O'Keefe didn't know what his ma's first name was.

—Agnes.

That was Ian McEvoy's one.

—Gertie, said Liam.

That was his and Aidan's ma's name.

—Does it say that on the grave?

—Yeah.

It was James O'Keefe's turn.

—Don't know.

I didn't believe him, but then I did. I'd thought he wasn't telling us because it was a name we'd laugh at, but we were laughing at them all, except Gertie. We tortured him, a Chinese burn on each arm at the same time, and he still didn't know his ma's name.

—Find out, said Kevin, when we let him up cos he was coughing.

—How?

—Just find out, said Kevin. —That's your mission.

James O'Keefe looked panicky.

—Ask her, I said.

—Don't give him hints, said Kevin. —You'd better know by after dinner, he told James O'Keefe.

But then we forgot all about it.

Missis O'Keefe wasn't that bad.

—George Best elbows Alan Gilzean in the face.

—I didn't touch him, I said.

I kicked the ball away to stop the game.

—I didn't touch him. He ran into me.

It was only Edward Swanwick. He was holding his nose so we wouldn't see that he wasn't bleeding. His eyes were wet.

—He's crying, said Ian McEvoy. —Look it.

I wouldn't have done it if it had been any of the others.

171

They knew that, they didn't care; it was only Edward Swanwick.

—And, really, said the commentator. —Alan Gilzean seems to be making a bit of a meal of his little knock.

The funny thing was, Aidan was never like that – that funny – when he was just himself, when he wasn't commentating. Forty-two, thirty-eight to Northern Ireland. Kevin's neck was getting red; he was going to lose. It was great. It was getting dark. Missis O'Keefe was the final whistle. Any minute now.

—Barrytown United.
  —Barrytown Rovers.
  We were thinking of names.
  —Barrytown Celtic.
  —Barrytown United's best.
  I said that. It had to be United. We were sitting in O'Keefe's back garden. Mister O'Keefe was sitting on a brick. He was smoking a cigarette.
  —Barrytown Forest, said Liam.
  Mister O'Keefe laughed but none of us did.
  —United.
  —Nev-er.
  —Let's have a vote for it, said Ian McEvoy.
  Mister O'Keefe rubbed his hands.
  —That sounds the best way alright, he said.
  —It'll be United.
  —No, it won't!
  —Shhhh, said Mister O'Keefe. —Shhhh, now. Right, okay; hands up who wants Barrytown Forest.
  Liam lifted his hand a little bit, then put it back. No hands. We cheered.
  —Barrytown Rovers?
  No hands.

172

—Barrytown——United.

The Manchester United and Leeds United fellas put all their hands up. There was no one left, except Sinbad.

—Barrytown United it is, said Mister O'Keefe. —By a handsome majority. Which one did you want? he asked Sinbad.

—Liverpool, said Sinbad.

It was so brilliant being in a team called United that we didn't bother getting Sinbad for saying that.

—Une-eye-ted!

Une-eye-ted!

I'd hold my arms out straight till they ached and I'd spin. I could feel the air against my arms, trying to stop them from going so fast, like dragging them through water. I kept going. Eyes open, little steps in a circle; my heels cut into the grass, made it juicy; really fast – the house, the kitchen, the hedge, the back, the other hedge, the apple tree, the house, the kitchen, the hedge, the back – waiting to stop my feet. I never warned myself. It just happened – the other hedge, the apple tree, the house, the kitchen – stop – onto the ground, on my back, sweating, gasping, everything still spinning. The sky – round and round – nearly wanting to get sick. Wet from sweating, cold and hot. Belch. I had to lie there till it was over. Round and round; it was better with my eyes open, trying to get my eyes to hang onto one thing and stop it from turning. Snot, sweat, round, round and round. I didn't know why I did it; it was terrible – maybe that was why. It was good getting there – spinning. Stopping was the bad bit, and after. It had to come; I couldn't spin forever. Recovering. Stuck to the ground. I could feel the world turning. Gravity sticking me down, holding me, my shoulders; my shins sore. The world was round and Ireland was stuck on the side; I knew that when I was spinning – falling off the world. The worst was when there was nothing in the sky, nothing to grab, blue blue blue.

I only ever got sick once.

It was dangerous to do things straight after your dinner. You could drown if you went swimming. I went up to my belly button to see if anything would happen – I wasn't going to go any further – just to check. Nothing did. The water was the same; the suck wasn't any stronger. That didn't mean much though. Standing in a bit of water wasn't the same as swimming. You weren't swimming until your feet weren't touching the sand for at least five seconds. That was swimming; that was when you drowned if you were full of your dinner. Your belly was too full and too heavy. Your legs and arms couldn't hold you up. You swallowed water. It got into your lungs. It took ages for you to die. Spinning was the same, only you didn't die, unless you were lying on your back when you were getting sick and you didn't turn over on your side because you'd fainted or something, or you'd walloped your head and you were unconscious with your mouth full of vomit. Then you suffocated, unless someone saw you in time and saved you; they turned you over and thumped your back to make room in your throat for some air to get through. You gasped and coughed; then they gave you the kiss of life to be on the safe side. Their lips would be touching your lips and your lips would be covered in vomit. They might get sick themselves on you. They might be a man, a man kissing me – or a woman.

Kissing was stupid. It was alright for kissing your ma when you were going to school or something, but kissing someone because you liked them – you thought they were lovely – that was just stupid. It didn't make sense. The man on top of the woman when they were on the ground or in a bed.

—Bed. Pass it on.

We snuck into Kevin's ma's and da's bedroom and looked

at their bed. We laughed. Kevin pushed me onto the bed and he wouldn't let me out; he held the handle on the other side.

When I got sick from spinning I didn't faint or anything. I just knew I was going to get sick when I was lying on the grass after I'd stopped – the grass was warm and stiff – so I tried to stand up but I fell back on one knee and then the sick came; not real vomit – food from the top of the heap in my stomach. My ma said that you should chew the food well before you swallowed it. I never did; it was a waste of time and boring. Sometimes my throat hurt after I'd swallowed something big; I knew it was going to be sore but it was too late to stop, it was too far down, there was nothing I could do. Boiled potatoes, big bits of bacon with fat on it, cabbage – that was what came out. Angel Delight, strawberry. Milk. I could name every bit of it. I felt better, sturdier. I stood up. It was in the back garden. My head moved a little bit – house, kitchen – but then it stopped. I looked at my clothes. They hadn't been hit. My runners were clean too. And my legs. It was all on the ground. Like stew off a plate. Did I have to clean it up? It wasn't on a floor or a path. But it was in the garden, not a field or someone-else-we-didn't-know's garden. I wasn't sure. I walked down to the kitchen door. I turned and looked. I couldn't make up my mind if I could see it there or not. I was looking there because I knew it was there. I could see it, but I knew it was there. I went around to the front and messed with the flowers. Then I went back down the side again and came around the kitchen and looked and I couldn't really make out anything. I left it there. I looked at it every day. It got harder and darker. I threw the bacon into the garden that backed onto ours, Corrigan's. I let it drop over the fence so they wouldn't see anything flying in the air if they were looking out. I waited for shouts. Nothing. I washed my hands. The rest of the sick disappeared. It was

175

slimy and real looking after rain. Then it was gone. It took about two weeks.

—Is it morning not to get up?
  —Yes, it is.
  —Go back to bed, lads.

The table was still dirty. The dishes were still on it, from dinner the night before. Ma put my cornflakes bowl on top of a dirty plate.

I didn't like it. The table should have been clean in the morning. With nothing on it except the salt and pepper in the middle, and the ketchup bottle with not too much dried ketchup up at the lid – I hated that – and the place mats, with a spoon on mine and Sinbad's. That was the way it always was.

I ate without letting any of my body touch the table. I swapped my spoon for Sinbad's. He was in the toilet. He'd probably wet the floor again. He was always doing that. He was afraid that the seat would fall down on him. It was only plastic, and not heavy, but it still frightened him. I was much bigger than him, so I could go into the bowl with only lifting up the hatch part of the seat. I never wet it much and I always dried it. Always. Diseases grew in toilets. If a rat ever got into your house it would go straight for the toilet.

Ma was humming.

It was stupid, not doing the dishes in the night. The food was still soft then and easy to get off; it came off in the water. Now, though, she was going to have to rub real hard. Loads of elbow grease. Blood, sweat and tears. She'd have her work cut out for her. It served her right. She should have done them the night before; that was the proper time to do them.

Morning was the start of a new day; everything should have been clean and tidy. I used to have to get up on a chair when I wanted to play at the sink – I remembered pushing the chair in front of me and the noise it made, like it was trying to stop me. I didn't need the chair any more. I didn't even have to stretch much to reach the taps. If the sink was too full my jumper got wet when I leaned over. With jumpers you didn't know you were wet for a while, unless you got really soaked. I didn't mess at the sink much any more. It was stupid. The neighbours could see you from the window and you couldn't pull the curtains over in the daytime. I was supposed to do the dishes on Tuesdays, Thursdays and Saturdays. I'd shown my ma how I could reach the taps and that was what happened; she said she'd let me do the dishes on those three days. Sometimes she let me off, sometimes without asking. I washed. Sinbad dried, but he was useless. He was as slow as anything. It took him years even to hold a plate when he was holding the tea-towel as well. He didn't trust his hands through the cloth. The only bit he liked was the cups, because they were hard to drop. He covered his fist with the tea-towel and put the cup upside-down on his fist and turned the cup round on his fist. I made sure that he got all the suds out of the bottom. Suds weren't supposed to be drunk; they tasted like poison.

He didn't want to let me see.

—Show.

—No.

—Show me.

—No.

—I'll get you.

—It's my job.

—I'm in charge.

—Who says?

—Ma.

—I don't want to do this.

—I'll tell her you said that. I'm the oldest.

He held the cup up for me to look into.

—Okay, I said. —Pass.

He always gave in when I told him I was the oldest. He made sure the cup was flat on the table before he let go of it and he jumped back when he took his hand away, so he wouldn't get the blame if it fell. When I was let do something and he wasn't all Ma and Da had to do was remind him that I was older than him and he stopped complaining. He got smaller Christmas presents as well sometimes and less money on Sundays and it didn't matter much to him.

—I'm glad I'm not you, I told him.

—I'm glad I'm not you, he said back.

I didn't believe him.

He held up the cup for me, without me asking him.

—Suds, I said.

—Where?

—There.

And I flicked them into his eyes. Ma came in when she heard him.

—I didn't mean to get his eyes, I told her. —He kept them open.

She stopped him crying; she was great at it. She could make him go from cry to laugh in a few seconds.

It was Thursday morning now. Wednesday wasn't our dishes night. She should have done them. I asked her.

—Why did you not do the dishes?

Something happened when I was asking it; it was in my voice, a difference between the beginning and the end. The reason – it fell into me. The reason she hadn't done the dishes. I'd been in a lift once – twice – up, then down. This was like going down. I nearly didn't finish: I knew the answer. It unwrapped while I was talking. The reason.

She answered.

—I didn't have the time.

She wasn't telling a lie but that wasn't the right answer.

—Sorry, she said.

She was smiling at me. It wasn't a real smile though, not a full one.

They'd had a fight again.

—You'll have your work cut out for you, I said.

One of their quiet ones.

She laughed.

Where they whispered their screams and roaring.

She laughed at me.

And she was always the first one to cry and he kept stabbing at her with his face and his words.

—I know I will, she said.

The first one hadn't been like that. She'd cried, and they'd stopped. It had been nice after that one.

—You'll have to use plenty of elbow grease.

She laughed again.

—You're a gas man, Patrick, she said.

It had been nice. We didn't have to creep, pretend we weren't hearing. Sinbad was no good at pretending. He had to look to listen. Like everything was television. I had to get him away.

—What's happening?

—They're having a fight.

—They're not.

—They are.

—Why are they?

—They just are.

And then when it was over Sinbad always said that nothing had happened; he wouldn't remember.

—Blood, sweat and tears, I told her.

She laughed again, not as good as the time before.

The first fight had ended. My da won because my ma cried; he made her. It ended; back to normal, but better. The fight was over, no more fights. I made the plates into a pile, all the knives and forks on the top plate, all of them pointing the same way. The fights didn't end now. There were breaks, long ones sometimes, but I didn't believe in them any more. They were only gaps. I pushed the plates slowly over to the edge until the slope part of the bottom plate and the ones on top of it were out past the end of the table. I wondered was my brain strong enough to get my arms to push them the rest of the way.

—They should be put in the thicks' class.

Kevin was right. We hated them. It was September, the first day back, and two of the boys from the Corporation houses got put into our class. Charles Leavy and Seán Whelan were their names. Henno was putting them into the roll-book.

—Tell him, I said.

I whispered it.

—What? said Kevin.

—Tell him there's room in the thicks' class for them.

—Okay.

Kevin put his hand up. I couldn't believe it. I'd only been messing; we'd be killed if Kevin said it. I tried to grab Kevin's arm without making noise.

Henno was looking down at the roll-book, writing real slowly. Kevin clicked his fingers.

—*Sea?** said Henno.

He didn't look up.

Kevin spoke.

—*An bhfuil cead agam dul go dtí an leithreas?***

—*Níl,**** said Henno.

—Fooled you, Kevin whispered.

We were having Henno for the second year, fourth class. I

* Yes.   ** Have I permission to go to the toilet?   *** No.

was ten. Most of the others were ten. Ian McEvoy was only nine but he was nearly ten and he was the tallest. Charles Leavy was two months younger than me; they had to call out their ages and Henno put them in the book. Seán Whelan was nearly the exact same age as me. He had to stop when he was telling Henno his date of birth; he knew the day and the month but he had to think before he said the year. I could tell.

—Thick.

He was put sitting beside David Geraghty. He nearly tripped over David Geraghty's crutches. We laughed.

—What's so funny now? said Henno, but he was busy; he didn't care.

Seán Whelan knew that the laughing was against him. His face was hurt but he tried to join in, but he was too late.

—D'you see him, laughing at himself?

Charles Leavy was next. Henno had to put him in a place. Henno stood up.

—Right.

Two of the boys were sitting by themselves. Liam was one of them. No one had sat beside him when he'd grabbed the seat at the back beside the window, the best desk. He'd looked delighted; he'd expected me or Kevin to charge over to him. He was by himself and so was Fluke Cassidy.

—Right, Mister Leavy. Let's see what we have for you.

Fluke tried to sneak over to Liam's desk.

—Stay where you are, Mister Cassidy.

He was going to put Charles Leavy beside Fluke for definite after that.

—Over there, Henno pointed to Liam's desk.

We laughed. Henno knew why.

—Qui-etttt.

It was great. Liam was finished now; Kevin and me wouldn't even talk to him any more. I was delighted. I didn't know why. I liked Liam. It seemed important though. If you were going to be best friends with anyone – Kevin – you had to hate a lot of other people, the two of you, together. It made you better friends. And now Liam was sitting beside Charles Leavy. There was just me and Kevin now, no one else.

David Geraghty was the fella with the polio. That was why there'd been no one sitting beside him. You had to help him with his school bag and there was a smell of medicine off him. I'd had to sit beside him one week after I'd done well in a spelling test and David Geraghty had done badly. It had been brilliant. I'd sat right at the edge of the desk, nearly off it, one half of my bum hanging over the ground. Then David Geraghty had started talking. And he never shut up. All day, out of the side of his mouth like the other side was paralysed. You could hardly hear it but it wasn't a whisper. Henno could hear it, I was sure he could, but he never did anything about it, probably because David Geraghty had to go around on crutches and was easily the best in the class.

—You can see the hairs in his nose, you can count them. Five in one hole and seven in the other.

Like that all day. When I realised that David Geraghty was never going to get into any trouble and that I wasn't going to get into trouble because I was sitting beside him I sat into the desk properly and started to enjoy myself.

—He has seventeen hairs on his arse. Divided by three equals five and two over. His wife combs them for him *gach maidin.**

All day.

He gave me a go on his crutches. My arms wobbled. I couldn't hold them straight for very long. They weren't like the metal crutches you got when you broke your leg. They

* Every morning.

182

were old fashioned, wood and leather, like the ones the boy on the polio poor-box had; you couldn't adjust them. David Geraghty's arms were as strong as legs. I sometimes hoped that I'd be put beside David Geraghty again but I was always glad when I wasn't.

Seán Whelan wore glasses. They were in a black case that he put at the top of the desk above the hollow for pens and pencils. Whenever Henno went near the blackboard Seán Whelan would pick up the case and when Henno wrote on the board he took the glasses out and put them on. Every time Henno stopped he took them off, and put them back on when Henno started again. I stopped looking at Henno for a while and just looked at Seán Whelan. I could tell where Henno was by looking at Seán Whelan's hand. It would creep towards the case, stop and go back to his side; up to the case again, pick up the case, open it and put on the glasses. He took them off and put both his hands to his sides. I waited for him to start moving again. Henno stopped talking. I kept my eyes on Seán Whelan, waiting for a signal. Seán Whelan just kept staring straight at the back of Thomas Bradshaw's head. He looked slightly towards me. And that was when Henno hit me, a hard slap on the back of the head. Seán Whelan jumped, I saw him just as I ducked and shut my eyes for more.

—Wakey wakey, Mister Clarke!

The class laughed and stopped.

Henno had held his open hand stiff; it was as hard as a plank. I was going to get Seán Whelan back for that. It was his fault. I was going to get his glasses case and do something with it, and the glasses. He had brown crinkly hair. It grew up straight but someone, probably his ma, was trying to make it grow to the side. It looked like half a hill on top of his head. He'd be easy to get. He wouldn't hit back. I'd get him. He wasn't rough looking.

Like Charles Leavy.

Charles Leavy wore plastic sandals, blue ones. We laughed at them but we were careful. He brought nothing into school the first day. When Henno asked why not he said nothing, he just looked at his sleeves on the desk. He didn't squirm. There was nearly a hole in one of his elbows. You could see lots of his shirt through it. His hair was very short, the same all over his head. Now and again he stretched his neck and sort of shot his head out to the side, like he was heading a ball but not bothering to look at it. He looked, and I looked away. I felt hot, scared.

—Irish books. *Leabhair Gaeilge.** Page – What page would you say, Mister Grimes?

—One, sir.

—Correct.

—*A h-aon,*** sir.

—Thank you, Mister Grimes. – *Sambo san Afraic.**** There he is in his canoe.

We laughed quietly; the way he'd said Canoe. The picture under the name of the story was black and red on top of the white of the page, a black boy with no shirt on in a red canoe under black trees, the jungle. I looked across. Liam was sharing his book with Charles Leavy. He was pressing his hand up the middle of the book so it would stay open. Charles Leavy waited till Liam was finished, then leaned forward to read the book. The other way: Seán Whelan had his own book, covered in wallpaper. He didn't wear his glasses for reading.

During little break, the eleven o'clock one, I pushed up against Seán Whelan when we were lining up to go back in.

—Watch it.

Seán Whelan didn't do anything or say anything. He just

---

* Irish books. ** One. *** Sambo in Africa.

looked like he was very determined not to look at me, and I was happy with that. I shoved so I could be beside Kevin.

—I'm going to get Whelan, I told Kevin.

—Sure you are, said Kevin.

I was surprised, nearly upset.

—I am, I said. —For definite. He pushed me.

I'd have to get him now. I looked back at Seán Whelan. He had a way of looking past you, looking ahead but around a corner.

He was dead.

The fight took me by surprise. I was going to wait for a good excuse but Kevin pushed me into Seán Whelan – this was outside the gate, across the road in the field that was being dug up – and Seán Whelan elbowed me or his elbow was just there and I was thumping him and being thumped and that surprised me as well. I swung my fists stiff-armed; I hadn't the time to ready myself, to remember to punch properly, and it was too late now. Seán Whelan's head got my chin; my teeth banged. I stepped back out of Seán Whelan's arms, and kicked. I drew back my left foot and kicked again. Seán Whelan tried to hold onto my foot, to knock me over. I got my foot back away from him and I didn't fall. Seán Whelan was going backwards, the boys behind him were letting him, because I was going to kick him again. I ran and kicked. I'd got him hard. A good bit over his knee. He skipped back like his legs had gone from under him. He grunted. I had him; I was winning. I was going to get his hair now, and knee his face. I'd never done it before. I'd nearly done it to Sinbad but pulling his head down had been enough; he'd screamed and I couldn't get my leg to go up hard; I could lift it but not to smash him. Seán Whelan wasn't Sinbad though. I'd grab a tuft of his stupid hair –

The pain knocked me sideways, buckled me for a second.

I'd just been kicked, just under my left hip and the tips of two fingers. Seán Whelan was in front of me. It took me a while to –

Charles Leavy had kicked me.

There was no cheering now. This was serious. I wanted to go to the toilet. My fingers stung like freezing cold. Seán Whelan was in the crowd now, looking in. I tried to pretend that I was still fighting him.

The same place. Charles Leavy kicked me again.

No one jumped in. No one said anything. No one moved. They knew. They were going to see fighting they'd never seen before. Blood and teeth, torn clothes. Things broken. No rules.

I couldn't pretend any more. I wished I hadn't kicked Seán Whelan. I couldn't kick Charles Leavy back. I couldn't do anything. I had to do nothing; it was the only way.

He kicked me.

—Here! None o' that!

It was one of the workmen. He was up on a wall. He was building it. Some of them ran when they heard him and stopped to see what was going to happen.

—No kicking, said the workman. —That's not the way to fight.

He had a huge belly. I remembered now: we'd shouted things at him and he'd chased us earlier in the summer.

—No kicking, he said again.

Kevin was further away from him than me.

—Mind your own business, Fatso.

We ran. It was brilliant. I was nearly crying. I could hear my books and copies shaking in my school bag, a noise like galloping horse feet. I'd escaped. The pain of the laughing was great. We stopped when we got to the new road.

No one had jumped in for me when Charles Leavy had been going to kill me; it took me a while to get used to that, to make it make sense. To make it alright. The quiet, the

186

waiting. All of them looking. Kevin standing beside Seán Whelan. Looking.

There was a huge brown suitcase under our parents' bed. It was like leather but it made a noise like wood. There were creases on it. When I rubbed it hard a brown stain came off on my hand. There was nothing in it. Sinbad got in. He lay down like he did in bed. I closed it over.

—What's it like?

—Nice.

I got the clasp on one side and shoved it in; it made a big click. I waited for Sinbad to do something. I did the other one as well.

—What's it like now?

—Still nice.

I went away. I stamped my feet on the floor, bang bang on the lino, and I got the door and I swung it so there'd be a whoosh and closed it with just less than a slam. My da went mad when we slammed doors. I waited. I wanted to hear Sinbad kicking, crying, scratching his hands on the lid. Then I'd let him out.

I waited.

I sang as I went down the stairs.

—SON YOU ARE A BACHELOR BOY –

    AND THAT'S THE WAY TO STAY-EE-AY –

I crept back up; I got over the creaks. I slid to the door. It was brilliant. But suddenly I was up on my feet, through the door; I was scared.

—Sinbad?

I pushed down the lock thing to release the clasp. It sprang out and hurt my hand.

—Francis.

The other one wouldn't come up, the lock thing. I pulled up a corner of the lid but it only came up a small bit; I couldn't see anything. I got about two fingers in but I couldn't feel anything and I scraped the skin. I kept the fingers there so air would get in, but then I felt teeth on them, I thought I did.

I heard a whimper. It was me.

I closed the door after me, so nothing could follow. I held onto the banister all the way. It was dark in the hall. My da was in the living room but the television wasn't on.

I told him.

He just got up; he didn't say anything. I didn't tell him I'd locked it, just that I couldn't unlock it. When he got into the hall he waited for me.

—Show me, he said.

He followed me up the stairs. He could have easily gone quicker than me but he didn't. Sinbad would be alright.

—Alright in there, Francis?

—He might be asleep, I said.

My da pushed and the lock clicked out. He lifted the lid back and Sinbad was still in there, wide awake; his eyes were open. He turned on his stomach, pushed up, stood up and stepped out. He didn't say anything. He stood there. He didn't look at us or anything.

Da thought he was great because he could sit in the same room as the television and never look at it. He only looked at The News, that was all. He read the paper or a book or he dozed. I watched the cigarette burning nearer and nearer to his fingers but he always woke up on time. He had a chair of his own. We had to get out of it when he came home from work. Me and Sinbad and our ma with the babies on her lap could fit into it. There was one day it was raining out, lashing; we all sat in the chair for ages just listening to the rain. The room got darker. There was a nice smell off my ma, food and soap.

When I called Sinbad Sinbad he wouldn't answer. Me and

188

Kevin got him and gave him a dead leg on each side for not doing what we told him. He was crying but he didn't make any noises. I had to look at his face to see that he was crying.

—Sinbad.

He closed his eyes.

—Sinbad.

I had to stop calling him Sinbad. He didn't look like Sinbad the Sailor now any more; his cheeks were flatter. I was still way bigger than him but it didn't matter as much. I could kill him in fights but the way he went scared me. He let me give him a hiding and then he just went away.

He didn't want the night-light on any more. When my ma turned it on before she turned off the main light he got up and turned it off. The light had been for him. He'd picked it. It was a rabbit that went red when the bulb inside him was on. The room was completely dark now. I wanted to turn the night-light back on but I couldn't; it was Sinbad's. I'd never needed it. I'd said it was stupid. I'd given out about it, said I couldn't sleep with it on. For a week my ma turned on the light and Sinbad turned it off. He turned off the light and I was trapped in the full dark.

Da had Sinbad. He was holding one of his arms, standing way over him. He hadn't hit him yet. Sinbad's head was down. He wasn't pushing or pulling to get away.

—Christ almighty, said my da.

Sinbad had put sugar in Mister Hanley's petrol tank.

—Why do you do these things? Why are you doing them?

Sinbad answered him.

—The devil tempts me.

I saw da's fingers open their grip on Sinbad's arm. He held Sinbad's face.

—Stop crying now; come on. There's no need for tears.

I started singing.

—I'LL TELL MY MA WHEN I GO HOME –
THE BOYS WON'T LEAVE THE GIRLS ALONE –
Da joined in. He picked up Sinbad and spun him. Then it was my turn.

The first time I heard it I recognised it but I didn't know what it was. I knew the sound. It came from the kitchen. I was in the hall by myself. I was lying on my stomach. I was charging a Rolls-Royce into the skirting board. There was a chip in the paint and it was getting bigger every time. It made a great thump. My ma and da were talking.

Then I heard the smack. The talking stopped. I grabbed the Rolls-Royce away from the skirting board. The kitchen door whooshed open. Ma came out. She turned quick at the stairs so I didn't have to get out of her way, and went upstairs, going quicker towards the top.

I recognised it now. I knew what the smack had been, and the bedroom door closed.

Da was alone in the kitchen. He didn't come out. Deirdre was crying in the pram; she'd woken up. The back door opened and closed. I heard Da's steps on the path. I heard him going from the back to the front. I saw his shape through the mountainy glass of the front door. The shape broke into just colours before he got to the gate and the colours disappeared. I couldn't tell which way he'd gone. I stayed where I was. Ma would come back down. Deirdre was crying.

He'd hit her. Across the face; smack. I tried to imagine it. It didn't make sense. I'd heard it; he'd hit her. She'd come out of the kitchen, straight up to their bedroom.

Across the face.

*

I watched. I listened. I stayed in. I guarded her.

Nothing happened.

I didn't know what I'd do. If I was there he wouldn't do it again, that was all. I stayed awake. I listened. I went to the bathroom and put cold water on my pyjamas. To keep myself awake. To stop me from getting cozy and warm and slipping asleep. I left the door a bit open. I listened. Nothing happened. I spent ages doing my homework so I could stay up longer. I wrote out pages from my English book and pretended I had to do it. I learnt spellings I hadn't been given. I got her to check me on them, never him.

—S.u.b.m.a.r.i.n.e.

—Good boy. Substandard?

—S.u.b.s.t.a.n.d.a.r.d.

—Good boy. Great. Have you more to do?

—Yes.

—What? Show me.

—Writing out.

She looked at the pages in the book I showed her, two pages with no pictures on them, and at the pages I'd done already.

—Why are you doing all these?

—Handwriting.

—Oh good.

I did it at the kitchen table, then followed her into the living room. When she was putting the girls to bed he was in the room with me, so it was alright. I enjoyed the writing out; I liked doing it.

He smiled at me.

I loved him. He was my da. It didn't make sense. She was my ma.

I went into the kitchen. I was alone. The noises were all upstairs. I slapped the table. Not too loud. I slapped it again. It was the right type of sound. It was duller though, hollow. Maybe it would be different from outside. In the hall where

I'd been. Maybe he'd done that, smacked the table. When he was in a temper. That was alright. I did it again. I couldn't make my mind up. I was tempted. I used the side of my hand. She'd come out of the kitchen, straight up to their bedroom. She'd said nothing. She hadn't let me see her face. She'd started going faster before she got to the landing. Not because he'd slapped the table. I did it again. I tried to lose my temper and then do it. Maybe because he'd lost his temper. Maybe that was why she'd gone past me up the stairs, hiding. Maybe.

I didn't know.

I went back into the living room. He wanted to check my spellings. I let him. I got one wrong, deliberately. I didn't know why I did it. I just did it when I was doing it; I left out the r in Submarine.

I listened. I watched. I did my homework.

I came home at Friday lunchtime.

—I'm in the best desk.

It was true. I'd made no mistakes all week. All my sums had been right. I'd got through the twelve-times table inside thirty seconds. My handwriting was

—Much improved.

I'd put my stuff in my bag and walked up to the front of the room and across to the top desk. Henno shook my hand.

—See how long you can stay there now, he said. —Good man, Mister Clarke.

I was beside David Geraghty.

—Howdy-doody.

—I'm in the best desk, I told my da later.

—Is that right? he said. —That's terrific.

He shook my hand.

—Put it there. Submarine?

—S.u.b.m.a.r.i.n.e.

—Good man.

*

The grass was wet though it hadn't been raining. The day was too short to dry it. School was over; it was going to be dark soon. There was a new trench. It was really huge, really deep. The bottom was gooey, no crumbly muck; everything was wet.

—Quicksand.

—No, it isn't.

—Why isn't it?

—It's only muck.

Aidan was in it.

Liam and Aidan sometimes didn't go to school. Their da let them stay at home sometimes if they were good. We saw the new white sticks sticking up over the grass. We knew they were markers and we went over to see what they were marking, and Aidan was in the trench. And he couldn't get out. He had nothing to cling to.

—He's sinking.

I watched.

One of his boots was under the goo, up to his knee. I looked at that leg; I counted to twenty. It didn't go down any further. Liam had gone for a ladder or a rope. I hoped it would be a rope.

—How did he get down?

That was a stupid question. It had happened to us all. Getting down was never a problem. It was too easy, always. You never thought about getting back up.

I checked Aidan's leg. His knee was covered now. He was sinking. He was trying to hold onto the side, trying not to fall, trying not to cry. He'd been crying earlier; you could tell from his face. I thought about throwing stones at him, but there was no need.

We sat on our school bags.

—Can you drown in mud? Ian McEvoy asked.

—Yeah.

—No.

—Say it louder, I whispered. —So he can hear.

Ian McEvoy thought about it.

—Can you drown in mud?

—Sometimes.

—If your boots are full and you can't get up.

We pretended Aidan wasn't there to listen. He was trying to lift a leg and keep the boot on it. We could hear the suck. Kevin made the noise with his mouth. We all did. Aidan slipped but he didn't go down.

Then I started worrying. He really could drown. We'd watch him; we'd have to. Suddenly the grass felt very wet. It would be like in my dream, the one I sometimes had, when my mouth was full of muck, dry summer muck; I couldn't wet it and swallow it. I couldn't close my mouth round it. It took over my mouth, deeper and deeper. My jaws really hurt, fighting it, and knowing I was losing and my mouth was going to get fuller, and I couldn't swallow. I couldn't shout, I couldn't breathe. Liam brought a ladder and his da and they saved him. Liam's da complained to the builders but he wouldn't let us come with him.

Keith Simpson didn't drown in the trench. He drowned in a pond. The pond was way across six or seven fields where the building hadn't started yet. It was great for frogspawn and ice. It wasn't deep but it was slimy; you'd never have put your bare feet into it. The ice growled when you leaned on it. It was too small for a lake.

Keith Simpson was found in it. He was just found. Nobody knew how he got there.

My ma cried. She didn't know Keith Simpson. Neither did I. He was from the Corporation houses. I knew what he'd looked like. Small and freckles. She snuffled and I knew she was crying. The whole of Barrytown went quiet, like the news had spread without anyone telling it. He'd slipped in face-

194

first and his coat and jumper and his trousers got so wet and heavy he couldn't get up; that was what they said. The water soaked his clothes. I could see it. I put my sock in the sink, hanging into the water. The water crept up the sock. Half the water went into the sock.

I looked at the house. I knew which one. It was a corner one. I'd once seen a man – it must have been Keith Simpson's father – up on the roof putting up the aerial. The curtains were closed. I went closer. I touched the gate.

Da hugged Ma when he came home. He went up and shook hands with Keith Simpson's ma and da at the funeral. I saw him. I was with the school; everyone in the school was there, in our good clothes. Henno made each of us say the first half of the Hail Mary and the rest joined in for the second half, and that took up the time before we were brought to the church. Ma stayed in her seat. There was a huge queue for shaking hands, down the side and around the back of the church, along the stations of the cross. The coffin was white. Some of the mass cards fell off during the Offertory. They slapped the floor. The sound was huge. The only other sounds were someone at the front sobbing and the priest's stiff clothes, then the altar boy's bell. And there was more sobbing.

We weren't let go to the graveyard.

—You can go and say a prayer by yourselves some other time, said Miss Watkins. —Next Sunday. That would be better.

She'd been crying.

—They just don't want us to see the coffin going in, said Kevin.

There was no more school. We sat on a flattened cardboard box in the field behind the shops to stop our clothes from getting dirty and to stop us from being killed by our mas. There was only room for three on the box and there were five of us. Aidan had to stand and Ian McEvoy went home.

—He was my cousin, I told them.

—Who was? said Kevin.

They knew who I was going to say.

—Keith Simpson, I said.

I thought of my mother crying. He must have been at least a cousin. I believed myself.

—Hari-kari.

—It's hari-kiri, I said.

—What's it mean? Ian McEvoy asked.

—Do you not know? said Kevin. —You're dense.

—It's the way Japs kill themselves, I told Ian McEvoy.

—Why? said Aidan.

—Why what?

—Why do they kill themselves?

—Lots of reasons.

It was a thick question. It didn't matter.

—Cos they got beaten in the war, said Kevin.

—Still? said Aidan. —The war was years ago.

—My uncle was in the war, said Ian McEvoy.

—No, he wasn't; shut up.

—He was.

—He wasn't.

Kevin grabbed his arm and twisted it behind his back. Ian McEvoy didn't try to stop him.

—He wasn't in the war, said Kevin. —Sure he wasn't?

—No, said Ian McEvoy.

He didn't even leave a gap.

—Why did you say he was, then?

It wasn't fair; he should have let Ian McEvoy go when he'd said No.

—Why did yeh?

He pulled Ian McEvoy's wrist closer to the back of his neck. Ian McEvoy had to bend forward. He didn't answer;

he probably couldn't think of anything, anything that would get Kevin to let go of him.

—Leave him alone, said Liam.

He said it like he was answering in school and he knew he was wrong. He still said it though. He was standing there. He'd said it. I hoped Kevin would get him, because he'd said it and I hadn't and Kevin getting him would make me right. Kevin pulled Ian McEvoy's arm up a little bit more till he bent him down – Ian McEvoy roared out – and then Kevin let him go. Ian McEvoy straightened up and pretended they'd been only messing. I waited. So did Liam. Nothing happened. Kevin did nothing. Aidan brought it back to normal.

—Do they have to kill themselves?

—No, I said.

—Why then?

—They only do it when they really have to, I said. —Or when they want to, I said, just in case.

—When do they have to? said Sinbad.

I was going to tell him to shut up and maybe hit him but I didn't feel like it. He had two snailers coming out of his nose even though it wasn't all that cold.

—When they lose a war and things like that, I said.

—When they're sad, said Aidan.

He said it like a question.

—Yeah, I said. —Sometimes.

—Very sad, only.

—Yeah.

—Not just down in the dumps.

—No. Sad that you can't stop crying. When your ma dies or something. Or your dog.

I remembered too late: Aidan and Liam's ma was dead. But they didn't do anything, look at each other or anything. Liam just nodded; he knew what I'd meant.

There were two other families with dead mas or das. The

Sullivans had a dead ma and the Rickards had a dead da. Mister Rickard had died in a car crash. Missis Sullivan had just died. The Rickards had moved after Mister Rickard got killed but they came back. They hadn't been gone that long, not even a year. They didn't go to our school, the three boys. There was a girl as well, Mary. She was older.

—A bit wild, my ma said.

She'd gone to London, run away. That was where they'd found her. She was a hippy, the only real one in Barrytown. The police in England had found her. They made her go home.

—They get a knife and they stick it in their belly, I told them.

It was impossible; their faces said that. I agreed with them. You couldn't stick a knife in your own belly. I had no problem thinking about swallowing loads of tablets. It would be easy. I'd get a bottle of something to wash them down, to make it even easier, Coca-Cola or milk. Probably Coca-Cola. Even jumping off a bridge when a train was coming was easy to imagine. I could do it. I'd be jumping, not hitting the train. I'd jumped off high things before. You couldn't smother yourself on purpose. If you jumped into the deep end of a swimming pool away from the sides and there was no one there to save you you'd drown, if you couldn't swim or you weren't a good swimmer. Or if you'd just had your dinner and got cramps. I couldn't imagine me sticking a knife into myself. I didn't even bother experimenting.

—Not a bread knife, I said. —Or one like that.

—A butcher's.

—Yeah.

It was easy to see how you could accidentally stab yourself with a knife. We'd seen the butcher using his one. He'd let us. He let us come round the corner. Missis O'Keefe, James O'Keefe's ma, was in her hatch where she took in the money and gave out the change, and she yelled at us for robbing the sawdust. We needed it for Ian McEvoy's guinea-pig. There was loads of sawdust. It was early in the morning so it was clean and fresh. We grabbed handfuls and put them in our pockets. It wasn't really robbing. Sawdust wasn't worth anything. And it was for the guinea-pig. She yelled at us; it wasn't even a word. Then she yelled a name.

—Cyril!

It was the butcher's name. We didn't run. It was only sawdust. We didn't think she was calling him for us. He came out of the big fridge at the back.

—Wha'?

She pointed at us. It was too late to run.

—Them, she said.

He saw the sawdust in our hands. He was colossal. He was the biggest, fattest man in Barrytown. He didn't live in Barrytown, like the other people who lived in the rooms on top of their shops. He came to work on a Honda 50. He made a face like he was annoyed with Missis O'Keefe. She was wasting his time; he'd been doing something.

—Come here, lads, till I show yis somethin'.

It was me, Kevin and Ian McEvoy and Sinbad. Liam and Aidan were at their auntie's in Raheny again. We went over to him.

—Stay there.

He went into the fridge and came back out with an animal's leg. It was over his shoulder. He was wearing a white coat. I thought it was a cow's, the leg.

—Over here.

We followed him behind the counter to the wooden block. It was clean. I could see scrape marks from the brush. I'd seen him with the brush before. It was the same shape as a brush but instead of bristles there was metal. He got the leg from his back to the block with just barely a flick of his hand. It slapped the wood. He let us feel it.

—Now, lads.

His knife was in a scabbard on a hook above the table. He took it out. It made a swish. He let us look properly at it.

—That cost me hundreds of pounds, lads, he said. —Don't touch it.

We weren't going to.

—Now look here, he said.

He slid the knife over the meat's skin – just slid it – and it came away; a chop. He made no effort; he leaned the edge on the leg, that was all. No noise, no tension. He was sweating though. He broke the chop's bone with a different knife, a cleaver. He thumped it onto the bone, once, twice, and the chop fell flat on the block.

—Now, he said. —That's all there is to it. And that's what I'll do to you feckers the next time I catch yis robbin' my sawdust.

He still looked nice and friendly.

—Sprinkle it all back on the floor on your way out. Bye bye, lads.

He went back into the fridge. I made sure that all my sawdust was even all over the floor. Sinbad ran away after he'd flung his sawdust out of his pockets.

—He did a jobby, I told them all. —Down his leg.

—IT'S ALL DOWN YOUR LEG –
    GICK GICK – LA LA –

—Down as far as his shoes, I said.

—IT'S ALL DOWN YOUR LEG –
    GICK GICK – LA LA –

Ian McEvoy's guinea-pig died because of a cold night. He came out to have a look at it before school and it was in a corner of its box covered in frost. He blamed his ma for not letting him bring it to bed with him.

200

—She said I'd've smothered it, he said.

—I'd prefer to be smothered than die from the cold, said Liam.

—It was sub-zero last night, I told them.

The life expectancy of a guinea-pig was seven years if you changed its water every day and gave it hot bran mash for its dinner every day in the winter. Ian McEvoy only had his one for three days. He didn't even have a name for it. He asked his ma but she wouldn't tell him what hot bran mash was; she said she didn't know.

—Grass will do him, Ian McEvoy said she said.

His da was no help either.

—Buy him an anorak, he said.

He thought he was funny.

We got his sister's doll and a pin. We brought them down to the field; we smuggled them down. The doll didn't look enough like Missis McEvoy.

—Doesn't matter, said Kevin.

—She doesn't have white hair like that, I said.

—Doesn't matter, said Kevin, —so long as we're thinking about her when the pins go in.

We were going to use Action Man for Mister McEvoy but Edward Swanwick wouldn't let us have his one and he was the only one that had one.

—Doesn't matter, said Kevin. —He'll be all in bits when Missis McEvoy dies and that's enough.

—He doesn't like her much, said Ian McEvoy. —I don't think.

—He'll still miss her, said Kevin.

We beat up Edward Swanwick anyway, but not in the face.

Kevin was the high-priest again but he let Ian McEvoy stick in the pin first because she was his ma and it was his sister's doll.

—Missis McEvoy!

Kevin held his hands up into the air.

—Missis McEvoy!

We held an arm and a leg each, like the doll was going to get away.

—You must die!

Ian McEvoy put the pin in her tummy, through her dress. I wondered was there a girl somewhere with white hair and big eyes screaming in agony.

—You must die!

I got her in the brain. Kevin got her in the gee. Liam got her in the bum and Aidan got one of her eyes. The pin marks were hardly there; we didn't do anything else to the doll. Ian McEvoy wouldn't let us. He brought it home. He went in to see. We waited for him outside. He came out.

—She's making the dinner.

—Damn.

—Stew.

It was Wednesday.

We weren't too disappointed but we pretended we were. We squashed the guinea-pig through Kilmartin's letter box and Missis Kilmartin never found out who'd done it. We wiped our fingerprints off it first.

She listened to him much more than he listened to her. Her answers were much longer than his. She did two-thirds of the talking, easily that much. She wasn't a bigmouth though, not nearly; she was just more interested than he was even though he was the one that read the paper and watched The News and made us stay quiet when it was on, even when we weren't making any noise. I knew she was better at talking than him; I'd always known that. He was good sometimes and useless others and sometimes you could tell that you couldn't go near him to ask him or tell him anything. He didn't like being distracted; he said that word a lot, but I knew what it meant,

Distracted, and I didn't know how he was being distracted because he wasn't doing anything anyway. I didn't mind, only sometimes. Fathers were like that, all the fathers I knew, except Mr O'Connell and I didn't want a da like him, only maybe for the holidays. Broken biscuits were lovely but you needed vegetables and meat as well even if you didn't like some of them. All das sat in a corner of a room and didn't want to be disturbed. They had to rest. They put the food on the table. My da came home on Friday with food, in a big huge canvas bag that he balanced on top of his shoulder. There was a cord at the top of the bag for tying it shut. It was the type of rope that hurt your hands. Tiny little bits of rope got into the skin of your fingers if you grabbed the rope too fast. Ma always emptied the bag. It was full of vegetables. He bought them all in Moore Street. My da paid for all the other food we got as well, everything. He had to get his energy back at the weekend. Sometimes I didn't believe that that was the only reason for not being able to go near him, for the way he got into his corner and wouldn't come out. Sometimes he was just being mean.

I won a medal. I came second in the hundred yards except it wasn't nearly a hundred yards; it wasn't even fifty. It was a Saturday, the school sports, the first one the school ever had. There were twenty in the race, right across the field. Henno was in charge of the start. He had a whistle. He had a flag as well but he didn't use it. The field was real uneven. It was hard to go straight, and the grass was longer in some places. I saw Fluke Cassidy falling. He'd been a bit ahead of me but I was catching up on him. I saw his leg going crooked. I went past. I heard the air rushing out of him. I threw my hands up at the finish, the way they did it. I thought I'd won; there was no tape and there was no one near me when I ran over the line. But Richard Shiels had won, over at the end of the field.

I came second, out of twenty – better than eighteen. Henno had something to say.

—Well done, Mister Clarke. If only you were as quick with your answers in class.

I was quick in class; I knew more about some things than Henno did. Henno was a bastard. A bastard was someone whose parents weren't married, or a child of illegitimate birth. Henno wasn't a child any more but he was still a bastard. He couldn't just give me my medal, he had to make a laugh out of it. Illegitimate wasn't in my dictionary but Legitimate meant In accordance with the laws or rules so Illegitimate meant the complete opposite of that. Hirsute meant hairy.

—His mickey is very hirsute.

—Hirsute!

—Hirsute hirsute hirsute!

The medal had a runner on it, no name or writing. The runner had on a white vest and red shorts and no runners. His skin was the same colour as the medal. I walked home; I didn't want to run. I went to my da first.

—Get out; not now.

He didn't look up. He was reading the paper. He always talked about Backbencher on Saturdays, telling my ma what Backbencher'd said, so he might have been reading Backbencher. He clicked the paper, straightened it up. He wasn't angry or anything.

I felt thick. I should have gone to my ma first; it would have been easier then, what had happened. I went to the door; the bones in my legs were rubbery. He was in the drawing room. Peace and quiet, that was what he got in there, the only place in the house. I didn't mind waiting, not really, but he hadn't even looked up. I was going to shut the door quietly.

He looked.

204

—Patrick?

—Sorry.

—No; come in.

The paper fell forward, folded over; he let it.

I let go of the handle. It needed oiling. I came back in. I was scared and pleased, bits of each. I wanted to go to the toilet; I thought I did, that kind of feeling. I asked him something.

—Are you reading Backbencher?

He smiled.

—What have you got there?

—A medal.

—Show us; you should have told me. You won.

—Second.

—Nearly first.

—Yeah.

—Good man.

—I thought I won.

—Next time. Second's good though. Put it there.

He held out his hand.

I wished he'd done it the first time. It wasn't fair the way he made you nearly cry before he changed and did what you wanted him to. It didn't always happen that way but it happened enough for him to have parts of the rooms to himself, for the house to be different at the weekends. I could never run to him; I had to check first. I blamed the paper. Newspapers were stupid, with their World War Three Looms Near when all that was happening was the Israelis milling the Arabs. I hated that. If someone said they'd kill you then they should have done it.

—I'll hurt you.

That were better.

Papers were boring. Da sometimes read out to my ma what

205

Backbencher said and it was stupid. Ma listened but only because my da was reading it and he was her husband.

—Very good.

That was what she usually said but it never sounded like she meant it; she said it the same way she said Go to sleep.

—The word was made flesh!

Swish.

—Backbencher!

They were big and the writing was tiny and they took all day to read, especially on Saturday and Sunday. I read a thing about a high-cross that was damaged by vandals. It was on the front page of the Evening Press, and it took me eight minutes. There was a picture of a high-cross but there wasn't any damage on it. I could always tell, when I was going down to the shops to get the paper, if it was a real nice day in the summer, sunny all day, there'd be a picture of girls or children at the beach on the front, usually three of them in a row; the children always had a bucket and spade in front of them. That was what happened my da: he started to read the paper and then he had to finish it – he thought he was being good doing it – and it took him all day. He became grouchy and dangerous; he was running out of time. The writing was small so he couldn't be distracted. Saturday afternoon: Ma was nervous, we hated him and all he'd done was read Backbencher.

I'll crucify you.

James O'Keefe's ma always said that to James O'Keefe and his brothers and sister. All she meant was Do what you're told. I'll leather you. I'll skin you alive. I'll break every bone in your body. I'll tear you limb from limb. I'll maim you.

They were all stupid.

I'll swing for you. I didn't know what that one meant. Missis Kilmartin roared it at Eric her mentler son. He'd opened up all the bags in six boxes of crisps.

My ma explained.

—It means that she'll murder him and then she'll be condemned to hang for it but she doesn't really mean it.

—Why doesn't she say what she does mean?

—It's just the way people talk.

It must have been great being mental. You could do anything you wanted and you never really got into proper trouble for it. You couldn't pretend you were mental though; you had to be that way all the time. No homework either and you could slobber your dinner as much as you wanted.

Agnes, the woman that worked in Missis Kilmartin's shop because Missis Kilmartin was busying spying behind the door, she spent ages every day with a scissors cutting bits off the front pages of the newspapers, the bit with the name of the paper and the date under it, only that.

—Why?

—To send them back.

—Why? I asked.

—Because they don't want the whole paper.

—Why not?

—They just don't. They don't need them. They're out of date, useless.

—Can I have them?

—You can not.

I didn't want them. I just said it because I knew she was going to say that and I was checking.

—Missis Kilmartin wipes her bum with them, I said.

Not loud.

Sinbad was there. He stared at the window door: she was behind it. Agnes spoke back quietly.

—Get out now, yeh pup, or I'll tell her.

She lived in the same house as her ma; she wasn't really a woman at all. They lived in a cottage that was stuck in the middle of the new houses. The grass in their garden was always perfect.

Da's face was different when he was reading the paper. It was pushed forward, his eyebrows were pushed up. Sometimes his lips were open but his teeth were closed. I heard him grinding his teeth and I didn't know what it was. I looked all around the room. I stood up. I'd been sitting on the floor beside him waiting for him to finish. I couldn't see anything. I looked at my ma. She was reading Woman; not really reading, turning the pages, still looking at the page when she was turning, her hand going with it, the exact same amount of time for each page. I looked at my da, to see if he was hearing what I was, strong things going to break, and I saw his mouth moving – I watched: it moved at the same time as the noise; it was the noise. I waited for the snap. I wanted to warn him. I hated him for doing it. Newspapers were bastards.

—I was thinking of getting pork for a change.

He said nothing; he didn't look.

—It might be nice.

His face was stuck to the page. His eyes weren't moving down. He wasn't reading. He made her say it.

—What do you think?

He cracked the paper. He folded it. He concentrated hard on it. He spoke but it was hardly like he was speaking; it was like the words came out with a sigh – not even a whisper.

—Do what you want.

Face on the paper, legs crossed and stiff, no rhythm.

—Whatever you want.

I didn't look back at my ma yet; not yet.

—You always do.

I still didn't look.

She didn't say anything.

I listened.

He was the only one I could hear breathing. He was pushing the air out, of his nose. Oxygen in, carbon dioxide out. Plants did it the other way round. I heard hers now, her breathing.

—Can I turn on the telly? I said.

I wanted to remind him that I was there. There was a fight coming and I could stop it by being there.

—Television, she said, corrected me.

There was nothing wrong. She'd never have said that if there had been. Ma hated half-words and bits of words and words that weren't real ones. Only full, proper words.

—Television, I said.

She didn't mind Don't and Amn't and shortened words like that. They were different. —It's a television, she'd say, not really giving out. —It's a wellington. It's a toilet.

Her voice was normal.

—Television, I said. —Can I?

—What's on? she asked.

I didn't know. It didn't matter. The sound would fill the room. He'd look up.

—Something, I said. —There might be, maybe a programme about politics. Something of interest.

—Like what?

—Fianna Fail versus Fine Gael, I said.

That made Da look at me.

—What's on? he said.

—There might be, I said. —Not for definite.

—A match between them?

—No, I said. —Talking.

The only programmes he didn't pretend he wasn't watching were ones with people talking in them, and The Virginian.

—You want the television on? he said.

—Yeah.

209

—Why didn't you say just that?

—I did say it, I said.

—Fire away, he said.

His leg was moving, the one on top of the one on the ground, up and down. He sometimes put Catherine and Deirdre on his foot and carried them up and down. He did it to Sinbad as well once – I could remember it – so he must have done it to me as well. I got up.

—Is your homework done?

—Yes.

—All of it?

—Yes.

—The learning?

—Yes.

—What did you get?

—Ten spellings.

—Ten of them; give us one?

—Sediment. Do you want me to do it?

—There's no point, but yeah.

—S.e.d.i.m.e.n.t.

—Sediment.

—C.e.n.t.e.n.a.r.y.

—Centenary.

—Yeah. That's the name for a hundredth anniversary.

—Like your mother's birthday.

I'd done it. It was alright. Normal again. He'd cracked a joke. Ma had laughed. I'd laughed. He'd laughed. Mine lasted the longest. During it, I thought it was going to change into a cry. But it didn't. My eyes blinked like mad but then it was okay.

—Sediment has three syllables, I told them.

—Very good, said my ma.

—Sed-i-ment.

—How many has Centenary?

I was ready; I'd done that one for homework.

—Cen-ten-ar-y. Four.

—Ver-y good. How many has Bed?

I got the joke just before I said the answer; my mouth was nearly open.

I stood up quick.

—Okay.

I wanted to go while it was nice. I'd made it like that.

There were two teachers not in because they were sick so Henno had to mind another class. He left us with a load of sums on the board. He left the door open. There wasn't much messing or noise. I liked long division. I used my ruler to make sure that my lines were absolutely straight. I liked guessing if I'd have the answer before I got to the end of the page. There was a screech and laughing. Kevin had leaned over and drawn a squiggly line all over Fergus Shevlin's copy, only he'd used the wrong end of the pen so there was no mark but Fergus Shevlin got a fright. I didn't see it. I was at the top of the second row that week and Kevin was in the middle of the third row.

You could always tell when Henno came back. Everything in the room went really still for a few seconds. He was in the room; I could tell. I didn't look up. I was near the end of a sum.

He was standing beside me.

He put a copy under my eyes. It was open. It wasn't mine. There were wet streaks in the ink all the way down the pages. They'd made the ink a lighter blue; there were bars of light blue across the page where someone had tried to rub the tears away.

I expected to be hit.

I looked up.

Henno had Sinbad with him. They were Sinbad's tears; I could tell from his face and the way his breath jumped.

—Look at that, Henno said to me.

He meant the copy. I did what I was told.

—Isn't it disgraceful?

I didn't say.

All that was wrong was the tears. They'd ruined the writing, nothing else. Sinbad's writing wasn't bad. It was big and the lines of his letters swerved a bit like rivers because he wrote very slowly. Some of the turns missed the copy line but not by much. It was just the tears.

I waited.

—You're damn lucky you're not in this class, Mister Clarke Junior, Henno said to Sinbad. —Ask your brother.

I still didn't know what was wrong, why I was supposed to be looking at the copy, why my brother was standing there. He wasn't crying now; his face was the proper way.

It was a new feeling: something really unfair was happening; something nearly mad. He'd only cried. Henno didn't know him; he'd just picked on him.

He spoke to me.

—You're to put that copy in your bag and you're to show it to your mother the minute you get home. Let her see what a specimen she has on her hands. Is that clear?

I wasn't going to do it but I had to say it.

—Yes, Sir.

I wanted to look at Sinbad, to let him know. I wanted to look around at everyone.

—In your bag now.

I closed the copy gently. The pages were still a bit wet.

—Get out of my sight, Henno told Sinbad.

Sinbad went. Henno called him back to close the door after him; he asked him was he born in a barn. Then Henno went over and opened the door again, to listen for noise from the other class.

I gave the copy to Sinbad.

—I'm not going to show the copy to Ma, I told him.

He said nothing.

—I won't tell her what happened, I said.

I needed him to know.

She didn't get up one morning. Da was going down to Mrs McEvoy to get her to take the babies for the day. Me and Sinbad still had to go to school.

—Get your breakfasts here, he said.

He unlocked the back door.

—Are you washed yet?

He'd gone before I could tell him that I always washed myself before I had my breakfast. I always made my own cornflakes, got the bowl and put in the flakes – never spilt them – put in the milk. Then the sugar. I used to flick my fingernail under the spoon so the sugar would be sprinkled evenly all over. But I didn't know what to do this morning; I was all mixed up. There was no bowl. I knew where she kept them. I put them away sometimes. There was no milk. It was probably still on the front step. There was only the sugar. I went over to it. I didn't want to think. I didn't want to think about my ma up in their bedroom. About her sick. I didn't want to see her. I was afraid.

Sinbad followed me.

If she wasn't sick, if she was just up in the bed, I'd have to know why she hadn't got up. I didn't want to know. I couldn't go up there. I didn't want to know. It would be back to normal when we came home from school later.

I had a spoon of sugar. I didn't keep it long enough in my mouth for it to become nice. I wasn't hungry. I wouldn't bother having any breakfast. I'd make toast. I liked the gas.

—What's wrong with Mam?

I didn't want to know.

—Shut up.

—What's wrong with her?

—Shut up.

—Is she sick?

—She's sick of you; shut up.

—Is she not well?

I liked the hiss the gas made and the smell for a little bit. I grabbed Sinbad. I made his face go close to the gas. He pushed back. He wasn't as easy to control as he used to be. His arms were strong. He couldn't beat me though. He'd never be able to do that. I'd always be bigger than him. He got away.

—I'm telling.

—Who?

—Da.

—What're you goin' to tell him? I said, moving towards him.

—You were messin' with the gas, he said.

—So what?

—We're not allowed.

He ran into the hall.

—You'll wake Ma, I said. —Then she'll never get better and you'll be to blame.

He wouldn't tell anything.

—There must have been the pair of you in it.

That was what Da nearly always said.

I opened the back door to get rid of the smell of the gas.

If Ma wasn't really sick; if they'd had another fight – . I hadn't heard anything. They'd laughed before I went to bed. They'd talked to each other.

I closed the door.

Da was coming back. I could hear his feet. He opened the door and came in, both steps at once. He left the door open.

—Nice day out, he said. —Have your breakfast?

—Yes, I said.

—Francis as well?

—Yes.

—Good lads. Good man. Missis McEvoy is going to look after Cathy and Deirdre. She's very good.

I watched his face. It wasn't tight or white; I couldn't see veins in his neck. He looked nice and calm: nothing bad had happened. Ma was sick.

—It'll give your mammy a chance to get better, he said.

I wanted to see her now; it was alright. She was only sick.

—I'll hardly have time for breakfast myself, he said, but he seemed kind of delighted. —No rest for the wicked.

—Can I go up to her? I said.

—She'll be asleep.

—Just to look.

—Better not; you might wake her. Better not. D'you mind?

—No.

He didn't want me to. There was something.

What about your lunch? he said. —You'll have to stay in.

—Sandwiches, I said.

—Can you manage? I can get the girls ready.

—Yeah.

—Good man, he said. —Francis's as well, right?

—Okay.

The butter was hard. I'd seen my ma doing it, scraping the top with the knife. I couldn't do it though. I just put pats of butter in each corner of the bread. There was nothing in the fridge to put in the sandwiches, not that I could see, except cheese, and I hated that. So I just made bread sandwiches. I made Sinbad's as well, just in case Da checked. There was nothing wrong with my ma. If he was smiling when he came back down I'd ask him for money for crisps for the sandwiches.

He smiled.

—Can we get crisps for the sandwiches?

—Good idea, he said.

He knew I was asking for the money to buy them. He had the girls in his arms; he had them laughing. Crisp sandwiches. I'd have to sneak out of the school at break because we weren't supposed to leave the yard, unless we were going on a message for one of the masters. There was definitely nothing wrong with her. Except she was a bit sick; I could tell for definite now. She had a tummy or a headache, that was all, or a bad cold. Da put Catherine down so he could get money from his pocket. Nothing that would stop her from being downstairs when we came home.

—Now.

He'd found the money.

—There now.

Two shillings.

—One each, he said. —Make sure now.

—Thanks, Da.

Sinbad had come back.

—Da gave us a shilling for each of us, I told him.

—Will Mam be better when we come home? he said.

—Probably, said Da. —Maybe not; probably.

—Crisp sandwiches, I told Sinbad.

I showed him the two shillings. I got out my hankie, put the two shillings in and stuffed the hankie right down, down into a corner of my pocket, the two shillings locked under it.

I took my time getting home, on purpose. I put my bag between Aidan and Liam's hedge and the wall and we went looking for the Weirdy Fella. The Weirdy Fella lived in the fields. There were hardly any fields left but he was still out there. I'd seen him once. He jumped into a ditch just when I was looking. He had a big black coat on him and a cap. He was all dirty and his back was crooked. He had no teeth, just two black stumps, like Tootsie's. I didn't see his teeth – he was too far away – but that was what they were like. I just saw his shape. We'd all seen him that day. We ran after him but he got away. We were going to kill him for all the things he did. He ate birds and rats and anything good he could get out of bins. My da always put the bin outside our gate on Wednesday night because the binmen came round on Thursday morning and he was in too much of a hurry in the mornings. One Thursday the lid was off the bin and there was stuff all over the path, bags and bones and tins and all the things that had been in the top half of the bin, the Monday, Tuesday and Wednesday stuff. I went back in and told my ma about it.

—Cats, she said. —Fizz it.

I went out again; I was going to school. I looked. There was a bit missing off a piece of bread. It was round, heel-shaped. I kicked the bread away; the shape stayed stuck to the ground. The weirdy Fella.

No one owned him. A girl in Baldoyle had had to be brought into hospital in Jervis Street after she fainted when she got home after the Weirdy Fella'd jumped up in front of her out from behind a pillar and had shown her his mickey. The guards never found him. He knew when you were on your own.

—He was in the army during the war, said Aidan.

There was just me and Aidan and Liam. Kevin had had to go somewhere with his ma and da; his granny was sick and he had to wear his good clothes. He had a note to let him out of school early. I was glad that Kevin wasn't coming, but I didn't say anything.

—How d'you know? I said.

I didn't say it the way I would've if Kevin had been with us.

—He got shot in the head and they couldn't get the bullet out properly so that's why he's mad.

—We should still kill him.

—Yeah.

—I'd say Kevin's granny is dying, said Liam. —We had to wear our good clothes when Ma died. D'you remember?

—No, said Aidan. —Yeah. There was a party after.

—A party?

—Yeah, said Aidan.

—Yeah, said Liam as well. —Kind of. Sandwiches and the grown-ups had drinks.

—So did we.

—Some of them sang songs.

I wanted to go home.

—I don't think we'll find him, I said. —It's too bright.

They agreed. No Chicken or Scaredy cat or anything like that. I got my bag and slowed myself, made myself walk normal. I got a leaf off Hanley's tree and folded and watched the crease getting darker and where the leaf broke. I got to the gate.

She was still in her dressing gown. That was all.

—Hello, she said.

—Hi, I said.

Sinbad was already home with his shoes off. There was nothing wrong with her to see.

—Are you still sick?

—Not really, she said. —I'm fine.

—Do you want me to go to the shops?

—I don't think so, she said. —Francis was singing his new song for me.

—We had crisp sandwiches for our lunch, I told her.

—So I believe, she said. —Will you finish it for me, love?

· —TALLY-HO HOUNDS AWAY –

Sinbad looked sideways at the lino.

—TALLY-HO HOUNDS AWAY –
TALLY-HO HOUNDS AWAY
ME BOYS AWAY – –
Ma started clapping.

She was in her dressing gown the next day as well but that was only because she hadn't got dressed yet. She was better. She looked straighter. She moved quicker.

I'd stayed awake all night, as long as I could, most of the night. There was nothing. I woke up early – half bright. I got out of bed. I didn't make noise when my feet got to the floor. I got to their door, over the creak just on front of it. I listened. Nothing. Asleep. My da's noise. My ma's noise under it. I went back. Bed was nice when you got back in after you got out for a bit when it was still warm. I kept my feet up near me. I didn't mind being awake. I was the only one. I looked across at Sinbad. His head was where his legs were supposed to be. His feet were somewhere. I could see the back of his head. I looked. I saw his breathing. There were birds outside, loads of them; three different kinds. I knew: they were getting at the milk. There used to be a bit of a roof slate beside the step for the milkman to put on top of the bottles to stop the birds from getting at them but it was gone now. Then there was a biscuit tin lid and a big stone to put on top of it but they were gone as well; the lid was, I didn't look for the stone. I didn't know why everyone tried to stop the birds from drinking the milk. They only took the top bit, hardly any. I heard the alarm going off in their bedroom. I could hear the clock on the wood of the cabinet on my da's side. I heard the alarm being stopped. I waited. I heard her coming to the door. I'd shut it properly after me. I pretended I was asleep.

—Good morning, boys.

I still pretended. I didn't have to look; I knew it from her voice. She was better.

—Wakey wakey!

Sinbad laughed. She was tickling him. He was whinging as well, funny and annoyed. I waited for my turn.

That didn't mean that there was nothing wrong, that nothing had happened. All it meant was that if something had happened between them, if they'd had a fight, she was better now. It was the first time she hadn't got up, except for two days after she came home from the hospital after having Deirdre. She was in bed when we got home from our auntie's; that was where we'd been when she was in the hospital. Our Auntie Nuala. She was my ma's big sister. I didn't like it there. I knew what was happening but Sinbad didn't really, not really.

—My mam's in the hop-sital.

He didn't talk like that now. He was better at it.

She was in bed when we came home. We came home on the bus, two buses, with our uncle.

I kept watch. I listened.

—They had a party, I told Kevin. —After the funeral. In the house. Singing and all.

I went to the shops for Henno to get him two cakes for his lunch.

—A packet of Mikado if she's no cakes left.

He said I could have a ha'penny out of the change for doing the message so I got a gobstopper with it. I showed it to Kevin under the desk. I wished I'd bought something different now, something I could have shared with Kevin.

When Henno told us to go asleep Kevin dared me to eat the gobstopper without being caught. If I took it out of my mouth because Henno could hear noises or he was coming down to check our copies, if I chickened, I'd have to give the rest of the gobstopper to Kevin. All he'd have to do was run cold water from the tap over it.

Henno went out to talk to James O'Keefe's ma just after I put the gobstopper into my mouth. Missis O'Keefe was shouting. Henno warned us and shut the door. We could still hear her. James O'Keefe wasn't in school. I sucked like mad. She said that Henno was always picking on James O'Keefe. I made the gobstopper go round and round, rubbing it off my cheeks but mostly the roof of my mouth and my tongue. It got smoother. I couldn't take it out of my mouth. I got Ian McEvoy to look; I opened my mouth: the gobstopper was white. I'd licked the outside off it. He was every bit as intelligent as the other boys, she told Henno. She knew some of them and they were nothing to write home about. Henno opened the door and warned us again. Calm down now, Missis O'Keefe, we heard him saying. Then he was gone. There were no more voices outside. He'd gone somewhere with Missis O'Keefe. We started laughing because everybody was watching me trying to eat the gobstopper. They kept saying He's coming and pretending that he was but I didn't fall for it. He was gone for ages. When he opened the door the gobstopper was small enough to swallow if I had to. I'd won. I looked at Henno's face and swallowed it. I had to push hard; my throat was sore for ages after it. Henno was real nice for the rest of the day. He brought us out to the pitch and showed us how to solo the ball. My tongue was pink.

They were fighting all the time now. They said nothing but it was a fight. The way he folded his paper and snapped it, he was saying something. The way she got up when one of the girls was crying upstairs, sighed and stooped, wanting him to see that she was tired. It was happening. They probably thought they were hiding it.

I didn't understand. She was lovely. He was nice. They had four children. I was one of them, the oldest. The man of the house when my da wasn't there. She held onto us for longer, gripped us and looked over us at the floor or the ceiling. She didn't notice me trying to push away; I was too old for that. In front of Sinbad. I still loved her smell. But she wasn't cuddling us; she was hanging on to us.

He waited before he answered, always he did, pretended he hadn't heard anything. She was always the one that tried to make them talk. He'd answer just when I thought she'd have to ask again, to change her voice, make it sound angry. It was agony waiting for him.

—Paddy?

—What?

—Did you not hear me?

—Hear what?

—You heard me.

—Heard what?

She stopped. We were listening; she saw us. He thought he'd won; I thought he did.

—Sinbad?

He didn't answer. He wasn't asleep though; I knew the breathing.

—Sinbad.

I could hear him listening. I didn't move. I didn't want him to think that I was going to get him.

—Sinbad?——Francis.

—What?

I thought of something.

—Do you not like being called Sinbad?

—No.

222

—Okay.

I said nothing for a bit. I heard him change, move nearer the wall.

—Francis?

—What?

—Can you hear them?

He didn't give an answer.

—Can you hear them? Francis?

—Yeah.

That was all. I knew he wouldn't say any more. We listened to the sharp mumbles coming up from downstairs. We did, not just me. We listened for a long time. The silences were worst, waiting for it to start again, or louder. A door sort of slammed; the back door – I heard the glass shake.

—Francis?

—What?

—That's what it's like every night.

He said nothing.

—It's like that every night, I said.

Breath came out sharp between his lips. He did that a lot since his lips had been burnt.

—It's only talking, he said.

—It's not.

—It is.

—It's not; they're shouting.

—No, they aren't.

—They are, I said. —Quietly.

I listened for proof. There was nothing.

—They've stopped, he said. —They weren't.

He sounded happy and nervous.

—They'll do it again tomorrow.

—No, they won't, he said. —They were only talking, about things.

*

I watched him putting on his trousers. He always brought the zip up before he did the button at the top and it took him ages, but his face never changed. He stared down at his hands and made two chins. And he forgot about his shirt and his vest, so he had to do it all over again. I wanted to go over and help him, but I didn't. One move and he'd change; he'd back away, turn sideways and moan.

—The button should be first, I told him. —At the top. Do it first.

I just said it in a normal voice.

He kept doing what he'd been doing. The radio downstairs sounded nice; the voices.

—Francis, I said.

He had to look at me. I was going to look after him.

—Francis.

He held the two sides of the front of his trousers.

—Why are you calling me Francis? he said.

—Cos Francis is your name, I said.

His face said nothing.

—It's your real name, I said. —You don't like being called Sinbad.

He put the sides into one of his hands and did the zip with the other, still the old way. It annoyed me. It was just stupid.

—Sure you don't? I said.

My voice was still just normal.

—Leave me alone, he said.

—Why? I said.

He said nothing.

I tried a different way.

—Do you not want me to call you Francis?

—Leave me alone, he said.

I gave up.

—Sinnnn-badd – !

—I'll tell Ma.

—She won't care, I said.

He said nothing.

—She won't care, I said again.

I waited for him to say Why not. I was going to get him. He didn't. He said nothing. He turned sideways and got his trousers done.

I didn't hit him.

—She won't care, I said when I was opening the bedroom door. I tried again.

—Francis.

He wouldn't look at me. He hid himself in his jumper when he was putting it on.

—I kneed you, I said, and I gave him a dead leg.

He collapsed before he understood the pain, straight down like something heavy. I'd done it and seen it done so often it wasn't funny any more. It was just an excuse; pretending that hurting someone was for a joke. I didn't even know his name. He was too small to have one. His scream died out once he knew there was nothing else going to happen.

The other one was getting your finger and digging it into someone's ribs real hard, like a knife, twisting it and saying, Am I boring you? It was new, in school on Monday after the weekend. You couldn't relax. Your best friend could get you: it was a joke. Or grabbing one of your diddies and saying, Whistle. Some fellas tried to whistle. Sinbad got a pulled diddy and a dead leg at the same time. Everyone got it done to them, except Charles Leavy.

Charles Leavy didn't do it to anybody. That was weird. Charles Leavy could have made us all line up, like Henno on a Friday morning, and kneed all our legs dead. You wanted to show off in front of Charles Leavy. You wanted to say bad words. You wanted him to look at you the proper way.

*

They said nothing for long bits but that wasn't bad; they were watching the television or reading, or my ma was doing a hard bit of knitting. It didn't make me nervous; their faces were okay.

My ma said a thing during The Virginian.

—What did we see him in before?

My da liked The Virginian. He didn't pretend he wasn't watching.

—I think, he said, —I'm not sure; something though.

Sinbad couldn't say Virginian properly. He didn't know what it meant either, why they called him the Virginian. I did.

—He comes from Virginia.

—That's right, said my da. —Where do The Dubliners come from, Francis?

—Dublin, said Sinbad.

—Good man.

Da nudged me. I did it back, with my knee against his leg. I was sitting on the floor beside his chair. Ma asked him did he want any tea during the ads. He said No, then he changed his mind and shouted in Yes.

They always talked during The News; they talked about the news. Sometimes it wasn't really talk, not conversation, just comments.

—Bloody eejit.

—Yes.

I was able to tell when my da was going to call someone a bloody eejit; his chair creaked. It was always a man and he was always saying something to an interviewer.

—Who asked him?

The interviewer had asked him but I knew what my da meant. Sometimes I got there before him.

—Bloody eejit.

—Good man, Patrick.

My ma didn't mind me saying Bloody when The News was

226

on. The News was boring but sometimes I watched it properly, all of it. I thought that the Americans were fighting gorillas in Vietnam; that was what it sounded like. But it didn't make any other kind of sense. The Israelis were always fighting the Arabs and the Americans were fighting the gorillas. It was nice that the gorillas had a country of their own, not like the zoo, and the Americans were killing them for it. There were Americans getting killed as well. They were surrounded and the war was nearly over. They had helicopters. Mekong Delta. Demilitarised zone. Tet Offensive. The gorillas in the zoo didn't look like they'd be hard to beat in a war. They were nice and old looking, brainy looking, and their hair was dirty. Their arms were brilliant; I'd have loved arms like that. I'd never been on the roof. Kevin had, and his da had killed him when he found out about it when he got home, and he'd only been on the kitchen roof, the flat bit. I was up for the gorillas even though two of my uncles and aunties lived in America. I'd never seen them. They sent us ten dollars, me and Sinbad, one Christmas. I couldn't remember what I got with my five dollars.

—I should get seven cos I'm the oldest.

And I couldn't remember the names of the uncle and auntie who'd sent it, which ones; Brendan and Rita or Sam and Boo. I had seven cousins in America as well. Two of them were called the same as me. I didn't care though; I was still up for the gorillas. Until I asked.

—Why are the yankees fighting the gorillas?

—What's that?

—Why are the yankees fighting the gorillas?

—D'you hear this, Mary? Patrick wants to know why the yanks are fighting gorillas.

They didn't laugh but it was funny, I could tell. I wanted to cry; I'd given something away. I was stupid. I hated being caught, more than anything. I hated it. That was what school was all about, not being caught and watching others getting caught instead. It was alright now though; it wasn't school. He told me what a guerrilla was. It made sense now.

—Impossible to beat, he said.

I was still up for them, the guerrillas.

It went back to the man in the studio. Charles Mitchell.

—His tie's crooked, look.

Then it was Richard Nixon.

—There's a nose, said my da. —Look.

—He's a better-looking man than some of them.

It didn't last long. He just shook a few people's hands. When Charles Mitchell came back his tie was straight. They laughed. I did too. There wasn't much else; two dead cows and a farmer talking about them. He was angry. I heard the creak.

—Bloody eejit.

There was nothing in any of that, no hints, no edges, no hard voices. It was normal.

—Bedtime, sonny jim.

I didn't mind. I wanted to go. I wanted to lie awake for a while. I kissed them. He tried to tickle me with his chin. I got away. I let him grab me without him having to get out of his chair. I got away again.

—Do your ma and da have fights?

—No.

—Not fights like thumping and kicking, I said. —Shouting. Giving out to each other.

—Yeah then, said Kevin. —They have them all the time.

—Do they?

—Yeah.

I was glad I'd asked. It had taken me all day to get to it. We'd walked to Dollymount, had a mess – it was freezing –

228

and come home and I hadn't asked till we were back on Barrytown Road, nearly at the shops.

—Do yours? said Kevin.

—Have fights?

—Yeah.

—No.

—What did you ask for then? They must.

—They don't, I said. —They have arguments, that's all; like yours.

—What did you ask me for then?

—My uncle and auntie, I said. —My ma was talking about it to my da. My uncle hit my auntie and she hit him back and she called the guards.

—What did they do?

—They arrested him, I said. —They came for him in a car with a siren.

—Is he in jail?

—No; they let him out. He had to promise that he'd never do it again. On paper. He had to write it down and sign his name under it. And if he ever does it again he has to go to jail for ten years and my boy cousins get sent to Artane and my auntie keeps my girl cousins cos she wouldn't be able to afford to keep them all.

—What does your uncle look like?

—Big.

—Ten years, said Kevin.

That was as old as us.

—That's ages for just hitting someone. And what about her? he remembered. —She hit him as well.

—Not hard, I said.

I loved making up stuff; I loved the way the next bit came into my head, it made sense and expanded and I could keep going till I came to the end; it was like being in a race. I always won. I told it the second I made it up, but I believed

it, I really did. This was different though. I shouldn't have
asked Kevin in the first place; he was the wrong one. I should
have asked Liam. I'd escaped, but Kevin would probably tell
his ma now about my uncle and auntie and she'd tell my ma,
although they didn't like each other much; you could tell
from the way they kept moving when they met each other on
the street or outside the shops, like they were too busy to stop
for long, they were in a hurry. She'd tell my ma and then
she'd ask me what I'd said to Kevin about my uncle and
auntie and I didn't think I was good enough to get out of that
one.

—But why were you talking about mams and dads fighting
anyway?

I'd have to run away from home.

I hadn't named the uncle and auntie. I'd done that, hadn't
named them, on purpose.

—I was only messing with him.

I was thinking of running away anyway.

—Having him on.

I'd spent ages – Henno had gone off to have a chat with
another teacher – looking at the map of Ireland.

—Leading him up the garden path.

She'd laugh. She always did when I said things like that.
She thought I was brainy because of it.

—I'm leaving you for a few minutes, gentlemen, said
Henno.

We loved it when he said that; I could nearly hear it, backs
relaxing. Getting ready.

—A few minutes only, said Henno. —I'll be leaving the
door open. And you know all about my famous ears.

—Yes, Sir, said Fluke Cassidy.

He wasn't messing. If anyone else had said that he'd have
got walloped.

Henno went out the door. We waited. He came back to the

230

door and waited. We stayed looking at our books, not looking up to see if he was there. We heard his shoes. They stopped. We heard them again, going away.

—Fuck your famous ears.

We tried not to laugh too loud. It was better that way, trying not to. I laughed more than I usually did; I couldn't help it. I had to wipe my face. I got my atlas out of my bag. We hadn't used it much, only for learning the counties of Ireland so far. Offaly was the easiest one to remember because it was the hardest. Dublin was okay just as long as you didn't mix it up with Louth. With Fermanagh and Tyrone it was hard to remember which was which. I stared at the map of Ireland from the top to the bottom. There was nowhere I wanted to run away to, except maybe some of the islands. I was still going to do it though. You couldn't run away to an island; you had to sail or swim part of the way. It wasn't like a game though; there were no rules that you had to stick to. An uncle of mine had run away to Australia.

I opened up the map of the world in the middle of the atlas. There were places right in the middle that I couldn't read properly because the pages wouldn't flatten fully for me. There were plenty of other places though.

I was serious.

Henno had said that my eyes were red. He said I hadn't got enough sleep. Right in front of everybody. He'd given out to me, said he was going to phone my mother and tell her to make sure I was in bed by half-eight every night. Right in front. I was being allowed to watch too much television.

He bent down closer to my face.

—Were you drunk last night, Mister Clarke?

For a laugh.

We didn't have a phone but I didn't tell him that.

My uncle had gone to Australia, by himself. He hadn't run

away, but he'd been very young, still not eighteen. He was still there. He had his own business and a boat.

I'd stayed awake all night. That was why my ma'd said that my face was white and Henno'd said that my eyes were red. I'd kept myself awake; I'd done it, right through.

I didn't know what was happening when it started to get more grey than dark; it was more frightening than the dark. It was dawn. Then the birds started. I was on guard. I was making sure that they didn't start again; all I had to do was stay awake. Like St Peter when Jesus was in the Garden. St Peter kept falling asleep but I didn't, not even once. I made a corner in the bed, and sat up in the dark. I stopped myself from slipping under the blankets. I hit my head off the wall. I pinched myself; I concentrated on how hard I could go. I went to the bathroom and threw wet on my pyjamas so I'd be cold. I stayed awake.

The cock crew.

There was no more fighting. I went up to my parents' door and listened without breathing. I could hear my da's sleep breathing and my ma's – his noisy, hers trying to keep up. I got away and took a breath, and then I started crying.

Mission accomplished.

A cock really did crow; I wasn't making it up. It did go Cock-a-doodle-do, but the four sounds were joined together more. It was in Donnelly's farm, down the road, the bit of the farm that was left. I'd never heard it before. But I'd seen the cock loads of times, in among the chickens behind the wire. I'd never known that it was a cock, until now; I'd just thought that it was a big chicken, the king chicken. We'd put grass through the wire to get him to come nearer.

—He's dangerous.

—Chickens aren't dangerous.

—This one is.

—Look at his eyes.

232

—His eggs are bigger. They're blue.

He wouldn't come near us. We couldn't throw stones properly at him through the wire.

She'd screamed, words I couldn't make out. She'd broken something; I think it was her because it came just after the scream, like the end of it. He laughed in a way that meant nothing funny. Then sobs. I got up to shut the door but when I got there I opened it more.

—Patrick.

It was Sinbad.

—It's just talking.

—Get lost, I said.

He was asleep before he'd time to start crying again.

It was up to me.

They'd stopped. Nothing. They went to bed, one after the other, him first. He didn't go to the bathroom; his breath would smell dirty and meaty in the morning. I heard the bed creaking, his side. Then she came. I didn't know the television was on until she turned it off. Then her on the stairs, in to the side to miss the creak. She went to the bathroom. The tap. The swush of the toothbrush; she used a blue, him a red, me and Sinbad smaller green and red ones, me the red. She turned the tap off, and the empty bubble hopped back up the pipes into the attic. Then she went across to their room. She pushed open the door as far as it would go, bang into the bed – his side – and flapped it shut with a flick of her hand. Quiet on the stairs, noisy going into the room.

I stayed there, standing. I had to stay still. If I moved it would start again. I was allowed to breathe, that was all. It was like after Catherine or the other baby stopped crying; forty-five seconds, my ma said – if they didn't cry out inside forty-five seconds they'd go back asleep. I stood. I didn't count; this wasn't a game or babies. I didn't know how long.

233

Long enough to be cold. No voices, just shuffling and creaks, getting comfy; everyone except me.

I was in charge. They didn't know. I could move now; the worst bit was over: I'd done it. But I had to stay awake all night; I had to keep an all-night vigil.

Rhodesia. It was near the equator, the imaginary line around the middle of the world. There'd be elephants there, and monkeys and poor black people. Elephants never forgot. When they were dying they walked all the way to the elephants' graveyard and then they lay down and just died. On top of the ground. It was too far away. I'd go there when I was bigger. I knew something else about Rhodesia. It was named after Cecil Rhodes, but I didn't know why; I couldn't remember why. He might have conquered it or discovered it. There were no more countries left to be discovered; they all had colours in them. I looked at the other pink countries. Canada was huge, forty, fifty times bigger than Ireland. Canadian Mounted Police. Mounties. Policemen on horses. Thin men on fast horses. None of them wore glasses. Red jackets. Trousers that stuck out at the sides. Guns in holsters with a cover on them that clicked open and shut. So the gun wouldn't fall out when they were going fast. After rustlers. Not rustlers in Canada; smugglers. Eskimos that wouldn't obey the law. Killing bears. Mushing their huskies. Whipping dogs. Curly tails. Goggles.

—Come on; good man.

The map was right in my face. I could smell the paper and the desk.

Henno was there.

I didn't know what had happened, what was happening.

—Up; come on.

It didn't sound like Henno. There were hands at my sides, man's hands, under my arms. I was lifted. I stood beside the desk. I could only see the floor. It was dirty. Hands on my shoulders. Pushing me forward, holding me up. Up to the front. I saw no one. No noise. Out the door. The door closed.

Mister Hennessey's face.

Looking up at me.

—Alright?

A nod, only one.

—Tired?

A nod.

—Okay; happens us all.

Hands on my side.

Up.

Rough material.

Too tired to move my face, too heavy.

A smell.

Nice.

I woke up. I didn't move. I wasn't in bed. The smell was different, leather. I saw the arm of a chair. I was lying in the chair. Two chairs, front to front to make a bed. I was in it. Two leather armchairs. I still didn't move. There was a blanket over me and something else, a coat. The blanket was grey and hard. I knew the coat. I knew the ceiling, the colour of it, the cracks like a map. The window over the door that had to be opened with a window pole. I knew the smoke rising up out of the ashtray, thin and flattening at the top. It took a while: I was in the headmaster's office.

—Awake?

—Yes, Sir.

—*Maith thú.**

He separated the two chairs to let me sit up. He took his coat and put it back on its hanger with his hat.

—What came over you at all?

* Good for you.

235

—I don't know, Sir.
—You fell asleep.
—Yes, Sir.
—In class.
—Yes, Sir. I don't remember.
—Did you sleep properly last night?
—Yes, Sir. I woke up early.
—Early.
—Yes, Sir. I heard the cock crow.
—That's early.
—Yes, Sir.
—Toothache?
—No, Sir. Pains in my legs.
—Tell your mother.
—Yes, Sir.
—Back to class now. Find out what you missed.
—Yes, Sir.

I didn't want to go back. I was scared. I'd been caught. They'd be waiting for me. I'd been caught. I was alone. I still felt tired. And stupid. There were bits missing.

Nothing happened. I knocked at the door first. Henno wasn't at the front when I opened the door. I saw Liam over at the window, Fluke Cassidy. Henno walked up the aisle. He said nothing. He nodded to my desk. I went down. No one looked at me hard. No one smiled or nudged. No notes landed on my desk. They all thought I was sick; there was something really wrong with me, the way Henno hadn't battered me but had nearly carried me out. They looked at me when I came back into the class as if they were waiting for something, for me to do it all over again. They said nothing, not even Kevin.

I still felt stupid.

I wanted to go asleep again. At home. I wanted to sleep awake, to know I was asleep.

For the rest of the day Henno only asked me questions when I put my hand up. He didn't try to catch anyone out. He hit no one. They knew it was because of me.

—Which of the tropics is north of the equator?

I knew. I put my hand up. I used my other hand to hold it up.

—Sir Sir.

—Patrick Clarke.

—The Tropic of Cancer, Sir.

—Good.

The bell went.

—Stay seated – ! —— Stand – First row . . .

They were waiting for me outside, not in a gang or a circle. They were pretending they weren't. They wanted to be with me.

I didn't like it much.

—Mister Clarke?

Henno was standing at the door.

—Yes, Sir?

—Come here.

I went. I wasn't nervous.

—Go home, the rest of you.

He moved back and let me in. He didn't shut the door. He stepped back and sat on the top of one of the desks.

He tried to smile and look serious.

—How are you feeling now?

I didn't know how to answer.

—Feeling better?

—Yes, Sir.

—What happened you?

—I fell asleep, Sir; I don't know.

—Tired?

—Yes, Sir.

—No sleep last night?

—Some, Sir. I woke up early.

He put his hands on his knees and leaned towards me a bit.

—Is everything alright?

—Yes, Sir.

—At home?

—Yes, Sir.

—Good. Go on.

—Yes, Sir. Thanks, Sir.

—Find out the homework you missed and do it for tomorrow.

—Yes, Sir. Will I close the door?

—Yes. Good man.

The door was bigger than the space for it. The damp had expanded it. I pulled the handle and the door scraped into its place.

They were outside the gate, pretending they weren't waiting for me. They all wanted to be with me; I knew. It didn't make me feel good. It should have. But it didn't. They didn't want to leave me alone, and I knew why: they didn't want to miss anything – they wanted to be the ones to run for help. They all wanted to save my life. They hadn't a clue.

—What eccer did I miss?

There was a race to get their school bags off their backs the first.

They were saps. Charles Leavy wasn't there. David Geraghty wasn't there either. He'd probably had to go straight home for tablets for his legs or something. All the rest of them had their homework diaries out. I got mine out and sat down against the wall. I let the railing touch my head. I let Kevin give me his diary.

Charles Leavy didn't care. He was the only one that knew what had happened: I'd fallen asleep. He stayed up all night all the time. Listening to his ma and da. Not caring. Saying cunt and fuck. Heading his ball.

They watched me filling in the day. I let my hand wobble a little bit, then gave up. I wasn't enjoying it. They were all there, and I didn't like them. I was alone.

We hadn't got that much eccer.

I realised something funny; I wanted to be with Sinbad.

—Francis. D'you want this?

It was a biscuit, only a biscuit. I wanted it as well but I wanted him to take it. I was giving it to him. He wouldn't even look at it.

I grabbed him.

—Open your mouth!

His lips vanished as he closed down his mouth. He got ready to be pulled around, stiff and dead.

—Open your mouth!

I held it in front of his eyes.

—See.

He shut them, crammed shut. I got the biscuit and I got his head and I pushed the biscuit at his mouth, and I pushed until it fell apart and I couldn't hold it. It was a fig roll.

—See! It was only a biscuit! A biscuit.

His face was still shut.

—A fig roll.

I got bits off the ground.

—I'm eating it; look.

I loved the fig bit, soft with little stones that broke. The biscuity outsides had all got crumbled. There were none left big enough to pick up.

His mouth and eyes stayed shut. He hadn't put his hands up to cover his ears but they were closed as well, I could tell.

—I'm finished, I said. —And I'm not poisoned, look.

I held my arms up in front of him.

—Look.

I danced.

239

—Look.

I stopped.

—I'm still alive, Francis.

I wasn't sure if he was breathing. Parts of his face were very pink and others, under his eyes were white. He wouldn't come out for me. I thought about giving him a dead leg – he deserved it – but I didn't bother; I just kicked him. Bang on the shin. My foot bounced back. He caught the noise; I saw his mouth bulge. I went to get him again, but I didn't.

He frightened me.

He could stop everything happening, and I couldn't.

—Francis –

Still, stiff.

—Francis.

I touched the top of his head, brushed his hair with my fingers. He didn't feel anything.

—I'm sorry for kicking you.

Nothing.

I went out and closed the door. I shut it hard enough for him to hear the click; I didn't slam it. I waited. I got down and looked through the keyhole. I couldn't see the space where he was. Keyholes were never any good. I counted to ten. I opened the door, the ordinary way.

He was still there, the same. The exact same.

I wanted to kill him. I was going to; it wasn't fair. All I wanted to do was help him and he wouldn't let me. He wouldn't even let me be in the room, and I was. And he was going to find out.

I closed his nose. I shut his nostrils with my fingers, not to hurt, not hard.

Now.

His nose was dry. It made it easier, holding on. The only air he had was the stuff already in him.

Now.

He'd have to die or do something.

—Francis.

He'd have to inhale oxygen and exhale the carbon dioxide, sooner or later. I watched the two colours on his face shifting. Something was happening.

His mouth opened – nothing else – real quick with a pop, and shut again, quick as a goldfish. He couldn't have breathed, not enough. He was bluffing.

—Francis, you're dying.

His nose still wasn't sweating.

—You'll die unless you inhale oxygen, I said. —Within a matter of minutes. Francis. It's for your own good.

He did it again. Open, pop, shut again.

Something happened: I started crying. I went to thump him and before I had a fist made I was crying. I hung on to his nose for a while longer, just to be holding him. I didn't know why I was crying; it shocked me. I let go of his nose. I put my arms around him. My hands touched around the back. He stayed hard and closed. I thought my arms would soften him. They'd have to.

I was hugging a statue. I couldn't even smell him because my nose was full of snot and I couldn't get rid of it. I stayed that way because I didn't want to give up. My arms got sore. My crying turned into a hum; no tears. I wondered did Sinbad – Francis – know that I'd been crying? Because of him, mostly.

I couldn't stop myself from crying these days.

I let go of him.

—Francis?

I wiped my face but most of the wet had gone. It had evaporated.

—I won't hit you again, okay; ever.

I didn't expect an answer or anything. I waited a bit. Then I kicked him. And I thumped him. Twice. Then I felt my back go freezing: someone was looking. I turned. No one. I couldn't hit him again though.

I left the door open.

I wanted to help him. He had to know; he had to get ready like me. I wanted to be able to stand beside him. He was warm. I wanted to get him ready. I was ahead of him; I knew more than he did. I wanted to get into bed beside him so we could listen together. I couldn't help it. When he wouldn't do what I wanted him to I couldn't help going back to annoying him, frightening him, hitting him. Hating him. It was easier. He wouldn't listen to me. He wouldn't let me do anything.

He ate his dinner like nothing had happened. So did I. Shepherd's pie. The Christmas cake potato top was perfect; the peaks were brown and crispy, the cover was like a skin. Ma's dinners nearly made me think that there was nothing wrong; they never got any worse. I ate it all. It was lovely.

I went over to the fridge.

K.E.L.V.I.N.A.T.O.R.

She'd taught me those letters. I remembered it.

I liked the way the handle tried to stop me from opening it and I always won. There were four pints, one opened. I carried the opened one, two handed – glass made me nervous – to the table. I filled my mug to an inch before the top. I hated spilling.

—Francis, I said, —d'you want me to put milk in your mug?

I wanted Ma to see.

—Yes, he said.

I didn't do anything, I'd been so sure he was going to say nothing or No.

—Yes, thank you, said Ma.

—Yes, thank you, said Sinbad.

I put the groove of the top of the bottle right on the rim of his mug and poured, the same amount as I'd given myself. There wasn't much left in the bottle.

—Thank you, Patrick, said Sinbad.

I didn't know what to say back. Then I remembered.

—You're welcome.

I got back from the fridge. Ma sat down. Da was at work.

—Have you two been fighting again? she said.

—No, I said.

—Are you sure?

—No, I said. —Yeah. Sure we haven't?

—No, said Sinbad.

—I hope you haven't been, she said.

—We haven't, I said.

Then I got her to laugh.

—I assure you.

And she laughed.

I looked over at Sinbad. He looked at Ma laughing. He smiled. He tried to laugh but she stopped before he could get going.

—I appreciate this dinner very much, I said.

But she didn't laugh much more.

I looked at him for a long time, trying to see what was different. There was something. He'd just come home, late, just before my bedtime. He was supposed to check my homework, to test my spellings. His face was different, browner, shinier. He picked up his knife slowly and then looked as if he'd just discovered the fork on the other side of the plate, and he picked it up like he wasn't sure what it was. He followed the steam coming off his plate.

He was drunk. It hit me. I sat down at the table with my spelling notebook for an excuse, English at the front, Irish at the back. I was fascinated. He was drunk. It was new. I'd never seen it before. Liam and Aidan's da howled at the moon, and here was mine. He was telling himself to do everything he did, I could see that, concentrating. His face was tight on one side and loose on the other. He was nice. He grinned when he had time to notice me.

—There y'are, he said.

He never said that.

—Have you spellings for me?

And he made me test him. He got eight out of ten. He couldn't spell Aggravate or Rhythm.

But that wasn't it. They weren't falling apart because my da was getting drunk. There was only a bottle of sherry in the house. I checked it. It was always the same. I knew nothing about it, how you got drunk, how much it took, what was supposed to happen. But I knew that that wasn't it. I looked for lipstick on his collar; I'd seen it in The Man From Uncle. There wasn't any. I wondered, anyway, why there'd be lipstick on the collar. Maybe the women were bad shots in the dark. I didn't really know why I was looking at my da's collar.

I couldn't prove it. I sometimes didn't believe it; I'd really think that there was nothing wrong – the way they were chatting and drinking their tea, the way we all looked at the television – but I'd swing back again before happiness could trap me. She was lovely. He was nice.

She looked thinner. He looked older. He looked mean, like he was making himself look mean. She looked at him all the time. When he wasn't looking; like she was searching for something or trying to recognise him; like he'd said he was someone whose name she recognised but she wasn't sure that she'd like him when she remembered properly. Sometimes her mouth opened and stayed there when she was looking. She waited for him to look at her. She cried a lot. She thought I wasn't looking. She wiped her eyes with her sleeve and made

244

herself smile and even giggled, as if the crying had been a mistake and she'd only found out.

There was no proof.

Mister O'Driscoll from the house at the top of the old road didn't live there any more. He wasn't dead either; I'd seen him. Richard Shiels's da sometimes didn't live in their house. Richard Shiels said he had to go to a job somewhere –

—Africa.

but I didn't believe him. His ma had a black eye once. Edward Swanwick's ma ran away with a pilot from Aer Lingus. He used to fly low over their house. One of their chimneys was cracked. She never came back. The Swanwicks –

—The ones that are left, said Kevin's ma.

moved away, to Sutton.

We were next. We never saw Edward Swanwick again. We were next. I knew it, and I was going to be ready.

We watched them. Charles Leavy was in goal, the gate closed behind him. Seán Whelan whacked the ball into the gate. It was his turn in goal. Charles Leavy got the ball, hit the gate. They swapped again. Charles Leavy's head was twitching. The ball made the gate bounce.

—He's not trying to stop it, said Kevin.

—He doesn't want to be in goal, I said.

Only spas went in goal.

There was just the two of them. Most of the new houses still had no one in them but their road looked more finished because the cement went all the way to Barrytown Road now; the gap had been filled. My name was in the cement. It was my last autograph; I was sick of it. The road had a name now as well, Chestnut Avenue, nailed to the Simpsons' wall cos theirs was the corner house. It was in Irish as well, Ascal na gCastán. When the ball skidded on the road you could

245

hear the stones and gravel. The dust was everywhere even though it was nearly the winter now. The turns off Chestnut Avenue didn't make any sense yet. You couldn't tell what shape it was all going to be when it was finished.

Charles Leavy was back in goal. He saved a shot because he couldn't help it, it went straight into his leg. Seán Whelan blemmed in the rebound. He was able to keep it low. The gate clattered.

We made our move.

—Three-and-in, said Kevin.

They ignored us.

—Hey, said Kevin. —Three-and-in.

Charles Leavy waited for Seán Whelan to get the gate properly closed again. His shot hit the pillar, the corner of it, and flew past us all. I ran after it. I was doing it for Charles Leavy. I kicked to him, careful that it went straight to him. He waited till it stopped, as if that meant that he didn't have to admit that I'd got it for him, because he didn't even look at me.

Kevin had another go.

—D'you not want to play three-and-in?

Charles Leavy looked at Seán Whelan. Seán Whelan shook his head, and Charles Leavy turned to us.

—Fuck off, he said.

I wanted to go; I'd never heard it like that before, like he meant it. It was an order. There was no choice. He'd kill us if we didn't. Kevin knew this as well. I could see him loosening to go. I didn't say anything else till Charles Leavy could see that we were going.

—We'll go in goal, I said. —Me and him.

We kept going.

—You can be out all the time.

Charles Leavy smacked the ball into the gate and Seán Whelan came out. Seán Whelan scored before Charles Leavy

246

had even got to the gate and they swapped again. This time Seán Whelan shrugged and Charles Leavy tapped the ball to me, to me, not to Kevin.

I let him win the ball off me. I let him win all the tackles. I put the ball too far ahead of me so he wouldn't have to tackle me. I nearly passed the ball to him. I wanted him to win. I needed him to like me. I went in hard on Seán Whelan. I was in my good clothes – my ma made us wear our clothes all day Sunday. I didn't have to go in goal even once, because I didn't win. I let Charles Leavy get past me when he was out, and Kevin when Charles Leavy was in. One of them was out all the time so I never won. I didn't mind. I was playing football with Charles Leavy. I was getting up close to him. I was pretending to try and get the ball off him. He was playing with me.

He was useless. Seán Whelan was absolutely brilliant. The ball stuck to his foot unless he didn't want it to. With the four of us playing, he was much better than when there'd only been two of them. He put it between our legs; he rolled the ball along under his foot, leaning out to stop you from getting at it; he tapped the ball against the kerb, it jumped, and he volleyed it into the net – the gate. He did that seven times. He took the ball off Charles Leavy, he elbowed him and pushed himself between Charles Leavy and the ball.

—Foul, I said.

But they ignored me. They were laughing, pushing each other, trying to trip each other up. The next time Kevin got the ball I pretended I was trying to trip him, and he kicked me.

Charles Leavy was bringing his foot back to shoot; Seán Whelan tapped it first, past Kevin in goal, and Charles Leavy kicked air and shouted from the fright. He fell over slowly – he didn't have to – and started laughing.

—Yeh fuckin' fucker, he said to Seán Whelan.

I hated Seán Whelan. He did the kerb trick again. Kevin got out of the way of the ball. The gate jumped. Missis Whelan came out.

—Get the hell out of it! she said. —Go on; break someone else's gate. And you, Seán Whelan, you mind them trousers.

She went back in.

I thought we'd go somewhere else but Seán Whelan didn't move, or Charles Leavy. They waited for Missis Whelan to close the door and then they started again. I looked at the gate every time the ball thumped it. Nothing happened.

The game died. We sat on the wall. There was a gap in the path where they were going to put something when the rest of the building was finished; you couldn't tell what. Whelan's garden had been dug; it was brown chunks of muck like the countryside.

—Why isn't there grass? I said.

—Don't know, said Seán Whelan.

He didn't want to answer; I could tell from his face. I looked to see what Kevin's face was like, what he was thinking.

—It has to grow, said Charles Leavy.

Kevin was looking around at the muck, like he was waiting for the grass to come up. I wanted Charles Leavy to keep talking.

—How long does it take? I asked.

—Wha'? I don't fuckin' know. Years.

—Yeah, I agreed.

Sitting beside Charles Leavy, on a wall. And Kevin.

—Will we go to the barn, said Kevin, —will we?

—Why? said Charles Leavy.

I agreed with him. There was nothing there any more, not even the barn properly since the fire. It was boring. The rats had gone off. They'd got into the gardens of some of the new houses. I'd seen a little girl with a rat bite; she was showing it to everyone. All you could do was throw stones at the corrugated iron walls that were left and watch the flakes jump off. The noise of it was good for a while.

Kevin didn't answer Charles Leavy. I felt good: he'd said it, not me. It was usually me. I felt even better.

—The barn's boring, I said.

Kevin said nothing. Neither did Charles Leavy. But it wasn't boring like this; I loved it, sitting there doing nothing. There wasn't even anything to look at except the houses across the road. Charles Leavy lived in one of them. I didn't know which one. I wondered was it the one with the big hill of broken bricks in the garden, bricks and muck and hard cement and bits of cardboard box sticking out of it. And huge weeds growing by themselves out of it with stalks like rhubarb. The one with the cracked window in the hall door. I decided it was. It seemed to fit. It scared me, just looking at the house, and thrilled me. It was wild, poor, crazy; brand new and ancient. The artificial hill would stay there for years. The weeds would creak, lean over, turn grey and become more permanent. I knew what the smell of the house was: nappies and steam. I wanted to go in there and be liked.

Charles Leavy was sitting beside me. He headed his imaginary ball, three times – boom boom boom, no noise – then his head settled. He was wearing runners. There was a split where the rubber joined the canvas. The canvas was grey and frayed. His socks were orange. On a Sunday. He said Fuck like – I wanted to say it exactly like him. It had to sound like no other word sounded, quick and sharp and fearless. I was going to say it without looking over my shoulder. The way Charles Leavy said it. His head shot forward like it was going to keep going into your face. The word hit you after his head went back. The Off was like a jet going overhead; it lasted forever. The Fuck was the punch; the Off was you gasping.

Fuck awfffffff.

I wanted to hear it.

—Did you do your eccer yet? I asked.

—Fuck off.

—Fuck off, I said across the dark to Sinbad.

I could hear him hearing it. It became more silent; he'd stopped breathing. He'd been shuffling around in his bed.

—Fuck off, I said.

I was rehearsing.

He didn't budge.

I watched Charles Leavy. I studied him. I did his twitch. I did his shoulder. I made my eyes go small. When my da left, or even my ma, I was going to head the imaginary ball. I was going to go out and play. I was going to go into school the next day with all my homework done. I wanted to be like Charles Leavy. I wanted to be hard. I wanted to wear plastic sandals, smack them off the ground and dare anyone to look at me. Charles Leavy didn't dare anyone; he'd gone further than that: he didn't know they were there. I wanted to get that far. I wanted to look at my ma and da and not feel anything. I wanted to be ready.

—Fuck off, I said to Sinbad.

He was asleep now.

—Fuck off.

He shouted downstairs, my da did, a roar.

—Fuck off, I said.

I heard tears being swallowed down in the hall.

—Fuck off.

A door slammed, the kitchen one; I could tell it by the whoosh of air.

I was crying now too, but I'd be ready when the time came.

*

He leaned against the pillar in the yard, in a bit so he wouldn't be seen when a teacher drove or walked in. He wasn't hiding though. He was smoking. By himself.

I'd smoked; a gang of us all round a butt, pretending to inhale more than we did and holding onto the smoke for ages. We made sure that everyone saw that the smoke coming out of us was straight and thin, smoke that had the cigarette stuff sucked out of it. I was good at it.

Charles Leavy was smoking alone. We never did that. Cigarettes was very dear and they were too hard to rob from the shops, even Tootsie's, so you had to smoke them in front of someone; that was the whole idea. Not Charles Leavy though. He was smoking by himself.

He terrified me. He was there, all by himself. Always by himself. He never smiled; it wasn't a real smile. His laugh was a noise he started and stopped like a machine. He was close to no one. He hung around with Seán Whelan but that was all. He had no friends. We liked gangs, the numbers, the rush, being in. He could have had his own gang, a real gang like an army; he didn't know. We pushed each other to get beside him in the line in the mornings in the yard; he didn't know that either. There were mills going on around him, fights that never touched him.

I was on my own. The steam came out of my mouth like cigarette smoke. I sometimes put my fingers to my mouth like I was holding a cigarette, and breathed out. Not now though, not ever again. That was just messing.

This was great. The two of us alone. The excitement made my stomach smaller; it hurt.

I spoke.

—Give us a puff.

He did.

He handed the cigarette to me. I couldn't believe it, it had been so easy. My hand was shaking but he didn't see because he wasn't really looking at me. He was concentrating on exhaling. It was a Major, the cigarette; the strongest. I hoped I wouldn't get sick. I made sure my lips were dry so I wouldn't put a duck's arse on it. I took a small drag and gave the fag back to him quick; it was all going to explode out of my mouth, it had hit my throat too fast, the way it did sometimes. But I saved it. I killed the cough and grabbed the smoke and sucked. It was horrible. I'd never smoked a Major before. It scorched my throat and my stomach turned over. My forehead went wet, only my forehead, and cold. I lifted my face, made a tube of my mouth and got rid of the smoke. It looked good coming out, the way it should have, rising into the roof of the shed. I'd made it.

I had to sit down; my legs weren't there. There was a bench in the back, the length of the shed. I got to it. I'd be fine in a minute. I knew the feeling.

—That was fuckin' lovely, I said.

Voices sounded great in under the shed, deep and hollow.

—I love smoking, I said. —It's fuckin' great, isn't it?

I was talking too much, I knew it.

He spoke.

—I'm tryin' to give the fuckin' things up, he said.

—Yeah, I said.

It wasn't enough.

—So am I, I said.

I wanted to say more, I was dying to, to keep talking, to make it last longer, up to the bell. I was thinking fast, something, anything not stupid. There was nothing. Kevin had come into the yard. He was looking around. He couldn't see us yet. He'd ruin it. I hated him.

Something formed in my head; the relief came before it was a proper thought.

—There's that fuckin' eejit, I said.

Charles Leavy looked.

—Conway, I said. —Kevin, I said to make sure.

Charles Leavy said nothing. He killed his Major and put it in his box and put it in his pocket. I could see the shape of the box through his trousers.

I felt good. I'd started. I looked across at Kevin. I didn't miss him. I was afraid though. I'd no one now. The way I'd wanted it.

Charles Leavy walked away, out of the yard, out of the school. He didn't have his school bag with him. He was mitching. He didn't care. I couldn't follow him. I couldn't even start and change my mind. There'd be teachers coming in, parents outside, it was cold. I couldn't do it. Anyway, I'd all my eccer done and I didn't want to waste it.

I got up and went out a bit from under the shed so Kevin could see me. I'd pretend I still liked him. I was going to mitch though. On my own; soon. I'd last the day. I'd tell no one about it. I'd wait till they asked. I wouldn't tell them much. I'd do it on my own.

I made a list.

Money and food and clothes. They were the things I'd need. I had no money. My communion money was in the post office but my ma had the book. It was for when I was older. It was a waste; you only bought clothes and school books when you were older. I'd only seen the book once.

—Will I put it away for safe-keeping?

—Yes.

It had three pages of stamps and each stamp was worth a shilling. One of the pages wasn't full. I couldn't remember how much they were all worth. Enough. I'd got money from all the relations and some of the neighbours. Even Uncle Eddie had given me threepence. My mission was to get the book.

Food was easy; cans. They lasted longer because they were

packed in a vacuum and that kept them fresh. They were only bad if there was a big dent in the can; it had to be a big one. We'd eaten stuff out of cans with small dents and nothing had ever happened to us. I'd waited to be poisoned once – I'd wanted to be, to prove it to my da – but I didn't even have to go to the toilet until the day after. Beans would be best; they were very nutritious and I liked them. I'd have to get a can opener. The one we had was one of those ones that was stuck to the wall. I'd rob one out of Tootsie's. We'd robbed one before, but not to use. We'd buried it. I'd never opened a can with one of them before. Cans were heavy.

There'd been another big fight, a loud one. They'd both run out of the house, him the front, her the back. He'd gone all the way; she'd come back in. She'd shouted this time as well. The smell on his breath, something about it. I didn't even see him when he came home, except out of the window. He came home, they shouted, he left. He was late. We were in bed. The door rattled. The air downstairs settled back to normal.

—Did you hear that?

Sinbad didn't answer. Maybe he hadn't heard it. Maybe he could decide to hear and not hear things. I'd heard it. I waited for him to come back. I wanted to go down to her. She'd hurt him this time though; that was what it had sounded like.

I'd only bring a few cans and I'd buy more when I needed them. I'd bring apples as well but not oranges. They were too messy. Fruit was good for you. I wouldn't bring anything that I'd have to cook. I'd make sandwiches and wrap them up in tinfoil. I'd never eaten beans cold. I'd pick them out of the sauce.

I didn't like it that she'd shouted. It didn't fit.

I'd eat a good dinner before I left.

Clothes was last. I'd be wearing some and I'd need some others; two of everything and my anorak. I'd remember to

254

zip the hood back onto it. Most fellas that ran away forgot about underpants and socks. They were on my list. I didn't know where my ma kept them. In the hot press, but I wasn't sure. There were clean ones of each on our beds every Sunday when we woke up, nearly like Santy'd put them there. On Saturday night in the bath we put the old underpants in front of our eyes to stop the suds from getting in when our hair was getting washed.

He came back a good bit later. I heard his echoes around the side and then the slide of the back door. The television was on. Ma was in the living room. He stayed in the kitchen for a while, making tea or waiting for her to notice him; because he dropped something – it rolled. She stayed in the living room. He went out into the hall. He didn't move for a bit. Then I heard one of the creaky stairs; he always stepped on them. Then I heard the same creak: he'd turned back. The lino along the edge hung on to the living room door as he pushed it. I waited. I listened hard.

I made a belch. My back had lifted up off the bed, like I was trying to stop someone from pinning me down. Another belch got out. It hurt my throat. I wanted a drink of water. I listened for their voices; I tried to hear them behind the television noises. I couldn't get up and go nearer; I had to hear them from the bed, exactly here. I couldn't. The television was up louder than it had been before; I thought it was.

I waited, and then I couldn't remember.

They were both to blame. It took two to tango. It didn't take three; there was no room for me. I couldn't do anything. Because I didn't know how to stop it from starting. I could pray and cry and stay up all night, and that way make sure that it ended but I couldn't stop it from starting. I didn't understand. I never would. No amount of listening and being there would give it to me. I just didn't know. I was stupid.

It wasn't lots of little fights. It was one big one, rounds of the same fight. And it wouldn't stop after fifteen rounds like in boxing. It was like one of the matches from the olden days where they wore no gloves and they kept punching till one of them was knocked out or killed. Ma and Da had gone way past Round Fifteen; they'd been fighting for years – it made sense now – but the breaks between the rounds were getting shorter, that was the big difference. One of them would soon fall over.

My ma. I wanted it to be my da. He was bigger. I didn't want it to be him either.

I could do nothing. Sometimes, when you were thinking about something, trying to understand it, it opened up in your head without you expecting it to, like it was a soft spongy light unfolding, and you understood, it made sense forever. They said it was brains but it wasn't; it was luck, like catching a fish or finding a shilling on the road. Sometimes you gave up and suddenly the sponge opened. It was brilliant, it was like growing taller. It wouldn't happen this time though, never. I could think and think and concentrate and nothing would ever happen.

I was the ref.

I was the ref they didn't know about. Deaf and dumb. Invisible as well.

—Seconds away –

I wanted no one to win. I wanted the fight to go on forever, to never end. I could control it so that it lasted and lasted.

—Break –

In between them.

—Burr-rreak!

Bouncing; my hands on their chests.

Ding ding ding.

Why did people not like each other?

I hated Sinbad.

But I didn't. When I asked myself why I hated him the only reason was that he was my little brother and that was all; I didn't really hate him at all. Big brothers hated their little brothers. They had to. It was the rule. But they could like them as well. I liked Sinbad. I liked his size and his shape, the way his hair at the back went the wrong way; I liked the way we all called him Sinbad and at home he was Francis. Sinbad was a secret.

Sinbad died.

I cried.

Sinbad died.

There'd have been nothing good about it; I couldn't think of any advantage. Nothing. I'd have had no one left to hate, to pretend to hate. The bedroom, the way I liked it, needed his noises and his smell, and his shape. I really started crying now. It was nice, missing Sinbad. I knew I'd see him in a while. I kept crying. There was no one else. I'd see him and I'd probably hit him, maybe give him a dead leg for himself.

I loved Sinbad.

The tears on the left were going faster than the ones on the right.

Why didn't Da like Ma? She liked him; it was him didn't like her. What was wrong with her?

Nothing. She was lovely looking, though it was hard to tell for sure. She made lovely dinners. The house was clean, the grass cut and straight and she always left some daisies in the middle because Catherine liked them. She didn't shout like some of the other mas. She didn't wear trousers with no fly. She wasn't fat. She never lost her temper for long. I thought about it: she was the best ma around here. She really was; I didn't just reach that conclusion because she was mine. She was. Ian McEvoy's was nice but she smoked; there was a smell of it off her. Kevin's one frightened me. Liam and Aidan didn't have any. I thought about Missis Kiernan a lot but she wasn't a ma because she didn't have any children. She was only Missis because she was married to Mister Kiernan. My ma was best of them and all the others as well. Charles Leavy's ma was colossal, her face was all nearly purple. She wore a girl's raincoat all the time when she was out and she tied the strap in a knot instead of using the buckle. I couldn't even imagine getting a kiss from her when I was going to bed; trying to make it look like I was kissing her so I wouldn't hurt her feelings or get into trouble, getting my lips close enough without touching. She smoked as well.

Charles Leavy could kiss her.

My da had more wrong with him than my ma. There was nothing wrong with my ma except sometimes she was too busy. My da sometimes lost his temper and he liked it. He had black things across the top of his back, like black insects clinging onto him. I'd seen them; about five of them in a bendy row. I'd seen them when I was watching him shaving. His vest didn't cover up two of them. He was useless at lots of things. He never finished games. He read the newspapers. He coughed. He sat too much.

He didn't fart. I'd never caught him.

If you put a match to your hole when you were going to fart it came out like a flame; Kevin's da told him that – but you had to be older for it to work, at least in your twenties.

It was all him against her.

But it took two to tango. He must have had his reasons. Sometimes Da didn't need reasons; he had his mood already. But not all the time. Usually he was fair, and he listened when we were in trouble. He listened to me more than to Sinbad. There must have been a reason why he hated Ma. There must have been something wrong with her, at least one thing. I couldn't see it. I wanted to. I wanted to understand. I wanted to be on both sides. He was my da.

I went up to bed just after Sinbad, before I had to. I kissed my ma goodnight, and my da. There'd been no words so far; they were both reading; the television was on with the sound down waiting for The News. My lips hardly touched my da. I didn't want to disturb him. I wanted him to stay the way he was. I was tired. I wanted to sleep. I hoped it was a brilliant book.

I listened on the landing. It was silent. I brushed my teeth before I went into our room. I hadn't brushed them the proper way in a while. I looked at my da's razor but I didn't take the blade out. The bed was cold but the blankets were heavy on me; I liked that.

I listened.

Sinbad wasn't asleep; there wasn't a big enough gap between the in and the out breathing. I didn't say anything. I checked again, listened: he definitely wasn't sleeping. I listened further – I'd left the door a bit open. There was still no talking from downstairs. If there was none before we heard The News music there'd be no fighting at all. I still said nothing. Somewhere in the minute I'd been in bed, while I'd been listening, my eyes had learned how to see in the dark; the curtains, the corners, George Best, Sinbad's bed, Sinbad.

—Francis?

—Leave me alone.

—They're not fighting tonight.

Nothing.

—Francis?

—Patrick.

He was jeering me, the way he'd said it.

—Pah-trick.

I couldn't think of anything.

—Pahh-twick.

I felt like he'd caught me doing something, like I was falling into trouble, but I didn't know what. I wanted to go to the toilet. I couldn't get out of the bed.

—Pahhh –

It was like he'd become me and I was him. I was going to wet the bed.

—twick.

I didn't.

I got the blankets off.

He'd found out; he'd found out. I'd wanted him to talk because I was scared. Pretending to be protecting him, I'd wanted him close to me, to share, to listen together; to stop it or run away. He knew: I was frightened and lonely, more than he was.

Not for long though.

There was a small hole in the top sheet just at where my big toe usually was; I liked searching my toe in it, the rough feel of the blanket, and taking my toe away. Now, the sheet ripped there when I pulled it off. I knew why: he didn't. He'd heard it. I'd scared him. The ripping sheet.

—Sinbad.

I stood up out of the bed. I was in charge again.

—Sinbad.

I was going to the toilet but I didn't have to hurry now.

—I'm going to strangle you, I said.

I went to the door.

—But first I'm going to the toilet. There's no escape.

I wiped the seat. The bathroom light was off but I'd heard the wee smashing on the plastic. I wiped all around and threw the paper into the toilet. Then I flushed it. I got back into the bedroom without touching the door. I crept to his bed but I made one step heavier.

—Francis.

I was giving him one more chance.

—Move over.

It was even: we'd scared each other. There was no noise; he wasn't moving. I got right up to his bed.

—Move over.

It wasn't an order; I said it nice.

He was asleep. I could hear it. I hadn't scared him enough to make him keep awake. I sat on the bed and lifted my feet.

—Francis –

There wasn't room. I didn't push him. He was much heavier when he was asleep. I didn't want to wake him. I went over to my own bed. There was still some warm left. The sheet hole was bigger, too big. My foot got caught in it. I was afraid I'd rip it more.

I was going to sleep. I knew I'd be able to. In the morning I'd tell Sinbad that I hadn't woken him up.

I listened.

Nothing, then they were talking. Her, him, her, him for longer, her, him long again, her for a bit, him. It was only talking, normal talk. Him talking to her. Man and wife. Mister and Missis Clarke. My eyes had closed by themselves. I stopped listening. I practised my breathing.

—I didn't wake you up, I told him.

He was ahead of me. It was going all wrong.

—I could have, I told him.

He didn't care; he'd been asleep. He didn't believe me.

—But I didn't.

We'd be at the school soon and we couldn't be together there. I made myself get up beside him, and then in front. He didn't look at me. I got in his way. I spoke when he was going around me.

—He hates her.

He kept going, wide enough for me not to grab him, the same speed.

—He does.

We were into the field in front of the school. The grass was long where there were no foundations yet but there were paths worn through the grass and they all joined one path at the end of the field right opposite the school. It was all hay grass in the middle, and nettles and devil's bread and stickybacks where the ditches were left.

—You don't have to believe me if you don't want to, I said. —It's true though.

That was all. There were piles of boys coming through the field, joining up on the big path. Three fellas from the scholarship class were sitting having a smoke in the wet long grass. One of them was pulling the hay off the grass and spilling it into his lunch box. I went slower. Sinbad got past some fellas and I couldn't see him any more. I waited for James O'Keefe to catch up.

—Did you do the eccer? he said.

It was a stupid question; we all did the eccer.

—Yeah, I said.

—All of it?

—Yeah.

—I didn't, he said.

He always said that.

—I didn't do some of the learning, I said.

—That's nothing, he said.

The eccer was always corrected, all of it. We could never get away with anything. We had to swap copies; Henno walked around giving the answers and looking over our shoulders. He spot-checked.

—I'm analysing your writing, Patrick Clarke. Tell me why.

—So I won't write in any of the answers for him, Sir.

—Correct, he said. —And he won't write in any for you.

He thumped me hard on the shoulder, probably because he'd been nice to me a few days before. It hurt but I didn't rub it.

—I went to school once myself, he said. —I know all the tricks. Next one: eleven times ten divided by five. First step, Mister O'Keefe.

—Twenty-two, Sir.

—First step.

He got James O'Keefe in the shoulder.

—Multiply eleven and ten, Sir.

—Correct. And?

—That's all, Sir.

He got another whack.

—The answer, you *amadán*.*

—One hundred and ten, Sir.

—One hundred and ten. Is he correct, Mister Cassidy?

—Yes, Sir.

—For once, yes. Second step?

Miss Watkins had been much easier. We always did some of the homework but it was easy to fill in the answers when we were supposed to be correcting the ones we'd already done. Henno made us do the corrections with a red colouring pencil. You got three biffs if the point wasn't sharp. Twice a week, on Tuesdays and Thursdays, we were allowed, two by two, to go up to the bin beside his desk and sharpen them. He had a parer screwed to the side of the desk – you put the pencil in the hole and turned the handle – but he wouldn't let us use it. We had to have our own. Two biffs if you forgot to bring it in, and it couldn't be a Hector Grey's one, Mickey Mouse or one of the Seven Dwarfs or any of them; it had to be an ordinary one. Miss Watkins always used to write the

* Eejit.

answers on the board before nine o'clock and then she'd sit behind her desk and knit.

—Hands up who got it right? *Go maith*.* Next one, read it for me, em –

Without looking up from her knitting.

—Patrick Clarke.

I read it off the board and wrote it down in the space I'd left for it. Once, she stood up and came around the desks and stopped and looked at my page; the ink was still wet and she didn't notice.

—Nine out of ten, she said. —*Go maith*.

I always made one of them wrong, sometimes two. We all did, except Kevin. He always got ten out of ten, in everything. A great little Irishman, she called him. Kevin did Ian McEvoy in the yard when Ian McEvoy called him that; he gave him a loaf in the nose.

She'd thought she was nice but we'd hated her.

—Still awake, Mister Clarke?

They all laughed. They were supposed to.

—Yes, Sir.

I smiled. They laughed again, not as much as the first time.

—Good, said Henno. —What time is it, Mister McEvoy?

—Don't know, Sir.

—Can't afford a watch.

We laughed.

—Mister Whelan.

Seán Whelan lifted the sleeve of his jumper and looked under.

—Half-ten, Sir.

—Exactly?

—Nearly.

—Exactly, please.

* Good.

264

—Twenty-nine past ten, Sir.

—What day is it, Mister O'Connell?

—Thursday, Sir.

—Are you sure?

—Yes, Sir.

We laughed.

—It is Wednesday, I'm told, said Henno. And it is half past ten. What book will we now take out of our *málas*,* Mister —— Mister —— Mister O'Keefe?

We laughed. We had to.

I went to bed. He hadn't come home. I kissed my ma.

—Night night, she said.

—Good night, I said.

There was a hair growing out of a small thing on her face. Just between her eye and her ear. I'd never seen it before, the hair. It was straight and strong.

I woke up. It was just before she'd come up to get us out of bed. I could tell from the downstairs noises. Sinbad was still asleep. I didn't wait. I got up. I was wide awake. I dashed into my clothes. It was good; the curtain square was bright.

—I was just coming up, she said when I got into the kitchen.

She was feeding the girls, feeding one and making sure that the other one fed herself properly. Catherine often missed her mouth with the spoon. Her bowl was always empty but she never ate that much.

—I'm up, I said.

—So I see, she said.

I was looking at her feeding Deirdre. She never got bored with it.

—Francis is still asleep, I said.

* Bags.

265

—No harm, she said.

—He's snoring, I said.

—He isn't, she said.

She was right; he wasn't snoring. I'd just said it; not to get him into trouble. I'd just wanted to say something funny.

I wasn't hungry but I wanted to eat.

—Your dad's gone to work already, she said.

I looked at her. She was bent down, behind Catherine, helping her get the last bit onto her spoon, touching her arm, not holding it, aiming the spoon at the porridge.

—Good girl —

I went back upstairs. I waited, listened; she was safe downstairs. I went into their room. The bed was made, the eiderdown up over the pillows and tucked behind them. I pulled it back. I listened. I looked at the pillows first. I pulled it back more, and the blankets. She hadn't done the bottom sheet. Only her side had the mark of a body, the right creases; they matched the pillows. The other side was flat, the pillows full. I put my hand on the sheet; it felt warm on her side, I thought it did. I didn't touch his.

I didn't tuck the eiderdown back in; to let her know.

I listened. I looked in the wardrobe. His shoes and ties were there, three pairs of shoes, too many ties, tangles of them.

I changed my mind; I tucked in the eiderdown and flattened it.

I looked at her. She was cleaning the baby chair. She looked the same. Except for the hair, and I couldn't see that now. I tried hard, I looked at her, I tried to see what her face meant.

She looked just the same.

—Will I get Francis?

She threw the cloth and it landed hanging over the sink.

She never threw things.

—We both will, she said.

She got the baby up and fitted her into her hip. Then she

put her hand out, for me. Her hand was wet. We crept up the stairs. We laughed when they creaked. She squeezed my hand.

The funeral would be colossal. And a flag on his coffin. The saved person's family would give me and Sinbad money. My ma would have one of those veils on, right over her face. She'd look lovely behind it. She'd cry quietly. I wouldn't cry at all. I'd put my arm around her when we were walking out of the church with everyone looking at us. Sinbad wouldn't be able to reach up to her shoulders. Kevin and them would want to stand near me outside the church and beside the grave but they wouldn't be able to because there'd be so many people, not just the relations. I'd have a suit with long trousers and a good pocket on the inside of the jacket. The saved boy's family would get a plaque put up on our wall beside the front door. My da had died saving a little boy's life. It wasn't going to happen like that though; that was only stupid. Dreaming was only nice while it lasted. Nothing was going to happen to my da. Anyway, I didn't really want him to die or anything else; he was my da. I preferred to imagine my own funeral; it was a much better dream.

I saw Charles Leavy going out the school gate. I looked around – I didn't want anyone else – and followed him. I waited for a shout; we weren't allowed out of the yard for little break. I kept going at the same speed. I put my hands in my pockets.

He'd gone into the field. I kicked a stone when I was crossing the road. I looked back. The shed blocked most of the yard. There was no one looking. I ran. He'd dropped into the high grass. I kept my eyes on the place. I slowed down and walked into the grass. It was still wet. I whistled. I thought I was going right for him.

—It's me.

I saw a gap in the grass, a hole.

—It's me.

He was there. I had to sit down but I didn't want to. My trousers were already dark from the wet. He was sitting on a soggy cardboard box. There was no room for me. I kneeled on the edge of it.

—I saw you, I said.

—So wha'.

—Nothing.

He took a drag from his Major. He must have got it lit in the time it had taken me to catch up with him. He didn't pass it on to me. I was glad but I'd been hoping he would.

—Are you mitching?

—Would I leave me bag in the room if I was mitching? he said.

—No, I said.

—Then.

—That'd be thick.

He took another drag. We were the only people in the field. The only noise was from the yard, the shouting and a teacher's whistle, and a cement mixer or something far away. I watched the smoke coming out. He didn't. He was looking at the sky. I was wet. I was listening for the bell. How would we get back in? The quiet was like a pain in my stomach. He wasn't going to say anything.

—How many do you smoke a day?

—Twenty about.

—Where do you get the money?

I didn't mean it to sound like I didn't believe him. He looked at me.

—I rob it, he said.

I believed him.

—Yeah, I said, like I did too.

Now I looked at the sky too. There wasn't much time left.

—Did you ever run away? I said.

268

—Fuck off, would yeh.

I was surprised. Then it made sense: why would he have?

—Did you ever want to?

—I'd have done it if I'd wanted to, he said.

Then he asked a question.

—Thinkin' o' doin' it yourself, are yeh?

—No.

—Why were you askin' then?

—I was only asking.

—Yeah, maybe.

I was going to ask him if I could go with him the next time. That was why I'd followed him. It was stupid. I was stranded, away from the yard. I was with him but he didn't care. If Charles Leavy ever ran away from home he'd never have come back. He'd have stayed away. I didn't want to do that.

I didn't want to get caught. I stood up.

—See yeh later.

He didn't answer.

I crept to the edge of the field but it was no fun.

I wanted to run away to frighten them and make them feel guilty, to push them into each other. She'd cry and he'd put his arm around her. And his arm would stay there when I came home in the back of the police car. I'd be sent to Artane for wasting the police's time and money but they'd come to see me every Sunday while I was in there, not for long. They'd think it was their fault, Sinbad as well, but I'd tell them that it wasn't. Then I'd get out.

That had been my plan.

I stood up out of the grass. I looked around as if I was searching for something, looking worried.

—I lost a pound note, Sir. I was minding it for my ma for messages.

I shrugged, gave up. The money had blown away. I crossed the road. The worst bit, around the shed, back into the yard.

No one waiting. Mister Finnucane coming out the door with the bell. I got beside Aidan and Liam.

—Where were you?

—Having a smoke.

They looked at me.

—With Charlo, I said.

I couldn't help saying more.

—D'you want to smell my breath?

Mister Finnucane lifted the bell with his other hand holding the donger inside it. He always did it that way. He held it over his shoulders, then freed the donger and dropped the bell, and lifted it, and dropped it, ten times. His lips moved, counting. We had to be in our lines by the tenth one. Charles Leavy was in front of me, five places. Kevin was behind me. He kneed my knee.

—Lay off messing!

—Make me.

—I will.

—Go on.

I did nothing. I wanted to do something to him.

—Go on.

I kicked him backwards in the shin. It hurt him; I could feel it. He jumped and fell out of the line.

—What's going on there?

—Nothing, Sir.

—What happened you?

It was Mister Arnold, not Henno. He'd been counting the boys in his row. He didn't care too much what had happened. He was only looking over boys' heads. He hadn't bothered breaking a way through them.

—I fell, Sir, said Kevin.

—Well, don't fall again.

—Yes, Sir.

Kevin was behind me again.

270

—I'm going to get you, Clarke.

I didn't even look around.

—I'm going to get you. D'you hear me?

—No talking back there.

Henno had come out to get us. He marched down one side of us, counting, and up the other side. He passed me the second time. I waited for Kevin to hit. He thumped me in the back. That was all he had time for.

—That was only the start.

I didn't care. He hadn't hurt me bad. Anyway, I could get him back. He wasn't my friend any more. He was a sap, a spoofer and a liar. He hadn't a clue.

—*Anois,** Henno shouted at the front. —*Clé deas,*** clé deas* –

We marched into the main school, around to our room. Henno was at the door.

—Wipe your feet.

He only had to say it once. The fellas at the front did it and everybody copied them. Last in had to close the door quietly. Not a peep going through the school. Henno always kept us till last so our noises wouldn't mix in with the other classes. He made us stand for half an hour if he heard as much as a whisper. We had to wait till the two ahead of us were in the room before we were allowed to go in.

I was still going to run away, even without Sinbad or Charles Leavy. I'd wanted Sinbad most, like in Flight of the Doves, me in charge, carrying my little brother on my back when he was too tired, through the ditches and the bogs, over rivers. Looking after him.

—Next two boys.

I'd go on my own.

—Next two.

* Now. ** Left right.

Somewhere not too far. Somewhere I could walk to, and back.

—Next two.

Kevin was waiting. He'd told some of the fellas. They were waiting. I didn't care. I wasn't scared. He'd beaten me every other time. They were different; I hadn't wanted to win. Now I didn't care. If he hurt me I'd hurt him. It didn't matter who won. I didn't try to get around him, pretend he wasn't there or I'd forgotten. I walked right up to him. I knew what was going to happen.

He pushed me on the chest. The space between us and the crowd got smaller. It had to be quick; the teachers would soon be coming out. I went back a step. He had to follow me.

—Come on.

He pushed me harder, harder – an open-handed punch – to get me to do something.

I said it loud enough.

—I saw the gick marks on your underpants.

I saw it, the hurt, pain, the rage charge through his face in a second. He went red; his eyes got smaller and wet.

The crowd got closer.

He came at me with both fists up and tight; he just wanted to get at me. He didn't care; he didn't look. He hit against me. One of his fists opened; he was going to scrape me. He was groaning. I got around him. I punched the side of his face; it hurt me. He turned and was into me again; his finger in my nose. I kneed him – missed; kneed him – got him, over his knee. I held him to me. He tried to escape out of his clothes. I got my hand up to his hair; my hand was wet – his snot and tears. He couldn't let us separate: they'd see him crying. I tried to get his hands off and jump back – I couldn't. I kneed him – missed. He was squealing now, inside his mouth. I had his hair; I pulled his head back.

—Cheating!

Someone yelled that. I didn't care. It was stupid. This was the most important thing that had ever happened to me; I knew it.

His head came into my face, mostly my mouth. There was blood – I could taste it. The pain was nice. It wasn't bad. It didn't matter. He did it again, not as good. He was pushing me back. If I fell it would be different. I went back – I was going. I fell back against someone. He got out of the way – jumped back – but it was too late; I'd got my feet steady again. This was great.

He was pushing my jumper and my shirt and vest up into my chin, trying to knock me over. He must have looked stupid. I couldn't kick him; I needed my legs. I got my two fists and I thumped both sides of his head, once, twice, then I grabbed his arms to stop him from getting his hands closer to my face. He seemed to be much smaller than I was. His face was right in my chest, boring in, biting the bottom of my jumper. I grabbed the back of his hair and pushed. His head slipped to my tummy and he thought he had me, could push me back fast enough to get me down. I held onto his hair. He was getting set to heave – I got my knee up clean, bang in the face – harder than anything. There was shock in his groan, pain and defeat. He was gone. The crowd was quiet. They'd never seen this before. They wanted to see Kevin's face and were scared to.

It would never go back to the same again.

My knee had got bigger. I could feel it. I still had his head down. He was still hanging on to me, pushing, but he was finished. I tried to do it again, knee him, but I'd thought too much about it this time; it slowed my leg. It just reached his face. I couldn't let go till he did. I got one of his ears and twisted it. He screamed till he stopped himself. I didn't want

273

to end it the way we were supposed to; this was different. It was over but he couldn't admit it, so I said it.

—Give up?

—No.

He had to say that. I had to hurt him now. I got his ear again, twisted it, got my nails into it.

—Give up.

I didn't stop twisting to let him speak. He couldn't answer. I knew that. I turned his ear back to normal.

—Give up?

He said nothing.

And I didn't want to do any more. So I let go. I got my hands to his shoulders and pushed him back enough for me to walk away. I didn't even look at his face.

I walked across the road. I had a limp. He could come after me; I hadn't won; he hadn't surrendered. He could come after me and jump. I didn't look back. Someone threw a stone. I didn't care. I didn't look back. I had my limp and I was hungry. I had Kevin's blood on my trousers. I was on my own.

—I never gave up, he said.

After dinner, in the yard.

—You're dead, he said.

His nose was red, his chin was grazed, five thin cuts in a curving line. The skin beside his right eye was purpley red. There was dry blood on his jumper, not much of it. He was wearing a clean shirt.

—You didn't win.

I stopped and looked straight into him. I could see his eyes dying to look around, to make sure he could get away. I didn't say anything. I started walking again.

He waited.

—Chicken.

274

My ma had run towards me when she saw my trousers, the blood on them. Then she stopped and looked over my face and down.

—What happened you?

—I was in a fight.

—Oh.

She'd made me change them but she said nothing else about it.

—Where did you leave the dirty ones?

I went back upstairs and got them. I put them in the plastic basket in the corner between the fridge and the wall.

—They'll have to soak, she said.

She took them out. Sinbad saw them. It was hard to tell that there was blood. It wasn't red in the material.

Another voice.

—Chicken.

Ian McEvoy's.

—Hey, chicken!

There was a hole inside me for a bit; getting used to it.

—Pulling hair.

—Buwahh! Bu-ock-buock-buock!

That was James O'Keefe, doing a chicken. He was good at it. I went into the shed and sat down, by myself in there. They all stood out in the sun and looked in, searching because it was dark and the sun was behind the shed roof. It was cool. I could hear a fly or something dying.

—Boycott!

Kevin's voice.

—Boycott!

Them all.

—Boycott boycott boycott!

The bell rang and I stood up.

Captain Boycott had been boycotted by the tenants because he was always robbing them and evicting them. They

275

wouldn't talk to him or anything and he went mad and went back to England where he'd come from.

I went to the line. I stood behind Seán Whelan. I put my bag on the ground. No one stood beside me. Henno came.

—Straighten up; come on.

He started walking, counting. David Geraghty was beside me. He had a way of leaning on one stick. He twisted his head to look like he was watching Henno passing.

—There he goes.

He straightened up.

—Great job that; counting children.

I watched David Geraghty's lips. I couldn't see them moving. They were a little bit open.

Fluke Cassidy had to sit beside me. He didn't look at me. The only one who looked was Kevin. His mouth moved.

Boycott.

That suited me. I wanted to be left alone. Only, I didn't want all of them to spend all their time leaving me alone. Everywhere I looked the faces looked away. It got boring. I looked over to Seán Whelan and Charles Leavy; they weren't in on it. At David Geraghty; he blew me a kiss.

Everyone else.

I stopped looking. They could only boycott me if I didn't want to be boycotted.

—Did you win? she said.

I knew.

—What? I said.

—The fight.

—Yes.

She didn't say Good, but she looked it.

—Who was it? she said.

I looked at her shoulder.

—Not telling?

276

—No.

—Alright.

I got into the hot press. I had to climb up, over the tank. It was hot. I made sure my legs didn't touch it. I used a chair to get up into the first shelf; towels and tea-towels. I leaned out and kicked the chair away from the door. Then the tricky bit: I leaned further out and grabbed the door and pulled it in, closed. There wasn't a handle on the inside. I had to get my fingers into the slats of wood that made the door. The air whoofed out; click.

Pitch black dark. No light at all, none inside or through the wood. I was testing myself. I wasn't scared. I closed my eyes, held them, opened them. Pitch dark still and I still wasn't scared.

I knew it wasn't real. I knew that the dark outside wouldn't be as dark as this but it would be scarier. I knew that. But I was still happy. The dark itself was nothing; there was nothing in it to frighten me. It was nice in the hot press, especially on the towels; it was better than under the table. I stayed there.

He came home from work like normal. He had his dinner. He talked to my ma; a woman had got sick on the train.

—Poor thing, said my ma.

Nothing different. His suit, shirt, tie, shoes. I looked at the shoes; I dropped my fork. They were clean, like they always were. I got my fork back. His face wasn't as black as it usually was when he came home, the part that he had to shave. There were usually bristles where he'd shaved them off in the morning. He used to tickle us with them.

—Here comes Dada's scratchy face – !

We'd run but we loved it.

They weren't there. His face was smooth; the hair was in under his skin. He hadn't shaved in the morning.

It felt good: I'd caught him out. I ate all the carrots.

I stayed in the hot press and listened to my ma downstairs and the girls. The back door was open. Catherine kept climbing in and out. I listened for Sinbad; he wasn't there. My da wasn't moving. It stayed dark, just a tiny chink at the edge of the door. It would be different out in the open. There'd be wind and weather and animals, people and cold. But the dark was the thing to beat. I could dress to stay warm and bring my torch to keep away animals. Nocturnal creatures. My anorak – remember the hood – would keep me dry. The dark was the only thing to beat, and I'd beaten it. It didn't scare me a bit. I liked it. It was a sign of growing up, when the dark made no more difference to you than the day.

I was ready, nearly. I'd robbed the can opener. It had been easy. I didn't even put it in my pocket. I took the price off it and held it like I'd brought it into the shop, and walked out with it. I had two cans so far, beans and pineapple chunks. I didn't want to take too many at once; my ma would notice them missing. The pineapple chunks had been in the press for years. I'd found out where my ma kept the underpants, the socks, the jumpers and that; on the shelf above me in the hot press. I could get them any time I wanted to. All I needed was a chair. The only thing I didn't have was money. I had two and threepence saved up but that wasn't nearly enough. I just had to find the post office savings book, then I'd be completely ready. Then I was going.

The only bit I missed was the talking, not having anyone to talk to. I liked talking. I didn't try to get any of them to talk to me. They all followed Kevin, especially James O'Keefe. He always roared it.

—Boycott!

Aidan and Liam weren't as bad. They looked at me; they'd have answered back if I'd said anything. They looked nervous,

278

and sad. They knew what it was like. Ian McEvoy had a way of looking that I hadn't seen before. He sneered, with only half his mouth. He walked away in a loop when I was near, as if he was coming towards me, then changed his mind. I didn't care. He'd never been anything. Charles Leavy was the same as always. None of them talked to me, none of them.

Except David Geraghty. He wouldn't stop. We were beside each other on different sides of the first aisle. He leaned out, hanging onto the desk, right under Henno.

—Howdy.

Trying to get me to laugh.

—Howdy doody.

He was mad. I nearly wondered if he was crippled on purpose; he didn't want to have legs like the rest of us. He wasn't doing it to make me feel any better; he was just doing it. He was absolutely mad, completely on his own; much better than Charles Leavy: he didn't have to smoke or make us see him going off to mitch.

—Mighty fine day.

He clicked his tongue.

—Yessi-ir, Trampas.

He clicked his tongue again.

—Shit shit gick gick fuck fuck.

I laughed.

—Ad-a-boy.

It was little break. I stood on my own, away from everyone so we wouldn't have to bother boycotting each other. I was looking for Sinbad, just to see.

I heard it before I felt it, the zip of the air, then the thump on my back. It pushed me forward and I decided to fall. It was real pain. I rolled, and looked. It was David Geraghty. He'd whipped me with one of his crutches. I could feel the line on my back. The noise of it was still around me.

He was crying. He couldn't get his hand into the arm hole. He was really crying. He looked at me when he said it.

—Kevin said to give you that.

I stayed on the ground. He got his crutches right, and rode them across to the shed.

I never got the chance to run away. I was too late. He left first. The way he shut the door; he didn't slam it. Something; I just knew: he wasn't coming back. He just closed it, like he was going down to the shops, except it was the front door and we only used the front door when people came. He didn't slam it. He closed it behind him – I saw him in the glass. He waited for a few seconds, then went. He didn't have a suitcase or even a jacket, but I knew.

My mouth opened and a roar started but it never came. And a pain in my chest, and I could hear my heart pumping the blood to the rest of me. I was supposed to cry; I thought I was. I sobbed once and that was all.

He'd hit her again and I saw him, and he saw me. He thumped her on the shoulder.

—D'you hear me!?

In the kitchen. I walked in for a drink of water; I saw her falling back. He looked at me. He unmade his fist. He went red. He looked like he was in trouble. He was going to say something to me, I thought he was. He didn't. He looked at her; his hands moved. I thought he was going to put her back to where she'd been before he hit her.

—What do you want, love?

It was my ma. She wasn't holding her shoulder or anything.

—A drink of water.

It was daylight out still, too early for fighting. I wanted to say Sorry, for being there. My ma filled my mug at the sink. It was Sunday.

My da spoke.

—How's the match going?

—They're winning, I said.

The Big Match was on and Liverpool were beating Arsenal. I was up for Liverpool.

—Great, he said.

I'd been coming in to tell him, as well as getting the drink of water.

I took the mug from my ma.

—Thank you very much.

And I went back in and watched Liverpool winning. I cheered when the final whistle got blown but no one came in to look.

He didn't slam the door even a bit. I saw him in the glass, waiting; then he was gone.

I knew something: tomorrow or the day after my ma was going to call me over to her and, just the two of us, she was going to say, —You're the man of the house now, Patrick.

That was the way it always happened.

—Paddy Clarke –

Paddy Clarke –

Has no da.

Ha ha ha!

I didn't listen to them. They were only kids.

He came home the day before Christmas Eve, for a visit. I saw him through the glass door again. He was wearing his black coat. I remembered the smell of it when I saw it, when it was wet. I opened the door. Ma stayed in the kitchen; she was busy.

He saw me.

—Patrick, he said.

He moved the parcels he had with him under one arm and put his hand out.

—How are you? he said.
He put his hand out for me to shake it.
—How are you?
His hand felt cold and big, dry and hard.
—Very well, thank you.